D1601547

NEPTUNE

OTHER BOOKS BY NOEL B. GERSON

Fiction

ALL THAT GLITTERS
STATE TROOPER
SUNDAY HEROES
DOUBLE VISION
TEMPTATION TO STEAL
ISLAND IN THE WIND
TALK SHOW
CLEAR FOR ACTION
WARHEAD
THE CRUSADER
MIRROR, MIRROR
TR
THE GOLDEN GHETTO
SAM HOUSTON
JEFFERSON SQUARE
I'LL STORM HELL
THE ANTHEM
THE SWAMP FOX
GIVE ME LIBERTY
YANKEE DOODLE DANDY

THE SLENDER REED
OLD HICKORY
THE LAND IS BRIGHT
THE HITTITE
THE YANKEE FROM TENNESSEE
THE EMPEROR'S LADIES
THE GOLDEN LYRE
THE TROJAN
DAUGHTER OF EVE
THE SILVER LION
THE CONQUEROR'S WIFE
THAT EGYPTIAN WOMAN
THE HIGHWAYMAN
THE FOREST LORD
THE IMPOSTOR
THE GOLDEN EAGLE
THE CUMBERLAND RIFLES
THE MOHAWK LADDER
SAVAGE GENTLEMAN

Nonfiction

DAUGHTER OF EARTH AND
 WATER
THE PRODIGAL GENIUS
BECAUSE I LOVED HIM
FREE AND INDEPENDENT
THE EDICT OF NANTES
P.J., MY FRIEND
FRANKLIN: AMERICA'S LOST
 STATE
PASSAGE TO THE WEST
SURVIVAL JAMESTOWN
LIGHT-HORSE HARRY
MR. MADISON'S WAR

KIT CARSON
NATHAN HALE
SEX AND THE ADULT WOMAN
 (WITH ELLEN F. BIRCHALL,
 M.D.)
BELGIUM: FUTURE, PRESENT,
 PAST
ROCK OF FREEDOM
SEX AND THE MATURE MAN
 (WITH LOUIS P. SAXE, M.D.)
FOOD
VALLEY FORGE
THE LEGEND OF POCAHONTAS

NEPTUNE

Noel B. Gerson

DODD, MEAD & COMPANY
New York

Library of Congress Cataloging in Publication Data

Gerson, Noel Bertram, date
    Neptune.

    I. Title
PZ3.G323Nf   [PS3513.E8679]   813'.5'2   76–6876
ISBN 0–396–07325–5

For
GEORGE GREENFIELD

NEPTUNE

ONE

"Submerge with all possible speed," the commander ordered.

"Gas contraction pressure is now twelve point two percent," the bo's'n said as he monitored the instrument panel located aft in the cigar-shaped bathyscaphe. "Rate of descent is increasing, sir. We're about to hit eleven thousand feet. Now. Eleven thousand."

The commander of the heavy steel underwater craft nodded, and there was no sound but the hum of the generator that provided the electric current. The basic design of the bathyscaphe had remained unchanged since the first had been developed by Auguste Piccard prior to World War II. The generators pumped oxygen into the cabin, and electromagnets held the iron bars used for ballast firmly in place on the hull; when they were released the vehicle would rise to the surface.

The executive officer peered out of the thick glass porthole, adjusted the beams of the twin searchlights that cut through the dark sea and reported to the mother ship, the U.S.S. *New Haven*, which rode at anchor more than two miles above them in the South China Sea. "The school of fish has disappeared. No marine life. No obstructions."

The bathyscaphe shuddered slightly as it picked up additional speed, and all five members of the crew were aware of the change. "Keep an eye on the gas 'float,' " the commander told the engineering officer.

"Aye aye, sir." The order was unnecessary, but the routines followed on a dive to the bottom of deep sea trenches were unvarying. "We're holding our own." He stared at a rising column of mercury in a tube.

"Contraction is thirteen point one percent, sir," the bo's'n called.

The commander allowed himself the luxury of a tight smile and ran a hand through his short hair.

The gasoline stored in the so-called spherical "float" attached to the underside of the cabin had reached its maximum rate of compression. Its density, which rose considerably in comparison with that of the water as the bathyscaphe descended, provided the thrust that was sending the craft to the bottom.

"Thirteen thousand four hundred feet, sir!" the bo's'n said.

The commander turned to the one inactive member of the crew. "Prepare your cameras."

"Aye aye, sir." The young lieutenant checked his four automatic cameras, each attached to a porthole.

Suddenly the executive officer clasped a hand to his earphones. "Oh-oh!"

The atmosphere became tense.

"The skipper has picked up an unidentified aircraft on his radar. Approaching at eight hundred mph."

All five instantly understood the significance of the unexpected development. If the intruder was a Russian military plane it meant that Soviet intelligence had learned of the mission, and then the troubles would begin.

The commander kept his head. "There's nothing we can

do about it, so let's stay on the job. Let the skipper do his own worrying."

"Fourteen thousand three hundred feet, sir," the bo's'n said.

The executive officer again held a hand to his earphone, then slumped in his seat. "We're okay, sir," he said. "RAF reconnaisance aircraft on a routine mission out of Hong Kong. I don't know what the skipper told him, but everything is under control topside."

The commander had already dismissed the aircraft from his mind.

"Switch on your sonar at fourteen thousand eight hundred," he told the chief engineer.

"Aye aye, sir." The younger officer's reply did not reflect his surprise. Surface soundings had indicated that the object they were seeking was sitting on the seabed at a depth of more than three miles, so the commander obviously was taking no chances by directing that the bathyscaphe's underwater detection device be placed in use before they reached the trench.

"Fourteen eight," the bo's'n said.

The chief engineer pressed a red button on his console, pulled a switch and began to manipulate a set of sensitive dials.

A low, humming sound filled the small cabin.

"Fifteen thousand two hundred."

The executive officer spoke into a small microphone suspended from his neck, the hum of the sonar making his words inaudible to the other crew members.

"Fifteen seven."

"You may release one thousand pounds of ballast," the commander said, and the others knew he was slowing the craft's descent so it wouldn't crash into the ocean floor.

"Very good, sir." The bo's'n punched a tab with a practiced hand.

For a moment the hissing of the oxygen vents stopped as the bathyscaphe's rate of fall was checked, but the flow of pure air resumed again, and the crew breathed more easily. Any interruption of the air supply at this depth would mean certain death within minutes.

"Fifteen eight, sir," the bo's'n said.

At almost the same instant there was a jarring sensation as the craft touched bottom.

There was no change in the steady hum of the sounding device.

The commander moved to a place beside the chief engineer, gripped a wheel and pumped his right foot on a pedal. The bathyscaphe crawled slowly along the ocean floor.

The operation had reached a crucial stage, and two additional searchlights were snapped on, straining the craft's electrical power to its limits. Modern science enabled an undersea search vessel to perform miracles, but only men could guide it, and locating an object at a depth of three miles taxed the resources of even the most experienced crew.

"The skipper says we're heading off course," the executive officer said. "Veer two points to starboard, sir."

The commander made the necessary correction.

"Fifteen thousand nine hundred, sir," the bo's'n said.

The commander grinned. The ocean floor was sloping downward, so a heavy object would drift to the lower regions of the trench. If the original calculations were correct, all he had to do was to push forward.

"Fifteen thousand nine hundred and fifty feet, sir!"

"One point to port, if you please, sir!"

For the next quarter of an hour there was no sound in the cabin but the hum of the sonar.

"Sixteen thousand, sir. Sixteen thousand one hundred.

There's a sharp slope here. Sixteen two!"

The hum stopped abruptly, and was replaced by a sharp, intermittent beeping sound.

The commander donned a microphone and headset. "Captain," he said calmly to the skipper of the mother ship, "I've established contact with an unidentified object."

The executive officer moved to the forward porthole, located in the nose of the cigarlike vessel, and trained all four of the searchlights in a crisscrossing pattern.

The tension in the bathyscaphe mounted as the beeping sound grew louder.

"On target, sir!" the executive officer said, and could not keep his excitement from his voice.

"Commence photographing!"

"Very good, sir."

With the commander expertly manipulating the controls the bathyscaphe moved still more slowly.

The sonar beeps were so loud they became painful.

"Twenty feet ahead, sir!" the executive officer shouted.

"Turn off the sonar!"

"Aye aye, sir."

The silence in the bathyscaphe was deafening.

"Ten feet, sir!" The executive officer's voice trembled.

The commander halted the craft, then moved forward to the porthole, a remote control steering apparatus the size of a portable radio in one hand.

Directly ahead and caught in the crossbeams of the searchlights was a black metal object. In places the paint had peeled away, and the steel beneath it was covered with a coating of green slime.

The commander reported his find to the *New Haven,* then began to manipulate his craft around the object. Maneuvering with great delicacy he inched still closer, until no more than five or six feet separated his vessel from the object.

"My God," he murmured. "This is it!"

The last doubt was removed as they saw a name on the side of the sunken object: *ZOLÓTO 14–2967.*

"Mission accomplished, Captain," the commander said. "I have located the Russian submarine."

He spent more than an hour slowly making a circle around the sub, making certain that the hull was intact, that the ejection ports for all eight of the ship's atomic projectiles were tightly closed.

"I've run out of film, sir," the young lieutenant said.

"I think we've seen enough for one day," the commander said, and added under his breath, "for a lifetime, maybe."

Neither he nor his subordinates felt any sense of elation as they discarded iron ballast and the bathyscaphe began her slow ascent to the surface of the South China Sea. They had enjoyed complete success in the final phase of the intensive search conducted by the United States Navy for the Soviet atomic submarine that had vanished without a trace in the Pacific Ocean. Washington would rejoice: not only might it be possible to capture one or more Russian atomic weapons and learn precisely how they were made, but an even greater treasure, a copy of the Red Navy's secret communications code, also was on board.

If it could be retrieved—and the commander had no idea how the feat might be accomplished—the U.S. Navy would be in a position to decipher every message sent to and from the submarines of its Soviet counterpart. The superpowers might be enjoying what they called detente, but diplomatic cordiality didn't mean the American admirals could relax their vigilance, and the capture of the code, if it could be done, would be even more valuable than a Russian atomic projectile.

But the commander was depressed, and so were the members of his crew. As men who spent their professional lives in underwater searches and exploration, they knew that the *Zolóto* class of submarine carried a complement of more than 100 men. That meant a large number of human beings were entombed in the *14-2967,* victims of the cold war waged with relentless fury for more than thirty years.

TWO

The Eurasian girl was insatiable, and he started to make love to her for the third time when the telephone rang.

He rolled over, cursing silently, and plucked the instrument from its cradle. "Porter."

"The mountains of Szechuan are very high," the man at the other end of the line said.

Porter immediately became alert. "I've been told there is snow in the higher passes all through the year." His accent marked him as English, but was a curious mixture of Oxbridge and Redbrick, with the vowels flattened by long association with Americans.

"Your information is correct. It sometimes reaches a depth of twenty feet." The way the man slurred his consonants identified him as Chinese.

"In July?"

"Oh, yes. In August also, and sometimes in September."

"Then in winter," Porter said, "it must be at least forty feet deep. Remarkable, isn't it?" He replaced the telephone in the cradle.

The Eurasian girl pushed back a mass of long, blue-black hair, propped herself on one elbow and stared at him.

He was already on his feet, beginning to dress. "No more

time for fun and games, my love. I'm on my way."

Sulkily and without comment she climbed out of the other side of the bed.

Porter checked his Smith & Wesson .44 Magnum, strapped on his shoulder holster and donned his jacket. Then, wasting no motions, he packed his one valise.

The girl sat before a dressing-table mirror, carefully applying eyeliner and mascara.

He counted out an extra Hong Kong $100 beyond the agreed fee and placed it beside her. "You'll have to make yourself beautiful on your own time, my love. I'm in a hurry."

She was unaccustomed to such treatment, but the finality of his tone made further discussion impossible, so she stuffed the money into her shoulder bag along with her cosmetics.

"I'll call you when I'm next in town." He held the door for her.

She made a dignified exit into the hotel corridor.

Porter bolted the door before he took a second pistol from a bedside table. It was a Lilliput that fitted into the palm of his hand, and he smiled without humor as he dropped it into a jacket pocket. Placing his toilet articles in a leather case, he closed his valise, then glanced at his watch before moving to the window. Hong Kong harbor stretched out below, its calm waters creased by freighters and passenger liners, sampans and diesel-powered junks and the ferries that sailed endlessly between Victoria Island and Kowloon. He paid no attention to the civilian shipping, but concentrated for a few moments on the Australian cruiser and two American destroyers riding at anchor in the Royal Navy berths at the edge of the Wanchai nightclub district. He waited five minutes, then went down to the lobby, where he paid his bill with precisely the right amount of money before walking without undue haste to a small side entrance.

There he waited inside for another two minutes, waving away the attendant who wanted to relieve him of his luggage. He was of medium height and appeared to be in his late thirties, his inconspicuously tailored suit concealing an athletic build. His training enabled him to stand motionless, calling no attention to himself. Others who used the side entrance ignored him, and if asked would have said he was blue-eyed, perhaps, and that he was either very dark or very fair. Actually he was neither, and had hazel eyes, medium to short brown hair and chiseled features that showed no expression.

At the appointed moment he went through the revolving doors just as a dilapidated taxi pulled up to the entrance.

Porter dropped his valise on the floor of the car and sat in the far corner. "Okay?"

"Yes, sir. I'm sure I wasn't followed. Reasonably sure," the Chinese driver said.

"Let's make very certain of it, shall we?" There was a hint of amusement in Porter's tone.

The taxi shot away from the entrance, its powerful engine belying its appearance, and slipped into the mainstream of waterfront traffic. "Chang is waiting for you at Kai Tak Airport," the driver said. "He'll meet you at hangar number four with your ticket and instructions."

"Ah, then I'm traveling to the States."

"Apparently, sir." The man studied the traffic behind them through his rear-view mirror as he drove onto the overpass that would take them to the tunnel under the harbor.

Porter knew better than to ask why he had been summoned without warning. The Corporation discouraged unnecessary chat between its senior operatives and lower-level employees.

The taxi entered the tunnel, where two lines of cars were

10

moving at high speed in the same direction.

Reacting instinctively, Porter removed the safety catch from his Lilliput and hunched down in his seat to make as small a target as he could. Tunnels were convenient for ambushes.

The taxi emerged onto a new highway built over the slums of Kowloon, the concrete ribbon cutting a path through mazes of buildings, twelve to fifteen stories high, where hundreds of thousands lived in high-rise Crown Colony squalor. Entire families occupied single rooms; tomato plants were crowded onto tiny balconies beside drying laundry and one-burner alcohol stoves. The late afternoon heat softened the asphalt on the streets where pedestrians in vast numbers roamed, looking for bargains in cubicle-sized shops and markets, all with open fronts. There was no breeze, and the odors of cooking oil, garlic and humanity drifted up to the highway.

Ordinarily Porter liked Hong Kong, but wasn't sorry he was leaving. In late June, when the combination of the heat and the overcrowding made the place unbearable, he preferred to be elsewhere.

An airplane that had just taken off thundered overhead at a height of only a few hundred feet. Every millimeter of ground was so valuable that no one thought it strange to locate the airport near one of the heaviest population concentrations in the Orient.

The taxi entered the Kai Tak grounds, shot past the passenger terminal and approached a gate that separated the freight warehouse area from the other buildings. The driver slowed, and two uniformed Crown Colony policemen pushed open the gate, then closed it again behind the car.

At last they came to a hangar with the number four marked on its side, and beyond it stood a Boeing 747. Ground personnel were washing the windows and vacuum

11

cleaning the interior, while baggage handlers were loading luggage under the watchful eye of Hong Kong Preventive Service officials.

An officer in a khaki uniform with three stripes on each of his shoulderboards saw the taxi halt, watched the passenger disembark and immediately moved forward, intending to intercept Porter.

Chang, a slender, gray-haired man, materialized under the wing of the mammoth aircraft and waved the officer away.

Porter's face showed animation for the first time as he shook hands with Chang. They hadn't seen each other since their joint caper, several years earlier, when they had smuggled a prominent defector out of Canton, by way of Macao, and the adventure had formed a bond between them.

"You're flying direct to New York," Chang said, "with refueling stops in Tokyo and Seattle. You'll be met at JFK Airport by a yellow Cadillac. The license number is on your baggage stub. Drive straight up to Winthrop, Connecticut, and go to a hotel called the Inn, which overlooks Long Island Sound. Unless I'm very much mistaken, Davidson himself will meet you there."

Porter whistled under his breath. "The great man is personally involved in this assignment?"

"He even signed the cable asking for you."

"What's up, Chang?"

"Brian Davidson doesn't take me into his confidence. All I know is that I don't envy you. Any case that takes him out of Washington for as much as one day must be big."

"I need a drink," Porter said. "Let's go to the bar."

Chang shook his head. "You're under maximum security restrictions. Come along." He led the way into the empty hangar, and two other Chinese immediately appeared to stand guard at the entrance.

"Maybe you could send one of your lads for a beer," Porter said.

"My staff is shorthanded today."

"Oh, well. Before I forget it, I'd better turn over the Nancy Wing case to you. I was softening her up when you phoned me. I have a hunch, nothing more, that she isn't a Peking informer, but there wasn't time to develop hard evidence."

Chang grinned. "I've seen the film she made in Taipei. I think I'll give myself that assignment."

"You won't regret it. Any rumors that might give me a lead on what Davidson is up to?"

"Mac passed through here day before yesterday and said the Corporation brass is jittery. So something important must be under way, but the lid is screwed on tight."

Porter took a small sack of tobacco from his breast pocket, rolled a cigarette and struck his match on a *No Smoking* sign. "I thought I'd be making love to Nancy Wing for the next couple of weeks, but the job was too good to last. That's the breaks. Any special reason for the maximum security?"

"Not to my knowledge. I'd have been notified by now if you had been tailed coming out here."

"I don't suppose Davidson had the courtesy to tell you who might want to put me under surveillance. Russia, China, Yugoslavia, North Korea—or Andorra. I always enjoy knowing the nationality of potential assassins, particularly when I'm the target."

Chang shook his head. "Sorry."

Through the open door of the hangar they could see an airport bus discharge a load of passengers, and soon the stairs leading up to the passenger sections of the 747 were filled.

Porter was morose as he watched them. "I'll find out soon enough. Why don't we quit this rotten business while we're still healthy?"

13

"Because," Chang said, "we'd soon die of boredom."

Porter brightened. "I'm afraid you're right. On my last holiday I went to visit some relatives in Sussex, and after three days of looking at every bloody rose in their bloody garden I went off to Cornwall and spent the rest of the month alone. Fishing."

A second bus discharged its passengers.

A short time later the pilot opened a window and waved.

"Off you go," Chang said, and they shook hands without bidding each other goodbye. Even the least superstitious of the Corporation's field men knew better than to tempt fate by engaging in a formal farewell.

Porter knew without being shown that he was occupying a seat at the rear of the first-class section on the starboard side of the aircraft. He loosened his .44 Magnum in its holster, buckled himself into his seat and gave the stewardess specific instructions. "Two cans of beer, any brand, will make me very happy. I don't care what you bring me to eat, provided it isn't American beefsteak. My name is Porter, and if any cables come in on the intercom for me while we're in flight, bring them to me, but tell the captain not to call my name on the intercom." He twisted sideways in his seat so he could keep an eye on the other passengers, and settled down for the long flight to New York.

The journey passed without incident, perhaps because Porter observed every required precaution. During a two-hour stopover in Tokyo he locked himself in a men's room stall in the in-transit-passengers' lounge. In Seattle, where the crew changed, he went forward to the flight deck and stayed there until the aircraft was ready to take off. Neither there nor in New York was he required to observe immigration and customs requirements.

The yellow Cadillac, a two-door sedan, appeared on the

ramp when Porter emerged from the arrivals building, the driver turning the car over to him without a word and jumping into a taxi. The heavy traffic in the vicinity of Kennedy Airport made it difficult for Porter to check on surveillance, but before he reached the Connecticut Turnpike he had satisfied himself that he was not being followed. All the same, he looked frequently in his rear-view mirror. A senior operative stayed alive by reducing risks to a minimum.

After an uneventful two-hour drive he reached Winthrop, a manufacturing center and university town which he had never before visited, and stopped at a gas station, where he was given directions to the Inn. In another fifteen minutes he drove up a hill to a rustic, nineteenth-century hotel located on a bluff overlooking Long Island Sound. He parked and locked the car, then strolled into the tiny lobby, where a desk clerk interrupted a telephone conversation long enough to tell him he was expected and hand him a room key. He was not asked to sign the Inn's register.

Porter's third-floor room was large, comfortably furnished and equipped with the usual air conditioner. He was still English enough to prefer fresh air, so he opened the window and was rewarded by a sea breeze. Below, on the left, he could see water breaking over rocks, and on the right a bikini-clad blonde was sleeping on a small beach. He studied her with pleasure, then unpacked his belongings and went into the bathroom for a shower and shave.

Refreshed after the flight of more than twenty-four hours, he had nothing to occupy him until he was summoned, so he wandered downstairs and discovered a bar beyond the lobby. Seating himself on a stool, he ordered a beer. The young bartender seemed taciturn, and handed it to him without comment. There was only one other customer, a middle-aged man in a plaid jacket, and Porter avoided conversation by looking out of a picture window at the sea.

15

The man in the plaid jacket sat erect and straightened his necktie.

A moment later a girl came into the bar, and Porter would have known her figure anywhere. She looked as sensational in a dress of thin, soft material that clung to her body as she had in a bikini, and seeing her face for the first time, he realized she was lovely. Her green eyes were enormous, her lips were full and she wore makeup with the expertise of a model or actress. He wondered if she were someone he should recognize, but shrugged away the thought since he rarely went to a film.

The blonde showed no self-consciousness as she seated herself on a bar stool and ordered a Scotch and water.

Predictably, the man in the plaid jacket tried to strike up a conversation with her. "That's a great tan you've got, especially this early in the season."

She made no reply.

"You must have a head start. Tell me if I'm wrong, but I'll bet you were in the Caribbean, or down in Florida, maybe."

Porter could only see the back of her head now, but it was apparent she was not encouraging small talk with plaid jacket.

The man continued to chat as she drank, however, and was undeterred by her silence.

Porter wondered why the bartender didn't tell the boor to leave the lady alone. Certainly he himself had no intention of interfering. One of the basic rules of his profession was succinct: Thou shalt mind thine own goddam business at all times. He rolled a cigarette, struck a match on the underside of the bar and inhaled deeply.

The girl finished her drink.

Before she could either pay for it or order another, plaid jacket saw his chance. "Let me buy you one," he said, and moved to the stool beside her, with one hand gripping the edge of the bar only inches from her body.

The blonde picked up a heavy glass ashtray and brought it down on the man's hand.

His howl of pain filled the bar. "My God, you could have broken my hand!" he shouted.

Porter caught a glimpse of her face in the mirror behind the bar. Her expression was calm, her green eyes revealing no emotion.

Plaid jacket took some money from his pocket with his uninjured hand, threw it onto the bar and stalked out, muttering to himself.

"Another Scotch and water, please, and I'll sign for it," the girl said in a husky voice.

Porter ordered another beer, and signed, too. The incident amused him, but he told himself the blonde had given herself away. She had been too efficient, too calm, too precise. He rolled another cigarette.

Several couples drifted into the lounge, seating themselves at tables.

A short time later a man with salt-and-pepper hair strolled in, immaculate in a lounge suit with unfashionable, narrow lapels, a solid-colored, knitted tie and a shirt with a button-down collar. Brian Davidson had dressed in no other way since he had been an Ivy League undergraduate a quarter of a century earlier. There was no recognition in his eyes as he looked at Porter, and a moment later he departed.

Porter knew what was required of him, and followed. He was not surprised when the blonde did the same.

Davidson climbed the stairs to the second floor, and Porter allowed the blonde to precede him. The charade was absurd, and only a man who had spent his entire Corporation career behind a Washington desk would have played it. Porter could imagine few ways of making themselves more conspicuous. Fortunately no one was on hand to watch the parade up the stairs.

Brian Davidson unlocked the door of a second-floor suite, waved the pair in and carefully closed the door behind him. "Welcome, both of you," he said, primly shaking hands. "Miss Adrienne Howard, Mr. Porter."

"I win a bet, ten to one odds," Porter told the girl. "You were so slick getting rid of that roué that I knew you had to be a member of the club."

Adrienne Howard bristled. "I didn't see you rushing to my defense, Mr. Porter."

He grinned at her. "I knew you could take care of yourself. By the way, the handle of your mini-Luger shows."

The blonde glared at him as she pushed her pistol out of sight.

Davidson was busying himself cutting a rectangle of cheese into small slices, arranging the bits on a plate with an assortment of crackers and pouring soft drinks into three glasses. It was one of his inviolable rules, totally ignored by field operatives, that employees of the Corporation should not drink while on duty. He placed the plate on a coffee table, handed them glasses and raised his own.

"Cheers," he said, and waved them to seats.

One sip of the insipid drink was enough for Porter, but he noted that Adrienne Howard went through the motions of enjoying hers.

"On behalf of the Director and all members of the Council," Davidson said, "I offer the Corporation's congratulations to Miss Howard and Mr. Porter."

That was all Porter had to hear. Without any question a horrendous assignment loomed ahead.

"You two have been chosen to lead our counterintelligence forces in the most important, vital operation the Corporation has ever undertaken."

"I'm flattered to death," Porter murmured, his voice dry.

The blonde remained silent, but a corner of her mouth twitched, and she bit her lip.

"Your one deficiency, Porter, is your misplaced sense of humor." Davidson was aggrieved. "Under the circumstances, I shall overlook your comment. I trust you're both comfortable here. The Corporation owns this place. Through a dummy setup, naturally, so we can speak with complete freedom."

"I hope the chap Miss Howard bashed wasn't a deputy director," Porter said.

Davidson did not smile as he shook his head. "No, a salesman who happens to be a guest here. We do take in outsiders." He passed the cheese and crackers, then became solemn. "It is my privilege to tell you about Project Neptune, an operation so secret that almost nothing concerning it has been reduced to paper. What does the name *Zolóto,* fourteen dash twenty-nine sixty-seven, mean to you?" He looked at Adrienne Howard, challenging her.

She thought hard, then shrugged.

Davidson turned to Porter.

"Give me a minute. *Zolóto* means 'gold' in Russian, of course, and with the numbers it must be the serial identification of a *Zolóto* class of Soviet atomic submarine."

Davidson looked crestfallen.

"It comes back to me," Porter said. "About two years ago a Russian atomic submarine was lost. Somewhere in the Pacific. I was on temporary duty as head of the Singapore station, and I was relieved so I could chase up leads. The Russians never made any announcement, and most of the KGB field people never even heard of the sub. As I recall it, I chased all over the Far East for a month or two, but I came up with zed-e-r-o. A great cipher."

Davidson perked up. "That was only the beginning, Porter. The Russians spent a year searching for their submarine. So did we. And we found her."

Adrienne Howard pushed back a strand of her shoulder-length hair, but betrayed no feeling.

Porter rolled a cigarette.

"We used our most advanced bathyscaphe diving techniques, our most modern sonar. We found the ship, resting at the bottom of the sea, more than three miles down. The precise location is irrelevant at the moment. Suffice it that within days a decision was made at the highest level to raise the sub. Our scientists will have eight Red atomic weapons to take apart, and for the first time we'll know what makes them tick."

"Wow!" the blonde said.

Davidson was smug as he held up a hand. "Wait," he said. "We also want, desperately, the Red Navy communications code on board that sub. We know that every captain and every communications officer has a copy, so there must be two of them in that tight shell at the bottom of the ocean. I need hardly tell you how valuable it would be to us if we could decipher every message received and sent by every submarine in the Red Navy."

"*Zolóto* submarines," Porter said, "have a gross weight of more than six thousand tons. You just said she's sitting at the bottom more than three miles down. The benefits of recovering her are so obvious we needn't waste time enumerating them. But how, in God's name, can you haul up a ship of more than six thousand tons without breaking her to pieces and sending her to the bottom again, this time with her codes destroyed and her atomic weapons ruined?"

"We believe it can be done and will be done," Davidson said. "That, my friends, is Project Neptune."

"Brian," Adrienne Howard said, "if I didn't know you never touch anything stronger than ginger ale, I'd be prepared to swear that you've been drinking."

"I'm listening to you, Davidson," Porter said, "but I'm not believing you."

"The White House," Davidson said, "is convinced that the recovery of the *Zolóto* will influence the course of our current arms limitation negotiations with Moscow. The President," he continued, intoning the words, "has given Project Neptune the highest priority."

"That still doesn't mean the submarine can be salvaged," Porter said.

His superior ignored the interruption. "More than seven hundred million dollars have been spent so far, and no one knows how high the bill will run before we're finished."

"I'm delighted I'm not an American taxpayer," Porter said.

"We in Gamma Division deal very little in technology. We leave that sort of thing to Theta. So you'll be filled in later on the details. It's enough for me to tell you now that some of the country's best scientists went to work on a crash program to design a salvage ship capable of bringing up the *Zolóto* intact. The keel of the *Neptune* was laid eleven months ago, and she'll soon be ready for launching."

Adrienne Howard frowned. "How big is this ship, Brian?"

"She has a gross weight of more than forty-two thousand tons!" Davidson said proudly.

Porter and the blonde exchanged glances, and for the first time their thoughts were the same. "Damn it, Davidson," Porter said, "thousands upon thousands of shipwrights, welders, carpenters, plumbers, electricians, steelworkers and God only knows how many others have had to work on this ship. The security problems are staggering. By now Moscow and Peking must know what you're doing, and so does every ha'penny Red satellite!"

"We've made no particular effort to keep the building of

the *Neptune* a secret, although we haven't publicized it, either." Davidson's giggle was unexpectedly high-pitched. "The U.S. government has no part in the project. The ship is being built by private industry for commercial purposes. Every last one of the workers believes she'll be used to explore the seabed for coal deposits. How's that for a cover?"

"Brilliant," Adrienne said, "but who would be stupid enough to swallow the story?"

Davidson played his trump card. "The builder is Franklin Richards."

Suddenly the wild scheme began to make sense. Franklin Richards, one of the world's wealthiest men, was a self-made billionaire who had accumulated his original fortune in coal, then expanded into real estate and built huge office complexes in New York, Chicago, Los Angeles and other major cities. It was well known, however, that his real love was the sea, and his shipyard on the Strait of Juan de Fuca in the state of Washington was one of the busiest on earth. It was said that one third of the freighters and tankers in the American merchant marine, as well as those flying the flags of Liberia and Panama, had been constructed in the Richards yards.

So Richards was the one man anywhere who could provide perfect cover for Project Neptune. His own fortune was so vast that he could finance it himself. He owned a yard where the *Neptune* could be constructed. His coal holdings were still extensive, and no one would question his desire to locate more deposits at the bottom of the sea.

There was one catch, however. The forty-five-year-old Richards and his French-born wife, Marie, were bona fide, charter members of the international jet set. They entertained extensively at their various homes, their names appeared constantly in society and gossip columns, and no list of Beautiful People would be complete without them. The risk of entrusting such key roles to a gregarious, socially active couple was great.

Adrienne was uneasy. "How reliable is Franklin Richards?"

Davidson's manner became severe. "He's a patriot. This isn't the first time we've worked with him. He and his wife dine at the White House frequently, you know. And," he added as a clinching argument, "he happens to be a close friend of the Director."

Porter saw a loophole. "Is Mrs. Richards safe? And how much does she know?"

Davidson shrugged. "We must assume her husband keeps no secrets from her. That's a basic rule of thumb in our business."

"Precisely," Porter said. "She's much younger than Richards—"

"She's thirty-two," Adrienne interjected.

"—and she's a foreigner. The French operate a clever little intelligence shop, so—"

"The Director," Davidson said, becoming glacial, "has full confidence in Marie Richards."

That ended the matter, and Porter shrugged.

"The hiring of the crew is about to begin," Davidson said. "We'll move in some of our own people, but there will be a lot of outsiders, too, and the FBI will investigate them for us. Naturally, we'll have to do our own umbrella job. That's where you come in. Miss Howard will be in charge of domestic counterintelligence for Neptune. Mr. Porter will run foreign counterintelligence. Decide what you'll need in the way of personnel, equipment, whatever, and you'll have it. You'll have to work together, of course."

Porter slowly rolled a cigarette. "Is there any indication that the Russians know what we're doing?"

"Not specifically."

"Assume they're wise, Davidson. Also assume we can pull off this stunt. The KGB knows a job like this is beyond their capacity. So what would we do in their position? Lie low, keep tabs on the operation and let the enemy salvage the submarine. Then you move in, fast and hard, and take it away from them. I'll need at least twenty men, including people with solid Russian connections. I'll want to select them myself, even if it means taking them off other assignments."

"You'll have all the priorities you'll need."

"The Chinese are a different problem," Porter said. "Nobody is in a class with them, and never has been. They'd go to any lengths to get hold of Russian atomic weapons and the Red Navy code, and if they learn of Project Neptune I'll have to borrow a couple of Marine divisions to protect the operation."

"I may be able to help you," Adrienne said. "I know something about the way the Chinese work."

Porter was curt. "Thanks." He refrained from telling her that he had spent half of his career in the Far East. Anyone who failed to give Chinese intelligence its due was a cretin.

"Make a preliminary estimate of your needs tonight," Davidson said. "I'm flying back to Washington this evening —I really can't afford to spend time away from my desk— so you can call me early in the morning, before you go off to Richards' island. I've ordered a cutter for you. He'll tell you all you need to know, so I'll expect your final requisitions early next week." He stood and nodded.

They knew they were dismissed, and left the suite.

"I wonder if there's a restaurant in this place," Porter said.

"There is. Come along." Adrienne led him back down the stairs.

They selected an isolated dining room table overlooking the water, and none of the other patrons were within earshot.

24

Adrienne ordered a Scotch, a steak and a salad.

"Ordinarily I don't care for hard liquor," Porter said, "but I need a double bourbon. What kind of pizza are you serving?"

"You have a choice," the waitress told him. "Sausage, onion, mushroom, cheese—"

"Put them all in one. A big one." When the waitress left he saw Adrienne looking at him. "Pizza is one of my weaknesses. I always gorge on them when I'm in America."

When their drinks arrived she raised her glass. "To the biggest headache the Corporation has ever dreamed up."

"May we survive it," Porter said, and drank.

She was still studying him. "You're cursing the luck that gave you a blonde for a partner."

"I can think of people I'd prefer."

"Apparently you haven't heard of me."

"Should I?"

"I was the agent in charge of the Budapest caper."

He was impressed in spite of himself.

"I was also responsible for cornering the Kubalov ring in Manila."

Porter returned her stare. "You behaved like an amateur when you got rid of that masher in the bar."

"I had other things on my mind," Adrienne said, "so I was a bit careless."

"When you work with me," Porter said, his voice hard, "be good enough to exercise full precautions in all matters at all times."

"Am I expected to genuflect?"

"Only if you feel compelled to," he said, rolling a cigarette and offering it to her as a peace gesture.

She recognized his intent, so she accepted it, but her first puff made her cough.

Her discomfort improved his mood, and he grinned at her.

25

"I'm already making out a list of the help I'll need. My first choice is the Deacon."

"I want him," Adrienne said.

"I dare say. But I mentioned him first."

"Suppose we give the Deacon his choice," she said.

He sighed. She was damnably attractive and knew it, which gave her a double advantage. "You get the Deacon," he said, "but Blackman is definitely mine."

Adrienne accepted her victory with a smile as tight as his. Regardless of the mutual antipathies they might feel, their joint assignment was staggering, making it imperative that they work together.

THREE

The cutter, one of a fleet owned by the Corporation, sliced through the calm waters of Long Island Sound en route to Franklin Richards' private island. Adrienne Howard was stretched out on a deck chair near the fantail, her eyes closed and the straps of her sun dress lowered so she could work on her tan. But Porter remained in the shade, removing neither his jacket nor necktie, and made an occasional notation in a small, looseleaf notebook. He had already put in requisitions for some members of the team he was forming, but there were others he wanted, and he could afford to make no errors.

What little he had gleaned of his new assignment frightened him, and he was afraid it would become even more complicated when he learned additional details. That, of course, was all to the good. On his very first field job for British MI-6, when he had been new to the business, his Berlin section chief had taught him something he'd never forgotten: "Espionage and counterespionage aren't romantic or mysterious. The spy who does his homework always wins, except when he's nabbed by the spy-catcher who has made even more thorough preparations." There was no substitute for hard work.

Certainly the KGB knew that the United States had been eager to find the missing *Zolóto* submarine. Whether they realized it had actually been located was anybody's guess, and he disliked guessing games. Then it would be even more difficult, but essential, to discover whether Moscow was aware of Project Neptune. The job he had been doing in Hong Kong had been child's play.

To admit the truth, he missed the Eurasian girl. Adrienne Howard was more attractive, with an even better figure, but long experience had taught him never to become involved with any woman employed by the Corporation. Without exception they were dedicated creatures, and the more reliable they might be on a caper, the less spontaneously would they react in bed. You can't have everything, he reflected.

A heavily wooded island, its shores and heights completely covered by tall pines, stood directly ahead, a mile or two from the shore of Long Island, and the cutter reduced its speed. Porter noted that Adrienne needed no one to awaken her; she was endowed with the sixth sense of a veteran agent, and was ready to debark long before the cutter nosed through a narrow channel into an inner, hidden bay.

Suddenly the view was different. A three-story house of limestone stood on a hill at the inner end of the U-shaped harbor, and beyond it were scattered several smaller buildings. An all-white, ninety-foot yacht rode at anchor offshore, and between the sandy beach and the house were terraced flower gardens, with two swimming pools standing side by side behind them. The very rich, Porter thought, really knew how to live.

As the cutter eased up to a stone dock a group of security men strolled toward it. All were in shirtsleeves, and made no attempt to conceal the .45 automatics they wore in shoulder holsters. Trust someone like Franklin Richards to have his own private army.

28

Porter jumped onto the wharf, then handed up Adrienne. "We're expected," he told the man who appeared to be in charge.

The security officer studied a pair of photographs, then looked intently at the pair before he nodded. "Welcome," he said, and directed an assistant to take their baggage.

No one spoke as they followed him up the hill, and finally Porter broke the silence. "Why two swimming pools?"

"Mr. Richards likes salt water. Mrs. Richards prefers fresh."

A faint gleam in Adrienne's eyes indicated her amusement.

A stunning redhead was poised on a diving board, and as the visitors approached she did a double backflip, then swam to the shallow end and climbed out of the pool.

"How do you do, Miss Howard?" Marie Richards had only a trace of a French accent. "Mr. Porter, we're so happy you could come."

Her charm was considerable, and her nearness in a string bikini was disturbing. Porter was proud of his ability to remain unflustered, but this was one time when his poise almost deserted him.

"Join me for a swim after you've been shown to your rooms, why don't you?" she asked, treating them as social guests. "Frank will be along for an aperitif before lunch."

Porter followed a butler to a guest bedroom. "I'm afraid I didn't bring a bathing suit," he said.

"You'll find whatever you need in your dressing room, sir," the man said as he bowed himself out.

Porter searched through a pile of togs before he found a pair of trunks and a terrycloth robe that were his size, and after changing he dropped his Lilliput into the pocket of his robe. Not that he needed it on this closely guarded, private island, but there was a first time for everything, and he'd hate

29

to be embarrassed. Poor Bob Williams had lost his life in a Helsinki sauna because he had been unarmed.

Adrienne had already gone to the pool, and Porter remained in the shadows for a time, watching the two women before he joined them. He rarely read society and gossip columns, so he had been as unprepared for Marie Richards' charm as he was overwhelmed by her beauty. She was also a superb swimmer, traversing several lengths of the Olympic-sized pool underwater and seemingly not out of breath when she emerged.

He had to admit that Adrienne was the best-looking Corporation field operative he had ever encountered. The KGB frequently employed women agents, as did the French, but the Anglo-Saxons were more conservative, and British MI-5, like the Corporation, ordinarily used them only as lures. Adrienne, somewhat taller than their hostess, did not appear muscular, but she was an exceptionally powerful swimmer, and her crawl stroke sent her effortlessly up and down the pool.

At last Porter went to the water's edge and shed his robe, which he arranged pocket-side up. "I'm no competition for you mermaids," he said, and splashed as he jumped into the pool, then struggled slightly as he swam without grace.

Someone landed in the water beside him, vanished beneath the surface and headed toward the far end. Before Porter quite realized what was happening the newcomer and Marie Richards were playing a game of underwater tag, and they stayed below so long that his lungs ached.

Suddenly a tanned, dark-haired man, his boyish face belying his age, popped up beside him. "Frank Richards," he said, shaking hands. "We're going to see a great deal of each other. We're leaving for the West Coast in a few minutes, so we'll have lunch and talk during the flight." He was gone again, pursuing his wife under water.

30

It was difficult to believe that this playful figure was one of the wealthiest, most powerful men on earth, but Porter could see why he and his wife qualified as Beautiful People. He could only hope they weren't as frivolous as they seemed.

The fringe of trees concealed the landing strip, but it was more than long enough for the takeoff of the DC-9, which climbed rapidly as it headed west. The four passengers sat amidships in a handsomely furnished cabin that resembled a living room, and Adrienne joined her host and hostess in an apéritif.

Porter demurred, "Beer," he told the stewardess.

Franklin Richards wasted no time. "What do you know about undersea salvage?"

"Virtually nothing," Porter said.

"I'm guilty, too," Adrienne added.

"I'll spare you the early history of the diving bell, which was first mentioned by Aristotle and was used in a primitive form as early as the seventeenth century. We can also skip the gaseous embolism of the decompression sickness that attacks virtually all divers as they rise to the surface. Let's just say that John Scott Haldane, a British scientist, discovered that nitrogen bubbles form stoppages in the joints, lungs, spinal cord and brain. He worked out a set of tables that establish the speed at which a diver can resurface. These tables, modified, are used in every diving vessel today— excluding the submarine, where surface pressures are maintained. But they're even used in the bathyscaphe. You follow me so far?"

His guests nodded, and Porter rolled a cigarette.

"May I try one?" Marie Richards openly and unabashedly flirted with him.

He handed her one, then struck a match on the sole of his shoe.

31

"I like it!" she said. "It reminds me of French cigarettes."
Porter gave her a bag of tobacco and a packet of papers.
"You must show me how to make them," she said.

"Later." Her husband smiled indulgently. "A quick word
about the bathysphere, which President Theodore Roosevelt
first suggested to the zoologist William Beebe at the beginning of the present century. In its original form it was a steel
ball, attached to a cable, and oxygen was pumped into it. The
bathysphere was the direct ancestor of the modern bathyscaphe." He paused, then asked abruptly, "I assume you
know gasoline is lighter than water?"

Adrienne smiled. "I never thought about it one way or the
other, I'm afraid."

"Now that you mention it," Porter said, "petrol does float
on water."

"Precisely." Richards drew a rough sketch of a cigar-
shaped cabin, with a round container beneath it. "This bottom section is known as a float. For the simple reason that
it contains gasoline. The deeper a bathyscaphe submerges,
the stronger and more rapidly the gasoline inside this sphere
compresses. This provides the bathyscaphe with its own
power. To check the speed of descent or cause the bathyscaphe to ascend again, the pilot releases iron ballast held in
place by electromagnets. I'd like to stress that the bathyscaphe is capable of performing remarkable feats. It's a matter of public record that the *Trieste,* which was made by
Auguste Piccard and his son, Jacques, and was acquired by
the U.S. Navy, descended to a depth of thirty-five thousand
eight hundred feet in 1960, in the Pacific. In the so-called
Mariana Trench, to be exact."

Porter saw that Richards' face glowed, and decided he
looked even more boyish.

The conversation was suspended as the stewardess served
them a cold, jellied soup, followed by eggs benedict and a

bottle of chilled rosé wine.

"If you've grasped what I've told you so far," Richards said, "you'll have no problem understanding what we're doing at my Washington shipyard. Project Neptune consists of two parts. The mother ship and a float slightly larger than a football field. The ship is very large—forty-two thousand three hundred tons—because its equipment includes a very powerful electric generator. That generator will supply the power that will release tons of iron shot after the float reaches the bottom. It also will operate the cranes that will be used when the float approaches the surface and its own power wanes. The float, of course, will be powered by its own compressed gasoline." He sat back and smiled.

Porter would have preferred another beer, but sipped his wine. "You've left out one angle. Are you planning to send men to the bottom in a bathyscaphe? And how do they attach the sunken submarine to your float?"

"No bathyscaphe." Richards was enjoying himself. "And I know of no way that men could scoop up the submarine."

"That's what bothers me," Porter said. "It weighs more than six thousand tons!"

"That's the reason for the football-field float. The generator will supply the power for the electromagnets. The hull of the submarine, you must remember, is made of metal, and the pulling power of that metal is stronger than that of the iron shot we'll use as ballast. We've devised a set of delicate instruments—I'm proud to say I helped design them myself. The key to the operation will be the substitution of the submarine for the ballast. We'll use twelve thousand tons of shot when the float goes to the bottom. Gradually, as the magnets attach themselves to the submarine, we'll release ballast. Bit by bit. When the submarine has been trapped and made secure, the rest of the ballast will be released. The float should rise, with the submarine beneath it. At a depth of

33

about five hundred feet our underwater cranes will take hold and bring her the rest of the way."

"You make it sound simple," Adrienne said.

Franklin Richards' smile faded. "I have nightmares when I think of all the things that could go wrong. One of our problems is that we don't dare make any practice hoists. Anyone with a knowledge of submarines would know, seeing the equipment in action, that we could possibly raise the *Zolóto*. Which means we'll have to do it the first time. Without a single rehearsal."

"You're going on the expedition yourself?" Porter asked.

The financier reached for his wife's hand. "Marie and I wouldn't miss it for anything in the world."

They waited until coffee was served before they resumed the conversation.

"There's one minor matter that needs to be settled before we arrive," Richards said. "Our Washington house is located only a few miles from the yards, so the security there is much looser than it is on the island. And the yard itself is a relative sieve. We try to keep out dissidents, of course, but it isn't easy to guarantee the loyalty of more than fourteen thousand people. So we've arranged a cover for you. With the approval of your Mr. Davidson. I spoke to him this morning."

"Anything Davidson approves will be fine with us, I'm sure," Porter said in a dry voice.

"Because it'll have to be," Adrienne added.

"You'll pose as a British banker, Mr. Porter. A colleague of mine. Miss Howard will pose as your wife." Richards betrayed a trace of nervousness. "Mr. Davidson thought it was a splendid idea."

"Mr. Davidson would," Adrienne said. "I didn't know when I left my apartment that I'd be making this trip, so I didn't bring anything with me that will make me look like a banker's wife."

34

Marie was delighted to be of help. "I have dozens of things you can wear."

"And I'm sure, Mr. Porter," her husband added, "that I can take care of you, too."

Davidson, damn him, has already taken care of me, Porter thought. My mind is whirling with facts about compression and electromagnets and electric power. I'm going into a plant of fourteen thousand people, any of whom could be Russian or Chinese agents. And now I must waste time and energy putting up a domestic front with Adrienne Howard. Desk men never have the good sense to let field people do their own work in their own way.

It was small consolation to see that Adrienne shared his annoyance.

Woods of towering fir trees surrounded the house, remarkably similar to the Long Island property, that overlooked the Strait of Juan de Fuca. Franklin Richards explained that all seven of his homes around the world were virtually identical, giving him and Marie a feeling of permanence even when traveling. As nearly as Porter could judge, the large double bedroom to which he and Adrienne Howard were shown was furnished like the chamber in which he had changed clothes on Richards' island.

He retired to the dressing room to don one of the London-tailored suits and shirts that a butler brought him. A silk handkerchief in his breast pocket added a final touch, and he decided he actually resembled an off-duty English banker.

Adrienne was dressed in a tailored tweed suit that was an almost perfect fit, although the skirt was a trifle short, and when they descended the central staircase together they found their host and hostess waiting for them.

Richards took the wheel of a Rolls-Royce Silver Cloud sedan, and they set out for the shipyard. "We've been fortunate," he said. "Shipyards all over the world have been going bankrupt in recent years, but our business is better than ever."

"That couldn't be accidental," Porter said.

"It isn't." The financier looked like a child who had just eaten a large slice of chocolate cake. "We build our ships in sections, using reinforced aluminum and other lightweight metals, and then we fuse the sections to each other in a patented process. This system not only reduces the work force by about one third, but we can build a ship—anything from a ferry to a supertanker—in about half the time it takes under the old method."

"What he's too modest to tell you," Marie said, "is that he invented the fusion process himself."

"Oh, I enjoy tinkering in a lab," he said. "It's a form of relaxation, and I was lucky."

His "luck," Porter thought, was consistent, both as a businessman and as a scientist. His guise of gregarious playboy served him in good stead, concealing his genius and making people less gifted comfortable in his presence.

They followed a road on a cliff high above the Pacific, and in places patches of fog obscured the sea. Thick clouds rolled in from the northwest, and the air was twenty degrees cooler than it had been on Long Island; the weather was typical for this section of the country in late June.

After a drive of a quarter of an hour they turned a bend, and in the distance could see the superstructures of four ships rising above the scaffolding of drydocks. "The second from the right is the *Neptune,*" Richards said.

The fore section looked like a sleek passenger liner, with portholes on five or six decks, but it was the aft section that interested Porter. This portion resembled a container ship, the hull cutting off abruptly about twenty feet above water level and surmounted by two mammoth cranes, one on the

36

port side and the other starboard.

"The cranes," Richards said, "will be equipped with electromagnets, but they won't be installed until we're ready to sail. We're making the sensitive instruments and tools in a special lab the Navy built for me at the San Diego Navy Yard, where they can be kept under close watch more easily than they can here, and we'll fly them north at the last possible minute."

A high steel fence topped by barbed wire surrounded the shipyard compound, and as the car pulled to a halt at the gate Richards and Marie pinned on identification badges bearing their photographs. The proprietor of the plant signed in his guests, who were provided with special visitors' badges. Only then did the uniformed, armed guards open an inner gate.

"I like your security," Adrienne said.

"We do what we can, but it isn't perfect. Most of our workers have been with us for years, but a turnover is inevitable when you have fourteen thousand people on the payroll. Everyone is investigated before we hire him, but I doubt if we're as thorough as the Corporation."

They drove past the main administration headquarters, machine shops, warehouses and the research and development building, then approached the drydock where a delegation, warned by telephone from the gate, awaited them. The general manager was presented to the visitors, as was the plant security chief, Henry Kaspar, a burly, middle-aged man. A flicker of recognition appeared in his guarded eyes as he shook hands with Adrienne, then with Porter, but he made no comment and ostensibly accepted them as a couple from London.

Porter knew him well, and approved of Richards' choice. Kaspar was a retired Corporation man, a former head of the Trieste section, who had served previously in Naples and

37

Marseilles, so he knew ships and yards.

Kaspar fell in beside them as the general manager led the party on board the *Neptune,* and then an eager Franklin Richards took charge as guide.

Work on the passenger section of the ship and crew quarters was almost completed, and Porter was surprised to find the cabins spacious and comfortably furnished, those on the upper decks the equal in both quality and size of the accommodations found on most passenger liners. Members of the party who would take part in the expedition to the South China Sea would suffer no personal hardships.

There were four dining rooms, one for the officers, another for the crew and two for the passengers, the smaller of them obviously intended to shield the scientists and other experts who would try to raise the sunken Russian submarine. Porter counted three large lounges, all furnished with couches and easy chairs, and saw two bars. There was even a small gymnasium in the aft portion of the officers' deck.

Directly below the captain's quarters was the suite Richards had installed for his own use. It consisted of a living room, bedroom and dining room, and was even equipped with a small galley, making it virtually self-sufficient.

It was the rear portion of the ship that fascinated the visitors. The electric plant was five decks high, and the cranes towered at least 200 feet above the superstructure. Each was made with automatically operated extensions that would plunge 500 feet below the surface to take hold of an object being raised to the deck. One aft section was a huge cavity, located below the waterline and similar to the open space on board a container ship. Neither Porter nor Adrienne needed to be told that, if the mission proved successful, this area would be used to store the *Zolóto* after it was salvaged. A sliding bulkhead could be utilized to cover the top, so it would be impossible to see the precious cargo from the air.

"Where is the float?" Porter asked.

"In the deep freeze at the San Diego Navy Yard," Richards said. "We've made it in sections, and they'll be flown to us and assembled after we put to sea. We're taking no chances of anyone catching a premature glimpse of it."

"How many of the *Neptune*'s officers, men and passengers will know in advance about the float?" Porter wanted to know.

Richards made some mental calculations. "No more than twenty-five or thirty."

"Can you cut that down to a maximum of ten?"

Henry Kaspar smiled appreciatively, and Adrienne approved, too.

"If I must," Richards said, "but it won't be easy."

"From what I've seen and heard," Porter said, "nothing connected with Project Neptune is easy. Don't even tell the technicians who'll assemble the float the real reason they're being taken on the voyage. Make up some other reason that will satisfy them until the time comes."

"We'll want an advance list of all those who will be told about the float," Adrienne added. "We'll put them through the Corporation's investigative wringer, and we must ask that you keep even these people in the dark until they pass a top-secret security clearance."

Richards thought they were taking unnecessary precautions, but was forced to agree. "Okay, we'll do it your way."

"Listen to these two," Kaspar told him, "and you won't go wrong."

The inspection of the *Neptune* took most of the afternoon, and dusk was falling when the Richardses and their guests drove back to the mansion on the bluff. Porter remained in the living room with his host while the women went upstairs to change for dinner.

"We have another guest coming for dinner," Richards

39

said. "Captain Humphries, the master of the *Neptune*. Mr. Davidson thought it would serve everyone's purposes best if you met him here. Privately."

"Who is he?"

"He's commanded several of the Navy's largest salvage ships, so I hired him a couple of months ago, when I learned he was retiring after twenty-five years of Navy service."

"A phony retirement," Porter said.

"Well, yes." Richards was surprised. "How did you know?"

"I've spent more years than I care to count with the Corporation, and I know how the so-called minds of their desk officers function. Captain Humphries will be recalled to active duty—with no loss of seniority—as soon as this mission is ended."

"That's my understanding."

"You're making just one mistake, Mr. Richards. It's one thing to help the country and provide cover for the Corporation in this operation. But you're asking for trouble by playing an active part in it."

The financier shook his head. "That was my one condition when your director came to me. I can do a more efficient job directing the salvaging of the *Zolóto* than anyone else they could find. Besides, it will be more fun that just making money."

Porter could think of no reply.

Captain Charles Humphries was announced, and was identifiable at a glance as a new breed U.S. Navy officer. Trim and tall, with graying, short-cut hair, he was completely at ease in the presence of the financier and the senior security agent. He had attained higher degrees at civilian universities after attending the Naval Academy, he had traveled extensively, holding a number of posts as a naval attaché, and he could hold his own in any conversation. Even when Adrienne and Marie arrived, both dazzling in low-cut dinner gowns, he remained unflustered.

The weather had cleared, so they went out to the terrace for cocktails. "I own all the property you can see from here," Richards said, "except for that horn-shaped little peninsula jutting out into the strait. That's state land, used mainly for picnics and camping, and so it isn't available for me to buy. Unfortunately. Tourists who know we live here often train binoculars on us, but there's nothing we can do to stop them."

If tourists could spy on the house so could others, Porter realized, so the security of the place was less than perfect. He kept his thoughts to himself.

No one referred to the business at hand during a pleasant dinner, but after the meal was finished Porter and Adrienne took Captain Humphries off to the library for a chat. He filled them in without prompting.

"I've asked the Navy for the loan of eight officers and forty-one enlisted men," he said, handing them a list. "Divers, bathyscaphe people—including the commander of the vessel that found the *Zolóto*—salvage experts. I need all of them in addition to a regular crew, and I believe the Office of Naval Intelligence is double-checking them for the Corporation."

"If you don't mind," Adrienne said, "I'll make my own check, too."

"You don't want to borrow them openly," Porter told the captain. "The concentration of that many first-rate salvage people on the *Neptune* would hint that the ship intends to go out on a special mission. I suggest you bring them in singly, as close to sailing time as you can. They'll be traveling here by commercial airlines and staying at hotels, so they

41

should be provided with false identities, and as an extra precaution they should use their assumed names until they're well out to sea."

"I'll attend to it," Adrienne said, showing a reluctant admiration for his thoroughness.

"Where do you intend to recruit your sailing crew, Captain?"

"I've had orders to go through the usual merchant marine hiring halls," Humphries said. "I've been told that to do it in any other way would arouse suspicions. The Corporation and the FBI will provide me with lists of merchant marine officers and men who have security clearance, so I'll take all of them from that group."

"I'll sit in on your hiring sessions with you," Adrienne said. "You can introduce me as an assistant personnel director of Richards Shipping. That way I can keep the whole procedure under close watch."

"You people sure don't take any risks," the captain said. Porter smiled.

"Are you expecting problems?"

"If we look hard enough ahead of time," Porter said, "we usually avoid them. This mission is the biggest intelligence enterprise ever attempted, anywhere, so we're not only closing doors, we're plugging keyholes."

They rejoined Marie and Richards for liqueurs and coffee, and the conversation again became general. Porter discovered that his host shared his enthusiasm for fishing, so they discussed trout lures for a time.

"Are you sailing with us on the *Neptune?*" Richards asked.

Porter shrugged. "That depends on more factors than I'm capable of analyzing at present."

"If you come, we can try our hand at deep-sea fishing from the float. It will be a long voyage across the Pacific."

42

It was too much for Porter to hope that he would have nothing better to do than fish.

When Captain Humphries departed, the Richardses went off to bed, so good manners forced Porter and Adrienne to retire, too. He changed into pajamas and a robe in the little dressing room, and when he returned to the bedchamber she was attired in a nightgown and semitransparent negligee that made her urgently desirable.

The circumstances permitted only one approach. "Will you go to bed with me?"

"No," she said.

Her refusal, combined with her proximity, made him want her all the more. "I could play rough."

"I have a karate black belt," Adrienne said. "What's your rating?"

"The same," he said and smiled. "Pointless to wear ourselves out in violent physical exercise that leads nowhere."

"All this nonsense because Brian Davidson wants us to put up a front for the Richardses' servants!" She sighed and sat on one of the twin beds. "If you were a gentleman you'd sleep in the dressing room."

"I'm not. Besides, the little chaise in there is too short for me." He removed his robe and climbed into the other bed. "It might be big enough for you."

"No, thanks. I've slept in so many strange places that I prefer a real bed whenever I have the chance to use one." Adrienne snapped off the lights. "Good night."

"Good night," Porter said, and tried to put her out of his mind, but it was difficult when he knew he could touch her if he extended an arm. She wasn't the coy type, so he doubted that she was playing hard to get, and her appearance, her sophistication and her status as a Corporation senior agent told him she had been around.

He could only conclude that he didn't appeal to her, which

43

was difficult to accept, particularly as he wasn't averse to combining pleasure with business. Certainly no one who knew him would believe they had slept apart, but he was reluctant to create a scene under Franklin Richards' roof.

Once Porter recognized Adrienne's unavailability he had no difficulty in falling asleep. His years in the field had taught him to empty his mind when he could, to rest whenever possible, and he slept soundly until a bright sun streaming through the blinds awakened him.

Adrienne was still asleep in the other bed, but he resisted the temptation to join her and take her by surprise. When he bedded her she would be wide awake—and willing.

He shaved, but a glance at his watch told him it would be another three quarters of an hour before coffee would be sent to the room, so he wandered out onto a balcony adjoining the bedroom to smoke. The sun sparkled in a clear sky, and the tourists' camping ground was partly visible through the fir trees on the horn-shaped peninsula. The air had the fresh scent of the woods, and as Porter inhaled deeply he told himself this was his favorite part of America. If he survived long enough to retire and decided to settle in the States, this was where he wanted to live.

Adrienne, clad in nightgown and negligee, joined him on the balcony. "Good morning," she said. "A day like this always makes me hate our kind of work."

"Don't waste your energy hating it. You'll need all your energy for this assignment." By gazing off at the peninsula instead of looking at her he was less conscious of her undress. "I don't care in the least for our situation. Thousands of people here have been working on the *Neptune,* Lord knows how many others in San Diego have been making the float and the other special equipment, and the sailing crew will be recruited from the merchant marine. Only a miracle will

44

prevent information leaks, in spite of all the precautions that have been taken."

"I'm sure you're right," she said, "but I find it hard to concentrate when all I want to do is spend the day sailing."

"There are only certain kinds of physical exertion I enjoy," he said, and catching a glimpse of motion on the peninsula, it occurred to him that people had been spending the night there. Still not looking at Adrienne, he offered to roll her a cigarette.

"Save them for Marie," she said, and lighted one of her own. "What do you think of her?"

"She reeks of charm. Tremendous sex appeal. A great hostess. She puts up a flirty-flirty front, but she's more intelligent than she appears."

"Reliable?"

"If she isn't," Porter said, "we're in for it. Her husband is crazy about her, and he's the one running this show, not the Corporation. He—"

Porter broke off abruptly as a bright light flashed on the horn-shaped peninsula.

An instant later something struck the wall above their heads, and chips of stone dropped on them.

Without hesitation Porter threw Adrienne to the floor of the balcony, falling on top of her and covering her body with his. In the same motion he drew his Magnum from the pocket of his robe, but the peninsula could be reached only with a high-powered rifle, so he didn't fire.

Adrienne remained calm even though his weight was suffocating her. "Bullet?"

"Definitely. I saw the flash. A silencer-equipped rifle." He peered hard at the end of the peninsula, but only the fringes at the tops of the firs were in motion in the wind.

45

"If you'd be good enough to move," she said, "I can look, too."

"I've been protecting you," he said, raising himself so she could crawl out from beneath him.

"Your gallantry leaves me breathless." She stayed low, too, and studied the point with him. "Shouldn't we sound the alarm?"

"I suggest you do that very thing, once we're reasonably certain it's safe to stand. But I'll bet a quid to a penny that our assassin will be gone long before the police or Franklin Richards' security people can seal off that property."

"You're probably right," she conceded.

"It's one of my more maddening traits." He took a deep breath. "Ready, steady, go!" In one quick bound he reached his feet.

The silence was all-encompassing.

"All right now, my love. You'll be safe." He hauled Adrienne to her feet.

While she hurried to the telephone he took a small knife of manganese steel from his valise and, returning to the balcony, chipped expertly at the hole. In a short time he recovered the bullet, which he wrapped in a tissue. "We'll see what our own ballistics lads think of this," he said. "I didn't want the locals to botch things."

The head of the private security detail and Franklin Richards himself were at the door.

Wasting no words, Porter told them what had happened, showed them the bullet hole and pointed to the spot where he had seen the flash.

They hurried away.

He closed the bedroom door after them, and his smile was wry. "That will keep them busy. As for us, now that we've awakened the household, I suggest we get dressed for breakfast."

46

Adrienne hesitated as she faced him, holding her low-cut negligee closed with one hand. "I was sharper than I intended to be. Ordinarily I'm not rude when someone saves my life."

"Think nothing of it," he said. "It just goes to prove that not even a lifetime spent in this rotten trade can ruin a good man's instincts."

She extended her hand.

Instead of grasping it he took her in his arms.

To his surprise she returned his kiss with a warmth and vigor that matched his.

Porter released her. "I offer you first use of the tub. If you don't accept, and quickly, we shall bathe together, and then we'll be here until lunch. Unfortunately, there's no time for sport this morning." He moved to the telephone.

Adrienne started toward the bathroom, then paused. "What's on the agenda?"

"You'll carry on at the shipyard as though nothing untoward has happened. Stay away from balconies, of course, and ride in closed cars."

"What will you be doing?"

"I'm ordering an aircraft that will take me to Washington as quickly as one of mine host's helicopters can deposit me at the Seattle-Tacoma airport."

He sounded so cheerful that Adrienne was puzzled. "I've never before met anyone who seemed to be enjoy being a target for an assassin."

Porter laughed aloud for the first time since they had met. "We're making progress, my love, and much sooner than I had hoped."

"We are?"

"You and I were given an impossible assignment. We were ordered to search for a pig in a poke. But we didn't know there was any pig, much less that a poke existed. Now a good friend—Russian or Chinese, or perhaps a domestic nut—has given us a genuine clue. I've lolled about long enough in the manor houses of the rich, and now I'm going to work!"

FOUR

When Brian Davidson was disturbed he polished his horn-rimmed glasses endlessly.

Porter paid no attention as he paced the length of his superior's office, and he ignored the view of the Washington Monument from the double windows, too. "The situation is basic," he said. "The killer missed my head by eighteen to twenty-four inches, which is unusual in a trained killer. Ballistics has established that he used a seven point six-two rifle. Certain to reach its target in the right hands. Except—and heed this, Davidson—he used a silencer, which requires a compensation of eighteen to twenty-four inches in one's aim. Always aim lower when using a silencer. I'll bet you didn't know that. Obviously my murderer didn't."

"I insist that the Corporation conduct its investigation of this matter in its own way." Davidson was indignant.

"You may insist until the Thames freezes in July," Porter said. "Aside from being personally aggrieved and seeking vengeance in my own way, I see an opportunity to learn how much may be known on the outside about Project Neptune. Give Adrienne Howard all the help she wants on the West Coast. She has her hands full there. Now, then. Show me a list of the known Chinese agents in this country."

"We have none." Davidson's voice was bleak.

"Chinese informers?"

"None."

"I am dazzled by the efficiency of the Corporation. Very well—Russian agents."

"This is highly irregular."

"So is my assignment, not to mention the attempt to kill me when I was Franklin Richards' house guest."

Davidson sighed, opened a small safe and removed a single sheet of paper.

Porter snatched it from him, and scanned a list of names. "Ah! Georgi Verschek!"

"We have reason to believe he's currently the head of clandestine operations in North America. He surfaced here months ago, and we keep him under constant surveillance."

Porter's eyes became dreamy. "Georgi and I are old friends. Pick him up for me so he and I can have a good old reunion."

Davidson was outraged. "Moscow will recall him, and we'll have the devil's own time identifying and locating his replacement."

"I suggest you start looking for my replacement on Project Neptune. In my letter of resignation, copies of which will be sent to all Council members, I shall underline your refusal to cooperate."

His superior's voice rose an octave. "This will require the Director's personal approval!"

"Get it. If you're afraid, I'll happily see him myself. One way or another, I want Verschek. Give him the distinguished prisoner treatment. No necktie, belt or razor. Lights in his cell day and night. The finest Corporation slop for his meals. No physical torture, however. Remember that. It just stiffens Georgi's backbone. Make him malleable for two or three days, and then I'll have my little tête-à-tête with him."

50

Porter sat at the bare table in the whitewashed basement room of the Virginia safe house. Heavy bars covered the window, which was only a few inches above ground level, and a naked light bulb burned in a ceiling socket. He rolled and lighted a cigarette, then looked up in simulated surprise as a tall, middle-aged prisoner was shoved into the room, the door closing behind him.

"Georgi! How very nice to see you again!"

Verschek sank wearily into the room's only other chair. "I might have guessed it would be you."

"Our last meeting was in Lubyanka Prison. Remember?" Porter's smile was solicitous.

"You were treated with consideration at Lubyanka."

"The service reminded me of Claridge's," Porter said. "I hope we've returned the compliment."

The prisoner stiffened. "I have no complaints."

Porter offered him tobacco and cigarette paper. "I wonder if you'd be interested in a deal, Georgi."

"These things are always possible."

"You'll get a free ride to Moscow. We won't blow your cover, so you can tell the KGB you were picked up in a minor case that makes your transfer necessary, but that we never found out you came over here to run clandestine operations. No salt mines for you, Georgi. Not even a demotion."

Verschek's expression was wary. "When Porter becomes Father Christmas and offers me gifts, I believe he wants something in return."

"Very shrewd of you. A couple of days ago somebody took a pot shot at me with a seven point six-two rifle. A Russian rifle, Georgi. Tell me who. And why. And you'll soon be on your way home."

The prisoner sighed.

"I'd hate to cancel your airline reservation. With a mem-

51

ory as poor as mine, you might stay here for years before somebody remembers to turn you loose."

"All right," Verschek said. "We make the deal. In Hong Kong you picked up the trail of Nancy Wing and became friendly with her. You did not know this, but she was one of ours. Andropov was afraid she talked too much, so he ordered her killed. You, too. Then both of you disappeared."

So the Eurasian girl had vanished. The Corporation would want to find her.

"The word went out," Verschek said. "For a few days no one knew where to find you. Suddenly you appeared at the shipbuilding plant of the millionaire Richards."

It could do no harm to offer a specious explanation. "That's what happens when you try to help a friend," Porter said. "You played hide-and-seek with our man Kaspar in Marseilles, as I recall. Well, he's out of the game now. In charge of security at the shipyard, and asked me to check out his system for him."

"You were seen at the yard," the prisoner said. "Do you remember Ravovsky?"

Porter thought for a time. "Young fellow. American-born. Not too bright. Changed his name to Rasmussen."

"That's the one."

Porter leaned back in his chair, yawned and gazed up at the ceiling. "I'm curious, Georgi. How did Ravovsky-Rasmussen happen to see me there?"

"A lucky accident, and he tried to take advantage of it. He has a cover job working at the plant. As a security guard."

The Director's office resembled a drawing room. There were no documents on the table he used as a desk, his private wall safe was concealed behind a portrait of the President of the United States, and even his telephones were hidden in a cabinet of inlaid teakwood. He looked like the amiable Midwestern members of Congress who were his close friends and supporters; and only his subordinates, men who had worked in the Corporation for enough years to be admitted to his august presence, were familiar with the coldly incisive side of his nature.

"The only conclusion we can draw is negative," he said. "We don't know whether the Russians are wise to Project Neptune."

"That's right, sir," Porter said. "I can accept Verschek's story that they put out the contract on me because of the Nancy Wing case. But there's no way of knowing whether it was accidental that I was seen at the Richards yard. I didn't mention Adrienne Howard and neither did Verschek, so we don't know whether she was recognized, too."

Brian Davidson, the third person present, cleared his throat preparatory to speaking, then changed his mind and subsided.

"The crux of the matter," the Director said, "is the presence of Rasmussen, a Soviet agent, on the Richards payroll as a security guard. Shocking. And although it may be coincidental, we can't afford to regard it as such. We must proceed on the assumption that the Russians know why we're building the *Neptune.*"

"Sir," Davidson said, "Verschek hasn't been released yet. We may find out all we want to know if we squeeze him."

"No," Porter said. "You don't reach his level in the KGB unless you can keep your mouth shut under torture. He'll die before telling us anything else. Besides, I made a bargain with him."

Davidson was annoyed. "Surely you don't expect us to abide by your deal."

Desk men rarely understood some of the more refined aspects of the trade. "I gave my word," Porter said, "and I expect it to be kept."

"Verschek will be returned to Moscow as soon as we settle the immediate problems at the Richards shipyard," the Director said. "I'll want a satisfactory explanation from Kaspar. How did a Russian agent land on his payroll?"

"I suggest we let Adrienne Howard handle that problem. Privately. Without notifying Franklin Richards," Porter said.

The Director glared at him. "I trust you aren't questioning the patriotism and integrity of Frank Richards! He's providing the Corporation with cover for Project Neptune. He's building the ship, the float and a great deal of the special equipment and instrumentation, which he helped design. And he intends to play a major role in the recovery of the *Zolóto*. No country could ask more of any citizen, Mr. Porter!"

"Granted." Porter was unflinching. "But are we as sure where Marie Richards stands?"

"You have a point," the Director said, backing down. "We've made a routine check on her, but I'm now ordering a discreet investigation in depth."

"Then my request makes sense," Porter said. "For the present, anyway, what Richards doesn't know may not hurt him. Let's tidy up our own house first."

"Fair enough," the Director said. "That leaves the Rasmussen problem."

Porter smiled. "He's mine."

Davidson was perturbed. "We should interrogate him."

"He's a hit man," Porter said. "On the bottom rung of the ladder. Nobody tells him anything, and nobody will miss him."

Adrienne spent the morning at the shipyard, still posing as a friend of the proprietor who had developed an interest in the *Neptune*. She was driven to the Richards mansion at

54

noon, and had just joined her host and hostess for a prelunch cocktail when she was summoned to the telephone.

"Hello, my love," Porter said. "Don't mention my name. Borrow a car—don't let anyone drive you—and meet me at the Palisades Motel, about fifteen miles down the main road. As fast as you can get here."

She followed the instructions without questioning them, and less than a half-hour later she pulled into the motel parking lot.

Porter was watching the entrance from the vantage point of a bar stool and, leaving his beer untouched, showed no sign of recognition as he walked to a room at the end of the corridor.

Adrienne remained a dozen paces behind him, and opened the unlocked door.

He bolted it behind her, and without preamble brought her up to date.

"Do you think Kaspar is a double agent?" she asked.

He shook his head. "The Director says he's okay. But private industry is sloppy when it hires people, so it couldn't have been too difficult for Rasmussen."

"There may be others, too!"

"I'm afraid you have a bit of a problem," Porter said. "So have I."

"I'll go straight to the yard for a chat with Kaspar. Obviously I'll have to bring in some of my own people and clean house. Quickly."

He nodded. "Richards is to know nothing until we get a green light on his wife."

"I understand. When will you return to the mansion, Porter?"

"I intend to remain incognito until I attend to a little unfinished business. Care to do me a favor?" The question was rhetorical, and he took a small photograph from his wallet. "Rasmussen may be using another name here. Get me a profile from Kaspar's files. Privately. And make certain that Kaspar says and does nothing that will alarm our friend prematurely."

She took the photograph and looked at him, her gaze steady. "Will you want help?"

"I feel no crying need for assistance," he said, "but I'm always delighted by the companionship of a lovely lady."

"Don't forget," she said, "that the bullet could have hit me."

"You're invited," Porter said. "I assume you're no stranger to these little celebrations."

Her smile was tight.

"Come straight back here after you've seen Kaspar, and make very sure you're not under surveillance."

"I should alert my team."

"I took the liberty of getting in touch with them on your behalf before I left Corporation headquarters. The Deacon will check in today, and the others will be on tap by morning, at the latest. Some of my people will be drifting in, too, so we could have ourselves a convention."

"You're all right, Porter," Adrienne said. "I haven't known many who live up to their reputations."

"We aim to please." His smile was fleeting. "One minor matter. What make of car did you borrow from Richards?"

"Cadillac. Eldorado convertible."

"Too flashy, and leather is sometimes hard to clean. The motel has a car rental desk, so I'll attend to the details. Now, before you go to the yard, you may want to call Franklin and Marie. Tell them you'll be busy the rest of the day, and drop a hint that you may bring me back with you this evening. To be on the safe side, tell them it may be rather late."

Adrienne attended to her call, then hurried off, and Porter waited for a time before he returned to the bar, ordered another beer and then sauntered into the small dining room for lunch. A sample case rested on the floor beside him, and he looked like a salesman.

That afternoon other Corporation employees began to arrive, one by one, and he conferred with each of them in his room. Most had been assigned to Adrienne's unit, so they waited until she returned to report to her, and she outlined their new duties. Two would join the shipyard security staff, one would work in the office and three others would become members of the yard labor force.

When Porter learned she had been too busy for lunch he brought her a sandwich from the motel dining room.

Not until their subordinates had gone did she tell him, "Kaspar was very upset. It will take months before he recovers."

"He'll cooperate, straight down the line?"

"Oh, yes. He wanted to confess all to Franklin Richards, of course, but I twisted his arm." She reached into her shoulder bag for a sheet of paper in her own handwriting. "Here's the Rasmussen data. That's the name he's using, by the way."

Porter studied the information in silence, then glanced at his watch. "Very neat timing. We'll be on our way after you finish your sandwich."

"I'm glad it will soon be night," Adrienne said. "Capers are so much cozier in the dark."

Port Angeles, Washington, was an unpretentious town, its summer population swollen by itinerant fishermen, longshoremen and lumbermen. Most of them lived in quiet rooming houses of weather-beaten wood on the edge of town, and because the atmosphere was conservative the local authorities led serene lives. The part-time workers saved their money and went to Seattle when they wanted to raise hell.

A single street light burned at the end of the block, and the few pedestrians paid scant attention to the couple locked in an embrace in the front seat of the modest, three-year-old sedan. A scarf covered the woman's blonde hair, her face was hidden by the man's bulk, and occasional passersby scarcely noticed the pair. They appeared to be engaged in nonstop necking, and anyone watching them might have guessed they were asleep.

When a dilapidated car turned onto the street behind them and slowed preparatory to a stop, however, they stirred.

"We're in business," Porter said, watching the other vehicle in the rear-view mirror.

Adrienne drew a snub-nosed .32 from her shoulder bag.

The other car halted, the lights were extinguished, and a husky young man with blond hair emerged. Still dressed in the uniform of a Richards Shipyard security guard, he took his time as he started past the other car en route to his rooming house.

Adrienne's pistol jabbed him in the small of the back, and at the same instant Porter approached him from the front.

"Palms up," Adrienne said. "All the way."

The young man obediently raised his hands over his head.

Porter frisked him with brisk efficiency. "If it isn't Rasmussen," he said. "The very chap we want to see. Come along, if you have nothing better to do."

Adrienne ordered him to place his hands behind his back before he entered their car, then snapped a pair of handcuffs on him. Porter climbed behind the wheel, Rasmussen was placed between the couple, and with the muzzle of Adrienne's gun pressed into his side, they drove off.

For at least a quarter of an hour no one spoke, and the silence made Rasmussen apprehensive. "Where are you taking me?"

"We'll ask the questions," Adrienne said.

Again a silence descended.

After a drive of almost forty-five minutes they turned onto the road that led to the state park on the horn-shaped peninsula that jutted into the Strait of Juan de Fuca.

Porter raised and lowered his headlights three times in rapid succession.

Flashlights that snapped on and off at either side of the road told him that the Deacon and Blackman were on duty, ready to turn away stray tourists who might wander into the area.

Porter drove to the end of the road.

"Let's stretch our legs, shall we?" Adrienne kept the prisoner covered as he climbed out of the car.

Porter led the way up a fir-lined path, and did not halt until he came to a cliff that overlooked the Strait. He wandered close to the edge and peered down at the sea, hundreds of feet below, that pounded on the rocks at the base of the precipice. "Dear me," he murmured, "no place for someone with vertigo."

"I'm told," Adrienne said, "that when weather conditions are right one can see Vancouver Island without difficulty."

"If you'll look inland, to your left there, through the trees," Porter said, "there's a splendid view of a gray limestone mansion. There's a slight fog this evening, but you can still make out the balconies on the second- and third-floor bedrooms."

Beads of sweat rolled down Rasmussen's face. "I had to do it," he said. "You know that. A guy like me has to follow orders."

Porter's tone remained conversational. "Whose orders?"

"My boss works out of Tacoma. His name is Eddie, and he lives—"

"Never mind," Porter said. "Eddie was picked up today, and he just follows orders, too. I don't suppose you've had the honor of making the acquaintance of Comrade Verschek?"

"Never heard of him," Rasmussen said.

"A pity. He knows you. But these Communist aristocrats are frightful snobs. Never mix with the hoi-polloi."

"I got nothing personal against you, Mr. Porter. You ought to know that. I'm just—"

Adrienne's pistol jabbed him in the ribs with such force that he gasped.

"Manners, manners," she said.

"I don't hate you, either," Porter said, "although I happen to loathe the system of government you represent. My feelings toward you might become positively benevolent if you'll tell me something I'm eager to know. Why have you been working in the Richards security department?"

Rasmussen seemed puzzled by the question. "We got to have jobs. Someplace in our assigned territory. Guys like me don't get paid all that much by the U.S.S.R. unless we do a special job, so we have to support ourselves."

"Why Richards?"

"Hell, Mr. Porter, they're the biggest outfit in the area. I applied last summer when they put on a big hiring campaign. I never been picked up by the police, so I got a clean record, and seeing I know how to handle firearms pretty good they put me in security."

"What were your duties?"

"Mostly keeping people out of restricted areas."

"And what's in those areas?"

"The same as there is every place else in the yards. Ships being built."

"Like the *Neptune?*"

"That's one of them."

"What do you know about the *Neptune?*"

"Me? I never even been near that ship. You got to have

60

a special pass for that. Don't take my word for it, Mr. Porter. Anybody at plant security will tell you."

As nearly as Porter could ascertain, Rasmussen was not lying. His story jibed with Kaspar's insistent claim that guards on his level did not have access to the *Neptune.* It was supremely ironic, if he was telling the truth, that a gorilla on the KGB payroll had been working, without his knowledge, within a stone's throw of an ultrasecret project. Porter was inclined to accept the man's account for the simple reason that he lacked the intelligence to pass along data of any significance concerning the ship.

But he had to try again. "You still haven't answered my question. What do you know about the *Neptune?*"

"Nothing!" Rasmussen was contemptuous. "I don't give a good goddam about any ship in the yards. All I know is Richards makes a fortune because he exploits the workers. He could pay us double what we get, and it still wouldn't be enough."

"I wonder if his memory needs jogging," Adrienne said.

"Perhaps." Porter nodded.

She reached for the young man's wrist and pressed a nerve.

Rasmussen's scream of pain echoed through the woods.

She pressed again, her face wooden.

He dropped to his knees, writhing in agony. "Cut it out! I'll tell you anything I know, but I can't make up stuff!"

"What other KGB people work at the Richards yards?" Porter asked.

"Maybe there's a thousand and maybe there's none. How the hell would I know?"

Adrienne approached him again.

Rasmussen became panicky. "Honest, lady. The way we work, I don't know anybody except Eddie. My boss. Unless he sends me special orders I meet him once a month, tell him what's going on in my territory and collect my pay."

Adrienne hovered behind him, her fingers close to his wrist. "Just what has been happening in your territory lately?"

"For three months I didn't get any orders at all, not one." Rasmussen was panting. "Not until a general alert went out to the whole network, telling us to kill Mr. Porter if we saw him."

"How did you know me?" Porter demanded.

"When Eddie called me to Seattle he showed me a couple of your pictures, and I studied them good."

Porter sighed. "I fear we're accomplishing nothing, my love. The KGB issues instructions to its peasants but gives them no information of substance."

"That's been my experience with them, too," Adrienne said. "The people at the bottom are acquainted only with their immediate superiors."

"That's so, lady!" Rasmussen, still on his knees, twisted around to keep an eye on the woman who hovered near him.

"I regret," Porter said, "that you can make no contribution to the land of your birth."

The young man became surly. "In another three years they would have made me a Soviet citizen. They promised."

"It was Carlyle, writing in *The French Revolution,* I believe, who said, 'O poor mortals, how ye make this earth bitter for each other.' I don't suppose you're familiar with Carlyle."

"No, Mr. Porter."

"A pity. Stand up, Rasmussen."

The young man struggled to his feet.

"Your education has been neglected," Porter said. "I doubt if you realize that fair play is an Anglo-Saxon concept. A practice in which only the chivalrous indulge. The British, the Americans, the Canadians, the Australians, the New

62

Zealanders. Do you know what I'm talking about, Rasmussen?"

"Sort of."

"There's no time like the present to improve your education." Porter removed his jacket, folded it with care and laid it on the ground, then took his Magnum from its holster and handed it to Adrienne, who looked at him in astonishment.

Rasmussen was bewildered.

"Like you," Porter said, "I am now unarmed. In a moment you'll have an opportunity to meet me in hand-to-hand combat. Do me in, and Moscow will give you your just rewards. Capitalist gold, Soviet citizenship and whatever else your heart desires."

"You're mad, Porter!" Adrienne said.

"What about her?" the young man asked. "She's got guns."

"I presume her grief over my passing would be so great it would spoil her aim. But you'd have to arrange your escape in your own way. Are you game?"

"Hell yes!" Rasmussen's grin bared his teeth.

"You can't do this," Adrienne said.

"Oh ye of little faith, remove his handcuffs. That's an order," Porter said.

She unlocked the cuffs and pulled them off with one hand while continuing to hold her .32 at the ready in the other. Then, so she couldn't be seized and used as a shield, she retreated rapidly to the edge of the clearing.

As soon as Rasmussen realized his bonds had been removed he raced across the open space and threw himself at the older, slighter man.

Porter sidestepped, and his antagonist brushed past him. "Easy does it."

Rasmussen whirled, came at him again and aimed a vicious kick at his groin.

"Fair play must be instinctive," Porter said. "I regret it can't be taught." Moving with great care he walked backward, step by step inching closer to the edge of the cliff.

A wild gleam appeared in Rasmussen's pale eyes as he lunged.

They were scant feet from the precipice as they grappled and swayed, and Adrienne caught her breath. If they lost their footing one or both could tumble from the ledge.

Porter's physical strength was no match for that of his opponent, and he had no intention of being overwhelmed. Holding the younger man at bay with his left hand he reached around Rasmussen with his right and, with a blow that traveled mere inches, struck the back of his neck smartly.

Rasmussen dropped to the ground, his head drooping at a grotesque angle. It was obvious that he had died instantly of a broken neck.

Porter rolled him over the edge of the cliff and watched as the body dropped to the rocks far below.

Adrienne was shaken as she came forward. "That was the most stupid—"

"You lack imagination, my love." Porter straightened his necktie, donned his jacket and took his Magnum from her. "In a short time one of my people will arrive with Rasmussen's car, which will be parked where ours now stands. In it will be a partly consumed sandwich and a half-can of beer. When the police find him in the morning they'll come up here. The verdict? Poor Rasmussen came to the park for a solitary picnic, lost his footing and fell. A bullet in the head would have been messy, and I dislike involving local authorities when we'll be hanging about the neighborhood for a time."

"I see your point," she said, walking beside him to their

waiting car. "All the same, it was an insane gesture. Suppose he—"

Porter chuckled, interrupting her. "For the sake of argument," he said, "I'm willing to concede I may have been showing off for your benefit. An adolescent trait I can't seem to overcome when I'm trying to impress a lovely lady."

The comment silenced her, and she realized it had been intended for that purpose.

"We'll turn in this rented machine, I'll pay my motel bill and we'll go on together to the Richards house, where I'm sure the charming Marie and the hospitable Franklin will offer us a late supper." Blinking his lights again as a signal when they left the park, he picked up speed on the highway.

"Are you always in this good a mood after an execution?" Adrienne asked.

"Hardly ever. But I've seldom been this fortunate. I haven't forgotten that in the eyes of the Richardses' household staff—if not of the Almighty—you and I are man and wife. And fair play, as I had cause to observe a short time ago, is a trait that can't be taught."

FIVE

The women went off to bed, and Porter stayed behind for a word with Franklin Richards. "Never mind the details," he said, "but the KGB is onto something. We don't know for certain whether they've figured out your connection, or have learned the purpose of the *Neptune*. So we're battening down the hatches."

"Meaning?"

"Adrienne and I have called in some of the Corporation's most experienced field people. Kaspar will be a front man, but we've taken charge of security on every level."

Richards bristled. "I would have appreciated advance notice so I could go through the motions of approving what's done at my yard."

"We didn't see it that way. I've been in Washington since I've last seen you, and the Director has given me supervision of all security.I've also been given carte blanche to handle matters as I see fit, so it will be my neck if anything goes wrong."

"Am I permitted to know the arrangements you're making?" There was a hint of sarcasm in the wealthy entrepreneur's tone.

Porter shrugged. "I don't agree with some members of the

Corporation, who believe in secrecy for its own sake. But the waters are a bit choppy, and for your own protection it won't pay to be too curious."

"If I were squeamish I'd have no empire."

"Suppose I tell you that one man has died within the past couple of hours, and I suspect that's only the beginning," Porter said with a sigh. "I don't tell you how to mine coal, or build real estate centers, or slap supertankers together. Let me run my business in my own way. With all due respect, Mr. Richards, you may think you're tough, but the stakes in this caper are higher than any even you have ever known. No holds are barred, and there are no rules."

"As a matter of principle," Richards said, "I've never trusted anyone."

"I'm not asking you to trust me. Just don't try to interfere. Your security operation is efficient according to the standards of industry, but your people are over their heads. That's why we've moved in." He refrained from adding that agents had been assigned to maintain a round-the-clock watch on both Richards and his wife to prevent their kidnapping or murder. The task would be simplified if the headstrong billionaire was kept in the dark.

"You give me no choice," Richards said.

"Right, sir," Porter said, and smiled. "Your job is hauling up that submarine and turning it over to government experts. Mine is making it possible for you to do it. Which reminds me, I'd like to go to San Diego tomorrow to see your football-field float."

The industrialist brightened. "Good. I'll fly you down myself. How many will be in your party?"

"You and I will be all we'll need," Porter said. "The float, even more than the *Neptune,* is the key to your success or failure, so I want to see for myself what I'm protecting. I work on the theory that what Adrienne and the others don't know, they can't be forced to describe if they fall into hostile hands."

They finished their drinks, and Richards looked at him with reluctant admiration. "What happens if you fall into trouble and they pump you for information?"

Porter's smile was bleak. "They've tried," he said, and walked with his host to the second-floor landing, where they parted.

The door of the suite was unlocked, and Adrienne stood on the balcony, sipping a drink and staring out toward the sea, which was shrouded in fog. She was wearing a thin negligee with a low-cut neckline, and Porter saw she was shivering.

"Either you enjoy looking at scenery you can't see," he said, "or you're trying hard to catch pneumonia."

She came into the bedroom, closing the balcony doors behind her and lighting a cigarette. "I was waiting for you," she said, "and I made the mistake—fatal in our profession —of wondering about the value of human life."

Her hair was tousled, her eye makeup looked smudged, and Porter wondered if she had been weeping. Perhaps the execution had upset her more than he had realized.

She seemed to read his mind, and laughed. "What happened tonight doesn't bother me. I was thinking about you. And me. Mostly about myself."

"What about us?"

"I'm ready to deliver," she said, and began to open a long row of tiny buttons.

Porter had always claimed he preferred sex without sentiment, but her approach was so matter of fact that he was startled. "Not so fast."

"If you've changed your mind, say so." She continued to undo the buttons.

"You know damned well I haven't!"

"Okay, you want me. I've decided I want you, too. So we do something about it."

He could not fathom her mood, much less her direct approach, and he hesitated.

Adrienne stepped out of the negligee and stood before him in the nude.

Her figure was perfect and she was his for the taking, but the mocking expression in her eyes halted him.

"Well?" she demanded. "Put up or shut up."

Porter realized she was challenging him, precisely as she had been doing vocationally from the moment they had first seen each other. He grinned at her and undressed slowly. "No karate, no judo and no broken bones, okay?"

"Agreed." She drifted to the nearer bed, stretched out on it and, using her own brand of necromancy, managed to look very fragile, very feminine.

The element of surprise was of paramount importance in hand-to-hand combat, and Porter expected her to struggle violently, but Adrienne surprised him by remaining totally passive as he took her in his arms.

Her lips parted for his kiss, and she was unmoving as he caressed her. Only the hardening of her nipples as he played with her firm, high breasts told him she was responsive to his touch. Her eyes were closed and her face was impassive as she allowed him to do as he pleased.

Gradually he became aware of her purpose: this was the ultimate challenge. Obviously she had used sex as a weapon too often to be aroused by casual lovemaking, and she was daring him to excite her. She was forcing him to accept her battleground, and he was pitting his masculinity against her far more subtle feminity.

Porter deliberately slowed his pace. Now that he understood the rules he would play the game accordingly, and his caresses became gentle, less demanding.

He could tell that Adrienne sensed the change in him, even though she was still seemingly indifferent.

Taking his time, he kissed her neck and breasts, gradually moving down the length of her body to her feet, then starting upward again and burying his face between her legs.

All at once she came to life, flipping him onto his back and mounting him. Her eyes were feverish, her lips were parted and she was determined to take command.

It would have been easy to allow her to dominate, but that would be an admission of defeat, so he rolled her over and assumed the superior position.

They struggled in earnest now, their erotic desire soaring, and finally, without saying a word, they achieved a compromise, slipping into a position on their sides. Unable to hold off any longer, they reached a climax together.

They rested in silence for a long time, and Porter was astonished to discover that although he could not claim to have mastered this extraordinary girl, he felt a tenderness toward her that was unique. He reached out to stroke her, opened his eyes and discovered that she was looking at him.

Adrienne's eyes were shining.

Porter searched for words that would express his feelings. "You're okay," he said lamely.

"You're more than that," Adrienne said.

"I am?"

"You're stronger than I am, and you know the same wrestling tricks, so you could have pinned me down. But you thought of my pleasure ahead of your own, and—frankly, Porter, you astonish me."

He was too flustered to reply, which was all the more disconcerting in a man who was proud of his ability to handle any situation.

Adrienne snuggled close to him, her body pressing against his. "Next time," she murmured, "it will be even better."

*   *   *

They flew to San Diego in one of Franklin Richards' small jets, with the industrialist himself at the controls. They landed on the grounds of the naval base, and a waiting limousine took them to an isolated corner, where Porter saw a large, three-story building of red brick. The place was surrounded by an electrified fence of steel mesh, topped by a deep roll of barbed wire. Marine guards armed with automatic rifles patrolled the outside of the perimeter and others manned watchtowers at each of the four corners.

They left the car outside the gate, and a lieutenant-commander, a pistol on his hip, examined the credentials of the pair at length before making a telephone call to confirm their identities. Then two Marines were assigned to escort the visitors to the building, and there the elaborate security check was repeated.

Porter noted with approval that closed-circuit television cameras were trained on them, too.

A captain from the Office of Naval Intelligence finally appeared and granted the pair permission to enter. The entire procedure had lasted more than a half-hour.

"Well?" Richards asked as the captain conducted them down a broad, soundproof corridor.

"The best security I've ever seen," Porter said, "although an enemy could land a helicopter on the roof."

"I think not, sir," the captain said. "We have antiaircraft gunners stationed there at all times."

After walking the better part of the way around the interior of the building they came to a steel door, where still another officer turned a set of combination tumblers. The captain opened one lock with a key, and Richards produced a key for another. At last the heavy door could be opened.

"I'll take charge inside," Franklin Richards said. "Come for us in an hour."

71

The steel door closed.

Porter followed the industrialist down a narrow hall, and then they climbed a steep flight of steps, coming at last to an observation platform overlooking a water tank with glass sides that was at least thirty feet deep, eighty feet long and perhaps fifty feet wide. At first glance it resembled a mammoth fish tank.

"As I've told you," Richards said, "the actual float we intend to use in Project Neptune is stored elsewhere in the building in separate sections and will be flown to us in the Pacific after we put out to sea. What you'll see here is the original scale model we constructed before we built the float itself."

At the far end of the tank Porter saw a heavy metal claw extending from a wall. "I assume that's electromagnetic," he said, "and represents the much bigger claws we saw on board the *Neptune.*"

"Correct." Richards opened a sliding board in the wall, which revealed a large panel of dials and switches. He began to push buttons, and soon lights in green, white and red were glowing.

"How many people have seen this gadgetry, Mr. Richards?"

"We've given demonstrations for the President, the Secretary of Defense, three admirals and the Director of the Corporation."

"No one else?"

"A number of scientists and naval architects, of course—"

"How many?"

"Perhaps eight or ten in all. Every one of them has a top security clearance, naturally, and—"

"I'd like Adrienne supplied with a complete list of names. Today."

"But they've already been checked."

"They'll be checked again," Porter said. "There must be no potential leaks, particularly if your machinery performs as you say it does."

"Watch," Richards said, and an overhead pair of cranes appeared out of the ceiling, each holding a thick metal bar. "We had to prove to ourselves that our float was capable of doing what we demand of it, so even this demonstration equipment is rather impressive. Each of those bars weighs a half-ton."

Porter watched as the bars were lowered into the water and dropped to the bottom of the tank. "American-Canadian or English?"

"The U.S.-Canadian ton, two thousand pounds. Only you English would invent a ton of twenty-two hundred and forty pounds. I'll be relieved when all of us switch to the metric system." Richards punched several buttons. "Here we go."

A sliding door just above water level opened, and Porter stared at a strange contraption that came slowly into view. About ten feet long and approximately five feet wide, it resembled an aluminum raft, with a thick lip of a darker, heavier metal.

Richards replied to his unasked question. "The iron shot we use as ballast is stored in the outer rim. The beauty of this design is its simplicity."

Porter leaned forward to examine the under portion of the float, a sturdy, tanklike contraption that looked somewhat like a torpedo with two rounded ends. "That's your power tank?"

"Right. We experimented with every known kind of gasoline, and finally settled on a high-octane aviation fuel. It compresses very quickly, and drags the float down. We're using the wrong terminology, actually, when we call this

73

machine a float. It would be proper to refer to it as a self-submersible."

The miniature football field settled on the surface of the water, and a long hose came out of the wall and attached itself to the underside.

"Wherever possible," Richards said, "we've automated. In this way we leave as little as possible to chance, and we minimize the possibilities that human error in a time of tension can cause improper functioning."

Porter said nothing as the tank was filled with gasoline.

"We're all set," Richards said, and when he tugged down a switch the hose disconnected itself and was swallowed up into the wall.

"You'll send down no observers in a bathyscaphe, or any divers?"

"That would complicate the operation. Remember we'll be hauling up an object from a depth of more than sixteen thousand feet, and if people are involved down there, the protection of their lives becomes our first consideration. The one piece of equipment the model lacks is the closed-circuit television cameras that we'll use on the real float."

"I'm sure television will be a help," Porter said, "but as a layman I can't understand how this raft can seek out—and find—an object at the bottom of the sea."

Franklin Richards laughed. "That was our most difficult problem, and we solved it by using a float. We wanted as large a surface as possible to create a field for our electromagnets. The entire underside of the float's surface is equipped with the most powerful, sensitive magnets ever made. As you'll soon see." He pulled a large switch.

The submersible float began to descend, gaining speed as it dropped toward the bottom of the tank.

"The magnets," Richards said, "seek their own target. In

an area the size of this pool there's no problem in locating the metal bars, while in the actual operation we'll need our television cameras to help guide us to the submarine."

Porter could scarcely believe what he was seeing. The float reached the bottom of the tank, then moved unerringly toward the two metal bars. In a few minutes it settled over them.

"Now," Richards said, "we need human intervention to guide the next step." He pressed several small buttons.

One side of the submersible's lip opened, and small pieces of iron were discharged.

"If the magnetic field is so powerful, why don't the chunks of iron cling to it?"

"They've been treated to make them antimagnetic. There will be special equipment on board the *Neptune* to perform that function just before the iron shot is loaded onto the float. Even treated iron remains antimagnetic for only a short time."

The float, with a load of shot released from one side, was now tilting.

"We've now come to the critical part of the operation," Richards said. "We must transfer the drawing power of the magnetic field from the bottom of the float to the top. This must be done gradually, so we don't lose physical contact with the object or objects we want to raise to the surface."

Porter watched him manipulating a series of plungerlike wires, and he looked like a puppeteer tugging at multiple, connected strings.

The two heavy metal bars, each weighing 1,000 pounds, inched toward the float.

Richards, totally absorbed in his operation, was perspiring heavily, even though the large chamber was airconditioned.

One of the metal bars seemed to hesitate at the lip of the

float, then rolled over it and settled on the top.

Richards held his breath as he manipulated the wires, his touch light.

The second bar reached the lip, fell away and then moved forward again.

"That's it, baby. Easy now." Franklin Richards had no idea he was speaking aloud.

The bar was drawn up over the lip, rolled onto the float and landed a few inches from its companion.

Porter discovered that he was sweating, too, and he wiped his upper lip and forehead.

"Now," Richards said, "we increase the electromagnetic pull to insure that the objects don't fall off when the submersible is raised."

He pulled yet another switch, and a humming sound filled the chamber.

Porter realized that, until this moment, the operation had been silent.

The wire plungers disappeared into their sockets.

"Next," Richards said, "we jettison the rest of the iron shot."

The three remaining sides of the lip opened, and small chunks of iron were expelled gradually. As they were propelled away from the submersible it began to rise.

"The gasoline decompresses as the float moves back toward the surface," Richards said. "That is another factor in the ascension. Theoretically, if we ran into serious trouble we could jettison the fuel, too, but I'd hesitate before I'd try it. The submersible might rise to the surface so fast that the magnetic field wouldn't be strong enough to hold the metal objects in place. If they fell off or slid off—or whatever—they'd sink to the bottom again, and we'd have to repeat the entire operation from scratch. I hate to think of what might happen to the *Zolóto* under such circumstances. Weighing as much as it does, it might be subjected to so much stress that it would crack and come apart. And that would mean the end of Project Neptune."

When the float was about three feet from the surface, a touch of a button activated the claw, which moved into place directly above the target, then slowly lowered itself, dipping beneath the surface and grasping the half-ton bars. Once it held them securely it lifted them into the air, then carried them out of sight into the wall.

The submersible continued to rise, and soon reached the surface.

"In the actual operation," Richards said, "at this stage we empty the float's fuel, and the *Neptune* will take it in tow. By that time the Russian submarine will be safely stored on board."

The ungainly little craft disappeared into its storage space, and the sliding doors closed. Franklin Richards pressed several buttons that turned off the power, and the demonstration came to an end.

"Very impressive," Porter said.

"Your tone indicates that you have reservations."

"I suppose I do. You work with this miniature equipment under controlled conditions. Ideal conditions, really. But in actual operation in the South China Sea, all sorts of things can go wrong."

"How well we know it. We're gambling with hundreds of millions of dollars worth of taxpayers' money, the lives of a great many people and my own time and efforts. There are no precedents to guide us, and we'll have to learn on the job. As you've seen, we're automating as much of the operation as possible, but machines are controlled by men, and one error in judgment can scuttle the whole project."

They left the chamber, and security officers locked it behind them.

"I'm not too worried about the Russians trying to get hold of the blueprints of your salvaging equipment," Porter said. "Even if they succeeded in duplicating it, they'd need years to build it. If they've caught on to the purpose of Project Neptune, they'll do one of two things. Sabotage your operation, so their submarine stays at the bottom of the sea. Or wait until you've raised the *Zolóto* and then try to take it away from you."

"Which approach do you think they'll take?"

Porter shrugged. "If I were in the KGB and given the assignment, I'd take a crack at both ways. Their object is to prevent the United States from learning some closely guarded secrets, so it doesn't really matter how they do it. As long as they bloody well see to it that they ruin Project Neptune."

They strolled down the corridor, in no hurry to leave the laboratory, and Richards was relaxing after his exertions. "I don't envy you your job."

"My business is similar to yours in one respect," Porter said. "No one works in a vacuum. The trick is picking up clues in time to do something about them."

The captain of Naval Intelligence approached them. "I have a telephone message for Mr. Porter," he said. "You're to call a Mr. Blackman in San Francisco. He left no number, but he said it's urgent."

"He's undoubtedly at Corporation headquarters there," Porter said. "Can you put me through on a scrambler?"

"I believe so. It'll take only a minute or two to set one up."

They went into an office, and as soon as the device was attached Porter made his call.

"I flew down here from Washington state a few minutes after you left for San Diego," Blackman said. "I had a tip that's turned out to be accurate. A friend of yours from Hong Kong has hit town and is looking for you."

"A lady friend?"

"Right. She's gone underground, so she won't be easy to locate."

"I'll come right up," Porter said. "Book me a room at the usual, the little place on the Hill, and I'll take over. Does Adrienne know about this?"

"Not yet."

"Phone her immediately, and tell her to establish a full alert until further notice. My friend's arrival could be a sign of trouble."

"I know," Blackman said. "Maybe I ought to hang around and go sightseeing with you."

"You're needed at the shipyard. And I'll function best in this situation if I work alone."

San Francisco's Chinatown had the largest Oriental population of any city in the world other than in the Far East, and when Porter left the cable car at the corner of California Street and Grant Avenue he could almost imagine himself in Hong Kong. The community and its people were Chinese, and the tiny, open-fronted shops, the restaurants and the atmosphere resembled the world their ancestors had known in Canton, Shanghai and Peking. But the dress of all but the elders was Western; rock music blared from transistor radios, and the streets were choked with oversized automobiles made in Detroit.

As in Hong Kong, the blend of cultures was successful but uneasy. The traditional values of the East and the mores of the West existed side by side without quite merging, and as a result the young respected neither. Their only gods were profit and pleasure, and the elderly men and women in black pajamas who sat on doorstoops and before open, ground-floor windows watched them in obvious, impotent disapproval.

Tourists relished the atmosphere, and Porter looked like all the others as he wandered through Chinatown, studying the architecture of Kong Chow Temple and window shopping interminably. After he had satisfied himself that he was not being followed, however, he walked a trifle more rapidly, and ultimately he slipped into a narrow alleyway on the side of a steep hill. Passing several tenements, he opened an unmarked door and went inside.

The interior was a small eating establishment, and every available foot of space was occupied by five rickety tables, all of them empty. The walls were bare, and the air was heavy with the scents of stale garlic, ginger and fried onions.

Porter sat with his back to the wall, lighted a cigarette and waited.

After a time a middle-aged Chinese woman came into the room, wiping her hands on her apron.

"Bring me some jasmine tea," he said, "and an order of noodles, Cantonese style."

She vanished through a swinging door, giving no indication that she had even heard him.

Again there was a long wait, and then a man in his forties, with razor-cut hair and wearing a suit of hand-tailored gabardine came through the swinging door. Like so many San Francisco Chinese he was short and slender, indicating that his ancestors had been Cantonese.

Porter returned his stare.

"Mac," the man said, "you came to the wrong place. This is a private club, not a public restaurant."

Porter's yawn was ostentatious.

"Get to hell out, Mac."

"Tell Tom Lee," Porter said, "that his old Macao gambling partner is here."

The man regarded him steadily before stalking off.

Porter rolled himself another cigarette and tilted his chair against the wall.

The man returned, beckoning, and led him through a crowded kitchen, then up a narrow flight of squeaking wooden stairs. Pausing outside a heavy door, he turned. "I'm going to frisk you."

"You'll keep your hands to yourself," Porter said.

They glared at each other, and the man lost the contest of wills. He opened the door and conducted the visitor through a small anteroom.

The inner chamber was incongruously furnished in Scandinavian modern, and four Chinese sitting at a table were engrossed in a game of Mah-Jongg. The eldest of them, a burly man with graying hair, looked up from his rack.

There were no tong wars in San Francisco any more, and Tom Lee was the primary reason peace had been restored, as the grateful police well knew. Occasionally the *Chronicle* or the *Examiner* referred to him as "the unofficial mayor of Chinatown," but he was successful in avoiding publicity. If he ran Chinatown's gambling and prostitution rings it had never been proved, and federal authorities, in spite of many investigations, had found no evidence connecting him with the sale of drugs.

He heaved himself to his feet, grinned and extended his hand. "I never expected to see you again in this world," he said.

"You're getting fat, Tom. Too much easy living."

The man in the gabardine suit was nervous. "He's armed, Mr. Lee. You can see the bulge."

"What else is new?" Lee waved his associates out of the room.

They hastened to obey.

Pulling his open-tailed sports shirt lower over his paunch,

81

Lee went to a corner cabinet and filled two thimble-sized glasses with *mao tai,* a sorghum-based, 180-proof liqueur made in mainland China. Handing one to his guest, he raised his own in a toast. "Here's to crime."

Porter hadn't forgotten their old joke. "And corruption."

Lee sipped his drink, then returned to his seat. "Still peddling cabbage?"

"They have me managing some of the carts now. If I'm not careful they'll give me a desk job, and that will be the end of me."

"Not with your will to survive, Porter."

"I try not to push my luck. Tom, I'm looking for a favor. Strictly personal, naturally."

"Of course."

"A girl I know has just arrived here from Hong Kong, and has passed the word that she wants to see me. It may not be healthy for her to stay in the clear, so she's gone underground. And I can't hang about for a week or so, just waiting for her."

"Particulars?"

"Eurasian. Tall. Attractive. She's been a starlet in a few films made in Hong Kong, and has done some others in Taipei. Earns pocket money on the side as an expensive call girl. There's a photo of her in front of the movie house around the corner, so she must be playing a bit part in it. She's the one with waist-length hair."

Lee nodded and looked at his watch. "It's now five o'-clock. If she's here we'll deliver her to your hotel room in time for dinner. With my compliments."

Mao tai was too strong for Porter's taste, but it would have been rude to refuse, so he emptied his glass. "There are complications. The world is full of baddies, and some of them may not want us to get together. I'd rather you take her to

82

a safe spot and then send for me."

"Sure," Lee said, "but will she cooperate with me?"

Porter grinned. "Damned if I know, but I've heard it said you can be persuasive."

The banalities and clichés of American television were too much for Porter, so he passed the time reading an inaccurate, romanticized history of the Corporation written by a former employee. Occasionally he glanced at the clock on the mantel over the imitation fireplace in his hotel room, and when the telephone rang he noted with satisfaction that it was 7:15 P.M. Tom Lee always kept his promises.

"This is the hotel desk, Mr. Porter. There's a gentleman here to see you."

"Tell him I'll be right down." Porter checked his Magnum, slipped his Lilliput into a jacket pocket and went down to the lobby.

The Chinese in the gabardine suit nodded curtly, then led him to a Jaguar limousine waiting at the main entrance.

"Tell Lee I admire his taste in cars," Porter said as they settled in the back seat.

The man made no reply.

Porter was silent, too, and after noting that they were driving across the bay to Oakland, he relaxed completely. It was a trick he had learned years earlier, when he had discovered that tension sapped a man's strength, and at his age he had to conserve his energy.

When the car reached Oakland they drove to a new residential district on the outskirts of the city, where large houses were surrounded by several acres of lawn. Probably he was being taken to one of Tom Lee's personal estates.

The driveway was long, and when the car pulled to a halt in front of a red brick Georgian house, the front door was opened by a Chinese houseboy. The effect of his traditional, pajamalike uniform was spoiled by a pistol he wore in a shoulder holster.

The servant bowed, then conducted the visitor to a set of marble steps that led down to a sunken living room.

The chamber resembled an indoor jungle, and Porter paused to appreciate it. There were several palm trees, a ten-foot-high grapefruit tree bearing fruit, and ferns of many varieties in large, lacquered pots. A tiny waterfall fed a pond in which goldfish were swimming, and soft music was being piped into the room through hidden stereo speakers. The overall effect was far more pleasant than anything he had seen in Franklin Richards' mansions.

A girl with blue-black hair hanging loosely to her waist was curled up in a chair, staring morosely into an adjoining porch that was also filled with plants. She wore a shirt unbuttoned almost to the waist, jeans and shoes with high platform soles, and she looked out of place in the elegant surroundings.

Porter descended the steps. "Waiting for someone?"

Nancy Wing jerked around at the sound of his voice, then leaped to her feet. "It's really you!"

He embraced and kissed her, and when she pressed close he did what was expected of him by letting his hands roam. At last he released her.

"They told me you'd join me, but I didn't believe them. They came for me at a horrid little furnished flat I'd taken by the day, and they wouldn't explain how they'd found me or knew me. I was frightened to death."

It would take a great deal more than that to frighten her, Porter thought. "We'll celebrate our reunion with a drink," he said, and went to a well-stocked bar, where he poured a Scotch for her and a bourbon for himself.

The Eurasian girl kept a hand on his shoulder. "Do these

people work for you, and whose house—?"

"You ask too many questions," Porter said, "but I see no harm in telling you the truth. No, they don't work for or with me, and this place belongs to an old friend of mine."

She didn't believe him, but that was unimportant, and settling close to him on a long divan, she took his tobacco pouch and papers from his pocket and rolled herself a cigarette.

She was damned clever, he thought. He had shown her how to make a cigarette at their last meeting, and she had picked up the knack with ease. "I heard you were looking for me."

"I called your office here from the airport as soon as I landed because I didn't know any other way to get in touch with you. I came because I've missed you, darling." She leaned her head on his shoulder.

He was amused. "Liar."

Nancy Wing sat upright, a hurt expression in her mascara-fringed eyes.

"One reason you came here—and went straight into hiding—is because Hong Kong isn't healthy for you, and neither is Taipei. Comrade Andropov has a long reach, and he's inclined to become a bit upset when he thinks someone on his payroll intends to sell him out. And one of the reasons you came all the way across the Pacific to me is because I'm one of the few people you know who might be able to offer you protection."

She sipped her drink, took a deep drag on her cigarette and stared at the plants on the porch. "I should have realized," she murmured. "You knew in Hong Kong that I was working for the KGB. But how you learned I was planning to leave them—"

"Oh, I have my sources, but it doesn't really matter."

"Quite right." She leaned against him, again placing her

85

head on his shoulder, and stretched out on the divan.

He had to give her credit, she used her sex appeal with more artistry than any agent he had ever encountered. "Don't tell me it was pure love that brought you halfway around the world."

"Love. And something else. I hope your people will be willing to pay for the information you wanted to pry out of me in Hong Kong."

"I'll check on that, but I'm fairly confident we can make a deal you'll accept."

"It goes almost without saying that I'll need to go into the deep freeze until this blows over, darling. I've never met Andropov personally, of course. I'm not that important. But I'm told he has a pathological hatred of double agents. I'll need your protection as a condition of the deal."

The manservant came to the door and announced that dinner was served.

"Let's talk about it after we eat," Porter said, and knew he had given her something to think about for the next hour or two. Her request for help was genuine, and there was no doubt in his mind that her fear of KGB retaliation was genuine. But she hadn't revealed all of her motives for seeking him, and a feeling of insecurity would make her more vulnerable.

A glass-topped table in a small dining room was set for two, and a second Chinese manservant served onion soup, a filet of beef with souffle potatoes, a salad with Roquefort cheese dressing and a spectacular cherries jubilee. Vintage wines were offered throughout the meal, and at its end the houseman placed a magnum of French champagne in an ice bucket.

Porter ate and drank sparingly. Tom Lee was making a gesture on his behalf, perhaps misunderstanding his interest in the Eurasian girl, and there was no way he would have known that Porter would have preferred beer and pizza, or even that exclusively American dish, chop suey.

Nancy Wing was ravenous, and Porter wondered how she kept her slender figure; he guessed she didn't eat this well very often. She drank steadily, too, which he interpreted as a sign of her nervousness, and he kept her glass filled.

She held her liquor with aplomb, however, and when they returned to the living room after dinner, the houseman bringing the bucket of champagne, she still looked and sounded sober. "What plans are you making for us, darling?" she asked when they were alone.

"I'll have someone pay my bill at the hotel and bring my luggage here," he said. "This is the safest place I know for tonight. Obviously, if my friends could find you in a furnished room, so could the KGB."

"I don't care where we stay, as long as we're together."

She was pressing too hard now, he reflected, so his strategy was working.

Nancy draped her arms around his neck and kissed him as they returned to the divan, her lips and tongue and teeth active.

Eventually he disentangled himself, increasingly convinced that she was going to great lengths to bind herself to him. "First thing tomorrow," he said, "I'll get Washington's approval for the deal, including the price ceiling."

"There is one other condition," the girl said. "I won't turn over the information to anyone but you. You're the only one I trust." She looked up at him, her dark eyes luminous.

She had been a minor cog in a machine, Porter reflected, but she had been an agent too long to trust anyone. "I'm sure my boss will be amenable to that," he said, and refilled her glass.

"Will they let you take me into hiding, do you suppose?"

"I don't know." Here was the crux of a delicate situation,

and he needed time to work out details. "I've been on holiday since I've come back from Hong Kong, but I never know when they'll put me to work again. Even if I can't stay with you, I'm certain they'll provide you with maximum security." Provided, he thought, the Corporation believed the data she fed them was authentic.

"I want to go with you." Even when she was being petulant Nancy was exceptionally appealing. "If you're still on holiday, I don't see why they wouldn't permit it."

"Did you have any special part of America in mind?"

"Well, the only places I know here are San Francisco and New York, and neither would be suitable, really."

"I suppose not."

"I don't see why we couldn't take a little place on the Strait of Juan de Fuca. It's isolated there, and you could go right on with your holiday."

At last she had given herself away, but he remained impassive. He had not mentioned to her that he was spending time on the northern coast of Washington state, and no one to whom she had spoken since her arrival in the United States had known where he was making his current headquarters.

So it was clear she had known his whereabouts before she had flown here, and was using flattery and sex to insure that he took her to the vicinity of the Richards shipyard. Was she aware of Project Neptune or was she on a fishing expedition? And for whom was she working? Porter's mind raced.

"When I speak to my boss in the morning," he said, hedging, "I'll try to find out when I'm being given a new assignment."

Nancy undid his necktie, opened his shirt and rubbed a hand back and forth across his bare chest. "I'm sure you'll arrange everything, darling. And right now let's find the bedrooms, or we'll do something right here. We haven't been together for ages, and I simply can't wait any longer."

88

Porter found a bell that summoned a houseman, who conducted them to a chamber on the second floor.

As they mounted the stairs together, their arms around each other, it occurred to Porter that as recently as a few days ago he would have welcomed this part of the job. If he had to sleep with Nancy Wing in order to discover the identity of her employers and how much she knew, he would sleep with her, and remembering her sexual proclivities he realized that any agent in the business would envy him.

But just last night he had gone to bed with Adrienne, and she was very much on his mind as he and Nancy went up the stairs.

SIX

Porter made an early morning telephone call to Adrienne, before Nancy Wing awakened. Several hours later he went into San Francisco, leaving Nancy at the Oakland house, explaining that he would pick up her belongings and call his superiors in Washington regarding her offer of a deal. What he did not tell her was that he had also scheduled a meeting with his principal associates, who were flying down from the Strait of Juan de Fuca.

He retrieved the Eurasian girl's luggage, then went on to the Corporation's local headquarters, which were located in one of the older office buildings. Chipped lettering on the frosted-glass door indicated that this was a firm of insurance adjusters.

A casual visitor would have found it difficult to identify the place as the office of an intelligence agency. A few calendars were pinned to otherwise bare walls, the plain wooden furniture was battered, and even the typewriters and filing cabinets were old. The middle-aged receptionist–switchboard operator seemed to spend most of her time filing and painting her fingernails.

The appearance of the innermost rooms of the suite was far different. One was equipped with a walk-in safe protected by a bank vault door. An operator was on round-the-clock duty at a shortwave sending and receiving radio console, and there was a small laboratory for on-the-spot investigative checks.

Porter made his call to Brian Davidson in Washington on a telephone with a scrambler device, and when he went into the adjoining, soundproof conference room, his colleagues were waiting for him. The impeccably dressed Blackman would have been at home at an Ivy League college class reunion, but he had been attending another type of school for the past decade and a half, and there was a veiled menace in his eyes. The Deacon, somberly attired as always in a dark suit, white shirt and solid-colored necktie, might have been mistaken for a clergyman, but his eyes, too, were hard and penetrating.

Adrienne, in a colorful print dress, appeared out of place in the gathering, but she was relaxed, and there was a hint of amusement in her expression when she greeted Porter.

He wasted no time, filling them in on what had happened since his arrival in San Francisco the previous day. "I've just now had a little chat with Davidson," he said. "The girl has offered us full information on the KGB naval observation station in Hong Kong. Location, personnel, everything. Davidson is putting through an immediate call to Chang in Hong Kong, and he'll turn the case over to British MI-six. If the information is accurate we'll pay the girl twenty-five thousand dollars."

The others were silent for a time, and Adrienne ran a comb through her hair. "This is tricky," she murmured. "It reminds me of the Budapest caper."

"Exactly," Porter said. "Here's how I see it. The information is probably accurate. I'll be surprised if it isn't."

"Meaning the Wing girl is selling out the KGB?" Adrienne asked.

91

"Possibly. Or the whole device could be a plant. The Russians deliberately sacrifice two or three agents, people who have lost their value and will be neatly out of the way at Stanley Prison in the Crown Colony. Meantime a more elaborate naval listening post has been set up, and is relatively safe. This possibility is based on the assumption that Nancy is actually still working for the Russians. We simply don't know. Yet."

The Deacon sat with primly folded hands. "The other possibility is that she's working for someone else, which points the finger at China."

"I'm not sure I buy that," Blackman said. "We know how subtle Peking can be. It doesn't make sense that they'd use someone who is half-Chinese and very attractive. They'd do better to use an inconspicuous Occidental, preferably an American."

"Not necessarily," Adrienne said, and her calm was extraordinary. "There are certain built-in advantages to utilizing the Eurasian woman as an agent. She had already slept with Porter, so she had a connection with him. As an agent supposedly on the run from the Russians, she wouldn't be suspected of having a Chinese connection. And an attractive woman is sometimes less obvious as an agent than someone who is easily lost in a crowd. It all depends on the point of view."

"The question," Blackman said, "is how to go on from here."

Porter smiled. "I've settled it already. First, we wait for word from Davidson, and then I pay Nancy the twenty-five thousand. Financial solvency—more money than she's ever had—may help make her careless."

"Your whole approach," Blackman said, "is predicated on the belief that she's on somebody's payroll and is on the trail of Project Neptune."

92

"I'm convinced of it," Porter said. "My popularity is limited, except in very exclusive circles, and only my fans in Moscow or Peking would know I'm making my base on the Strait of Juan de Fuca. Why did Nancy come to San Francisco instead of flying straight to Washington to propose her deal? Why did she make her pitch to me?"

"Probably," Adrienne said, venom showing for the first time, "because you're irresistible."

Porter ignored the jab. "She's working for people who either know or are guessing, and Moscow and Peking don't have to guess all that hard. I'm sure you remember the Zagreb headache, Blackman. Simple deduction tells as much as a dozen expensive field agents. There's nothing of interest within hundreds of miles of Port Angeles except the Richards shipyard. A bottom-drawer KGB man fell off a cliff. Andropov knows bloody well that something is happening in the neighborhood. They know me, they know Adrienne, and they damned well know we're not given routine assignments. I can hear Andropov giving the orders. 'Send someone who can get close to Porter and find out what he's doing.' We've used the same technique hundreds of times, and it succeeds because even the best agents have egos."

"You may talk in your sleep like the rest of us," the Deacon said. "I ran into Nancy Wing in Singapore a couple of years ago, and she can overwhelm any man. Just remember you're vulnerable, too."

"Not all that much," Porter said, and looked at Adrienne. "I have interests elsewhere that shield me."

She realized this was the closest he could come to an apology, and her faint smile indicated an acceptance. He could sleep anywhere he found necessary in the line of duty, and she would try not to let it influence their relationship. "Where do we go from here?"

"Your job," Porter said, "is hiring a clean crew and keep-

93

ing the shipyard windows closed. Concentrate on that, and leave the rest to us. The *Neptune* will be launched in about a month, and will sail straight away across the Pacific without even making any sea trials. So the next few weeks will be critical."

"If the KGB or Peking is going to do anything," Blackman said, "they'll have to do it in the coming month."

"One of them has already moved a pawn," Porter said. "Nancy Wing. Blackman, I want you to rent two houses on the Juan de Fuca coast, not too far apart, for a month's occupancy. We'll need one as a headquarters. The motel is a sieve, and the security is too lax at Richards' house and the shipyard. I want a complete command post with full equipment and manpower."

The Deacon chuckled. "Davidson will scream. He'll claim you're wrecking his budget."

"Project Neptune knows no budget limitations," Porter said.

"What's the purpose of the second house?" Blackman wanted to know.

"Nancy Wing and I are going to have a holiday in a love nest of our very own."

His assistant was startled. "You're really going to take her up to the strait?"

"If it's the last thing I ever do," Porter said. "She's the perfect decoy, so we can stop searching the haystack for invisible needles. Sooner or later her bosses will push her for information, or she'll send off a report. Either way we'll be ready with an intercept. Deacon, I want that house bugged, every last room of it. Also the car you people will get for me. And Blackman, I'll want surveillance teams who'll keep her under close watch every time she sets foot outside the house. Regardless of whether I happen to be with her."

"She's a smart bird," the Deacon said, "and she's no novice. She's bound to stumble onto some portions of that massive a surveillance."

"That will either inhibit her or make her reckless," Porter said, "and either way we'll benefit. With each day that passes we're that much closer to sailing time. Okay, does anyone find holes in the plan?"

"I can think of only one," Adrienne said. "You and I have been staying with Franklin and Marie Richards, ostensibly as a married couple. Now you'll be showing up in the neighborhood with a woman who, I gather, would call attention to herself during a hurricane. Doesn't that blow our cover?"

"To an extent," Porter said. "But we've had almost no social life at the Richardses' place, and if you continue to stay there we may get away with it. I hope Blackman will find me a house on the far side of the shipyard, so even fewer people will get wise. I'll grant you we're taking a small risk, but I don't see that it can be avoided. Nancy will lead us to her bosses only if I'm the bait."

"There's another angle that bothers me," Blackman said. "If you're going to remain in charge of Project Neptune security—"

"I am!"

"—the whole team will have hell's own time reporting to you with the Eurasian girl underfoot."

"I'll find ways to get over to our headquarters two or three times a day. That's why I want the two houses near each other. Also, I'll have to give Nancy enough time alone to send and receive messages. She's our only link with the people—identity unknown—who are breathing down our necks. Let's organize, shall we?"

Blackman and the Deacon went into other rooms to start making necessary arrangements by telephone, and Porter was alone with Adrienne.

He wanted to kiss her, but realized it would be inappropriate when he would be going off to live with another girl.

"You won't have much time to double-check my okays of the crew," she said.

"I'll have none, but you won't need me for that, will you?"

"I think not. The FBI is doing backgrounds on all the men we hire. Most of them are ex-servicemen with names like Rusty and Fats, and they're clearing easily."

"I'll stop at the yard whenever I have the chance. Tell Richards I haven't deserted him. And make certain his wife is kept under watch."

"I'm coming to know Marie, and I'm sure she's clean," Adrienne said.

"I've been around too long to be sure of anyone, including myself."

"Well," she said, "you've given yourself an assignment that every male in the Corporation will envy. I can't say I feel sorry for you."

"It's all part of the job," Porter said, "and I've never yet had a simple, straightforward assignment. The worst of this lunacy is that the success or failure of the most important, most expensive project in the entire history of the Corporation now depends on the whims and weaknesses of a high-class hooker."

Microphones were planted in a Corporation convertible, and Porter drove it back to the house in Oakland. He and Nancy Wing had nothing to occupy them until he was informed of the outcome of the Hong Kong investigation, so they spent the better part of the next twenty-four hours in bed. Her sexual appetites were still prodigious, and he was relieved, the following noon, when he received a telephone call summoning him to San Francisco.

He returned several hours later, carrying a briefcase. "You came through," he said. "Congratulations. The British

96

picked up two men in a Kowloon flat overlooking the harbor, and there's enough evidence to send them to prison for years. Shortwave radio transmitter, lists of British, American and Australian warships entering and leaving Hong Kong. They'll make a full confession." He refrained from saying that Davidson had told him the two Russian agents who had been apprehended were small fry. "So, my dear, this is for you."

Nancy opened the briefcase and, her eyes shining, counted out 250 bills, each of $100 denomination. "You're an angel," she said, hugging him.

"No, but I always keep my word. Get dressed, and we'll be on our way."

She removed the flimsy robe she had been wearing since he had departed in the morning, and began rummaging in her luggage. "Where are we going?"

"Why, the Strait of Juan de Fuca, of course. That's where you wanted to go. I've rented us a little house for a few weeks, and we'll start the drive up there as soon as you're ready."

"I want to buy some clothes!"

"We'll go to Seattle one day. Or up to Victoria. This area still isn't healthy, and I want us out of it. I do think we ought to stop at an Oakland bank so you can either open an account or put your money in a safety deposit box. You don't want to carry that much cash."

She agreed and, changing quickly, soon was dressed in a traditional Chinese *cheongsam,* a sheath with a high, stiff collar and slits at the sides of the skirt. "How do I look?"

"Gorgeous," Porter said, "but you'll wear your jeans and that shirt with the missing buttons. We'll be on the road for several days driving through northern California, Oregon and Washington, and if the KGB lads are looking for you there's no point in advertising your presence, is there?"

"You're quite right. I was so excited I forgot."

He had no way of knowing whether she was telling the truth or making a lame excuse. If she was still in the employ of the Russians she had nothing to fear from them.

"My big case is ready, darling. Why don't you put it in the car with your luggage, and I'll join you shortly."

Porter went downstairs, wrote a note to Tom Lee thanking him for his hospitality and packed the baggage in the car. He was just finishing when Nancy joined him, and he blinked at her.

She was dressed as he had suggested, but a dark blonde wig and westernized makeup totally transformed her appearance, and she looked like the thousands of Caucasian girls he had seen on the streets of San Francisco and Oakland. Well, not quite like them; her figure was still breathtaking.

They drove to a bank, where Porter parked and waited while Nancy made her deposit, and when she returned she told him she had kept out $1,000 in cash for a buying spree. "You've been wonderful, darling," she said, "and I hope I can return the favor."

He expected repayment, but not the kind she had in mind.

As they started out on the long drive Porter told the girl he had another surprise for her: he had hired a woman who would do the cooking and cleaning at their holiday retreat. He did not explain that the servant was an experienced Corporation agent being flown from the East Coast for the assignment.

"My boss is so pleased with the results of your information that my holiday is being extended," he said. "I'll have to check in by telephone a couple of times every day, and if they give me any little errand I'll rent myself a jeep so you can use this car for shopping." The jeep was already awaiting him.

Nancy sat closer to him as he drove, a hand across his lap. "You think of everything," she murmured.

In this situation, Porter thought, I must. I can't afford to leave any loopholes.

The two-story house was located on a small inlet, and boasted a tiny, isolated beach of its own, prompting Nancy to announce that she would sunbathe and swim in the nude, which she did. The house itself was plainly but comfortably furnished, Blackman had put in a substantial supply of liquor and wines, and the "cook" was as competent in the kitchen as she was in other areas.

For several days the couple on holiday lazed around the house, dividing their time between beach and bed. Every morning and again in the afternoon Porter went off in the jeep to the Corporation command post that had been established in a house only a mile away, but during his absences Nancy neither went out in the convertible nor used the telephone.

If his assessment was mistaken he was wasting time and energies needed elsewhere, so he set a trap for her on their third morning, returning to the house with an attaché case, which he left in their bedroom. Two very thin, almost invisible threads had been attached to the interior, and would snap if the case was opened more than a few inches, and he had lightly dusted talcum powder on the top layer of harmless papers in the case.

That afternoon he left the attaché case behind when he went off in the jeep, and it was in the same place, at the foot of the bed, when he returned.

Not until early evening, when Nancy went off for a bath, did Porter have the opportunity to inspect his handiwork. The threads were broken and the traces of powder had disappeared, offering positive proof that Nancy had opened the case and examined the contents. This act didn't necessarily indicate that she was an agent in the employ of a foreign power, however, and he realized it might be nothing more than a testimony to her feminine curiosity. He would have to prepare a more rigorous test.

Meanwhile there were other problems on his mind. The following morning, by prearrangement, he met Franklin Richards at the command post, and learned there was a malfunction in the electric generator that was scheduled to be installed on board the *Neptune* within the week.

"What's the significance?"

Richards was unworried. "Not much. Technical bugs often crop up in a major project. We'll find the fault and correct it. I doubt if this will delay us more than a week in putting out to sea."

"Suppose I were to tell you," Porter said, "that I'm virtually certain either the Russians or the Chinese are on our trail. Every day of delay doubles the odds against us."

The entrepreneur became grim. "In that case," he said, "I'll take charge and find the malfunction myself. I promise you we'll sail on schedule."

Porter stepped up the pace of his own investigation, and late that morning he received his first telephone call at the house. Blackman was calling, and by prearrangement they indulged in sheer gibberish, their cryptic conversation filled with non sequiturs that could keep a decoding office busy for days.

Thereafter he accompanied Nancy to the beach, where they went for a short swim, and when she stretched out on a towel to sunbathe, Porter strolled up to the house to fetch them drinks.

The "cook" awaited him in the kitchen.

"Well, Mrs. Stevens?"

The woman's face was grim. "I watched her on closed-circuit television, Mr. Porter. She attached a miniaturized tape recorder to the telephone extension while you were on the line. It's one of those new gadgets that records a conversation without the need to take the instrument off the hook."

His theory that Nancy Wing was in the employ of some foreign agency was correct, and he was elated.

"She stashed it away in that big leather shoulder bag she carries. I went through it when you two went down to the beach, and she also has a camera built into a ballpoint pen."

Porter smiled.

"You won't be all that pleased," the woman said with asperity, "when you hear she also carries a two-millimeter Kolibri automatic."

"I'm not surprised."

Mrs. Stevens' technical interest overcame her annoyance. "It's the first one I've seen. It looks too small to be effective."

"Oh, it's an effective weapon, but I prefer the Lilliput." Porter finished preparing the drinks and started toward the door.

"Hold on, sir," the woman said. "What are you going to do about all this?"

He laughed. "Feed her enough material so she'll choke on it. That reminds me. Call the command post and tell them I want some special blueprints made up for me by this afternoon. The electrical system of a supertanker. The plumbing system of a deluxe washing machine. And anything else Blackman can dream up that's useless but looks complicated."

There was no need for him to explain that he wanted to feed Nancy so much data that she would feel compelled to pass it along to her superiors in the immediate future. Now that he had confirmed her status as an agent it was imperative that he trace her employment to its source as soon as possible. She was a vital link in an otherwise invisible chain, so she had to be encouraged and nurtured.

Nancy's smile was lazy as she took her drink from him.

"You're spoiling me," she said.

"You deserve it," Porter said. "Look at all the credit I get in Washington for your Hong Kong tip. And that reminds me, we haven't yet celebrated. How'd you like to go somewhere for dinner tonight, if I can find a restaurant worthy of the name in these backwoods?"

"I'd love it," she said. "I suppose I ought to wear my wig?"

"A wise precaution. After I get back from my errand this afternoon I'll scout around the neighborhood and see if I can find a place to eat." The time he spent away from the house, he thought, would give her the opportunity to photograph the worthless blueprints he would bring back with him from the command post.

They strolled up to the house for a light lunch after they finished their drinks, and Nancy returned to the beach when Porter went off on his supposed regular afternoon errand. Blackman had a stack of blueprints waiting for him, and he packed them away in his attaché case.

"Tomorrow morning," Porter said, "the combination of her telephone tape and the photos she'll take of these prints will have become unbearable. I'll make it plain to her that I'll be away longer than usual, and that should prod her into passing along her tape and film to her contact. I want the surveillance team breathing down her neck if she leaves the house. As I'm certain she will."

"I'll take charge of the surveillance myself," Blackman said.

"Be careful," Porter told him. "Mrs. Stevens has discovered she carries a baby Kolibri."

"A nasty little gun," Blackman said. "We'll watch our step."

"Make certain you don't lose her contact," Porter said.

"He's the key to this situation, and we'll have to work quickly. It won't take long for her bosses to find out that we've fooled them with the blueprints, and it'll be easy enough for them to guess that we were talking on the phone in a mock code. That will be the tip to them that we're feeding Nancy rubbish, so they'll switch from her to someone else, and we'll have to start all over again."

"I know what's at stake," Blackman said.

As Porter anticipated, Nancy Wing photographed the documents he brought back to the house, and the following morning she told him at breakfast that she thought she might spend the morning at a shopping center about ten miles from the house. She would pick up some cosmetics and other items she needed, and if there were any dress shops there she hoped to find a few simple outfits that would lend greater variety to her wardrobe.

When Porter left the house he stopped the jeep at the edge of the woods beyond the end of the property, and alerted the waiting Blackman. "She's going off to the shopping center," he said. "She's taken the bait."

Two members of the surveillance team went off to mark time at the shopping center parking lot, and when the girl left the house she was followed by Blackman and another agent using separate cars.

It was obvious that Nancy was unfamiliar with the area. Twice she hesitated at crossroads to read the directional signs, and later she had to double back after turning in the wrong direction. But she reached the shopping center in a quarter of an hour, with the two vehicles trailing her taking turns in the lead so she wouldn't know she was being followed.

Blackman's report, written later in the day, was succinct:

103

Subject parked in lot at Northern Shores Shopping Center at 10:20 a.m. Checked her wristwatch as she left car, which she did not lock. Was in no hurry, and walked slowly to principal shopping area. Spent short time looking in windows of Today's Bestsellers Bookstore. Wandered on to Elite Dress Shop, where she examined everything in windows. Did not enter shop or exchange greetings of any nature with anyone. Contrary to expectations, subject made no attempt to use a telephone. This makes it likely that her contact, by prearrangement, would await her each day at specified time and place in shopping center. Before leaving Elite Dress Shop windows, subject again checked the time on her watch. Still in no hurry, went to Save Rite Drugstore, where she purchased 1 container Luxury Lash Lengthener mascara, 1 Dragon Red lipstick and 1 bottle Pearl Nail Lacquer. Paid for purchases with $10 bill, received $3.67 in change. Agent Wilson, who stood beside her throughout the transaction, is certain she did not pass recording tape, film or other material of any kind to clerk during or following the exchange.

When Nancy left the drugstore she looked at her watch for the third time, then increased her pace and walked more rapidly until she reached the Northern Shore Snack Bar. She entered and sat on a stool at the counter.

A pretty, expensively dressed girl sat two seats away, eating a toasted muffin and drinking coffee.

Blackman took the seat between them.

Nancy ordered a Danish pastry and tea.

Blackman was startled when he realized that the young woman on his left was Marie Richards. He signaled to one of his colleagues, who followed Mrs. Richards when she left the snack shop. His report indicated that she went to the bookstore, where she bought two volumes of fiction and three of nonfiction. Charging them, she went straight to her car, a two-door Jaguar sedan, and drove straight to her home.

Nancy ate about a third of her pastry, but took her time drinking her tea. In all, she spent 27 minutes in the establishment, leaving a tip of 25¢ and paying her bill of $1.12 with the exact change.

She passed nothing to the cashier, Blackman's report stated, and he emphasized there had been no contact of any kind between her and Mrs. Richards.

Leaving the snack bar, she returned to the convertible without pausing anywhere, and drove straight back to the rented house.

Before she had left the house, Mrs. Stevens had looked in her shoulder bag and had seen the tape and a roll of film. Examining the bag again when the girl went down to the beach after her return, Mrs. Stevens found that both the film and the tape were gone.

That afternoon, at the command post, Porter confronted the four agents who had participated in the operation. He allowed them to sit in silence while he read their reports, and then he stared for a moment at each in turn, his eyes cold. Blackman, who knew him well, realized he was seething.

"Gentlemen, one fact emerges from your exercise in futility." Porter's English accent was pronounced, as it always was in moments of stress. "Miss Wing had the tape and film in her possession when she left for the shopping center. They were no longer in her possession when she returned from the shopping center. So in some way unperceived by you, she passed the material to an accomplice."

"I don't see how that's possible," Blackman said. "I was thrown when I saw Mrs. Richards, and I still think there may have been some connection between those two chicks.

But nothing was passed by Wing to Richards, I'll stake my job on it."

"You may have to," Porter said. "I've just spoken to Washington and requested headquarters to bear down in its investigation of Marie Richards. But Adrienne swears she's clean, and I'm inclined to agree it was only a coincidence that she happened to be in the same eating place at the same time."

"A damn long shot coincidence," Blackman said.

"Granted." Porter jabbed a finger at one of the others. "Where were you during all this?"

"Sitting across the counter, sir, and Blackman is right. Mrs. Richards picked up absolutely nothing from the Wing girl. Nothing!"

"And where were you two?"

"Outside the snack bar, Mr. Porter. I was near the door, watching everyone who was entering or leaving, and Freddie stood near the plate-glass window so he could see everything going on inside."

Porter picked up the telephone beside him. "Get hold of Adrienne Howard at the shipyard," he said. "Tell her to drop whatever she may be doing and to hurry over here. As fast as possible." Replacing the instrument in its cradle, he took his time rolling a cigarette.

The others looked at each other, aware that he was fighting a losing battle in an attempt to control his temper.

"Blackman," he said, his voice barely audible, "you've been with the Corporation almost as long as I have, and you must have a half-dozen commendations on your record. Including that superb roundup of KGB people in the Baltic a few years ago. The rest of you, between you, must have twenty years of creditable service." A blood vessel in his temple began to throb visibly, and his voice rose to a shout.

"You bloody lunatics! You've been taken in by one of the most elementary tricks in the game!"

They glanced at each other in bewilderment.

"Four of you had the girl in the snack shop under observation. One other agent, according to these reports, stood outside the kitchen door, while two others stationed themselves at points some feet down the street. Who in hell was keeping watch on the car Miss Wing was driving?"

Blackman clasped his forehead. "Oh, my God!"

"Precisely." Porter's fury became cold. "Miss Wing left the tape and film in the car. All of you, without exception, followed her in a happy phalanx around the shopping center, noting such matters of vital importance as the exact sum she spent for cosmetics and tea. And while all this was happening, her accomplice quietly removed the film and tape from the unguarded car. You've muffed what may have been our only chance to trace this conspiracy to its source."

Blackman buried his face in his hands, and the others were shaken, too.

"I can't even begin to estimate how badly you may have placed Project Neptune in jeopardy." Porter waved them out of the room. "Go away. I need time to think."

They filed out the room, the stricken Blackman in the lead.

When Adrienne arrived Porter was chain-smoking as he paced the room.

He stopped short when he saw her. "We're up a gum tree," he said.

"Blackman just filled me in."

"I spent days setting up a perfect trap, and those bungling morons—"

Adrienne put a hand on his arm to silence him. "It isn't hopeless."

"Nothing is ever hopeless, but we've come close." Porter

107

sank into a chair. "There's only one thing we can do now."

"Take her into custody and interrogate her?"

He nodded. "It's dicey. Nancy is a tough chick, and she won't be broken easily or quickly. If she gives us false leads that need time to be checked, the Lord in His wisdom only knows the damage that can be done to Project Neptune!"

"The Deacon is a persuasive interrogator," Adrienne said. "What he didn't already know he learned in the year he spent in Lubyanka."

"This operation," Porter said, "requires finesse as well as firmness. First, I want you to take charge of the interrogation."

"Thank you," Adrienne said.

He knew she would waste no sympathy on the girl who had interrupted their affair and become his mistress. "No broken bones, mind you, and no permanently disfiguring marks. If Nancy's pride is destroyed she'll have no reason to cooperate voluntarily with us."

"You think she'll do that?"

"Here's the scenario," Porter said. "I'll give you eight hours to work on her—"

"That's all?" Adrienne was dismayed. "I've never yet seen an experienced agent who can be broken down in that short a time!"

"I don't expect you to break her down. Put the fear of God into her. I want her filled with terror. By tonight."

Adrienne smiled. "I'm reasonably sure I can accomplish that much."

"Good. Then the knight in the customary shining armor will ride to the rescue on his white charger."

"Why the rush?"

"Because," Porter said, "anyone with technological expertise will take one look at the blueprints and know we're thumbing our noses at them. We need to get the jump on our opponents, whoever they may be."

"Fair enough," Adrienne said. "But can the fearless knight persuade the lady to open her rosebud lips and pour out her little heart to him?"

"She isn't in this business out of patriotism, and I don't think she particularly craves adventure. She'd love to be a film star, but I've seen no sign that she has any great yearning for fame. The two things she appears to love most in this world are sex and money, although not necessarily in that order. If you put her in an amenable mood, I may be able to do the rest."

"I'll try. I brought the Deacon with me, not knowing what had come up, so he'll wait here with me." She went to the door. "Blackman!"

The pale agent came to her.

"Pick up the Wing woman and bring her here. If she's on the beach in a bathing suit, so much the better. Give her no chance to change."

"And if she asks for her shoulder bag," Porter added, "make certain you remove that cute little automatic before you give it to her."

"But she's to bring nothing else," Adrienne said. "Blind-fold her, handcuff her, and if necessary gag her. You needn't be too gentle, and give her the silent treatment in the car. Take as many men with you as you need to do the job efficiently and quickly. But don't hurt her, and above all, don't bruise her."

Blackman's mouth was set in a thin line as he left, and they knew this was one assignment he would not bungle.

"I think I'll leave," Porter said.

Adrienne nodded, and it was evident she understood. Under the best of circumstances no senior field agent enjoyed the utilization of psychological terror and physical force, and regardless of his private opinion of the Wing girl, he had been intimate with her.

The hours ahead would not be pleasant for anyone concerned.

SEVEN

The little room on the top floor of the rented house was empty except for two straight-backed chairs, the walls were bare and so was the wooden floor. Adrienne Howard entered, carrying an ashtray, and a moment later a blindfolded and handcuffed Nancy Wing, clad in a bikini, was led into the chamber. At a signal from Adrienne the bonds were removed, and the escort silently departed.

The two women looked at each other, their faces impassive, and finally Adrienne smiled. "Make yourself comfortable, dear," she said, and waved toward the unoccupied chair, which faced her.

Nancy sat.

Adrienne offered her a cigarette and a light.

Nancy exhaled in a thin stream, and managed to appear bored.

Adrienne placed the ashtray on the floor between them. "I hope we're going to have a heart to heart chat. If you'll cooperate, you'll have time for a swim before dinner."

Nancy broke her silence. "I can't imagine anything I know that would be of interest to you, whoever you are."

"Oh, I happen to have a deep personal interest in you, dear. Far more personal than you could ever guess."

The prisoner raised a thin eyebrow.

"You see, you stole my man."

"What man?"

"Porter."

A malicious light appeared in Nancy's eyes. "I didn't know he had another girl, but he couldn't have been all that involved. He didn't offer any resistance."

"I don't believe any man does, especially with you. I'll concede that you're exceptionally handsome, and I'd hate to see that beautiful body disfigured."

Nancy smiled. "Do you always kidnap girls who steal your boyfriends?"

"This is the very first time," Adrienne said. "I do hope you believe me. If we're going to get along together we'll have to establish a basis of mutual trust."

"Maybe you've come to the wrong person," Nancy said. "Maybe you should have kidnapped Porter so you could persuade him to leave me."

Adrienne's sigh was exaggerated. "We'll get nowhere if you misunderstand, dear. I've merely explained my personal interest in you, so you'll know why I'm not particularly patient, kind or gentle. I also have a deep professional interest in you."

"I have no profession other than that of actress."

"Who are your employers?"

"I'm not under contract to any studio. I'm what's known as a free-lance artist."

"Enough," Adrienne said. "We know you taped a telephone conversation of Porter's, and photographed some documents he carried in his briefcase. This morning you passed film and tape to a messenger at the shopping center. Strange activities for an actress."

Nancy adjusted a tie at the side of her bikini bottom. "If Porter is so concerned about his property, why doesn't he ask me about it himself?"

"Porter doesn't even know we've taken you into custody," Adrienne said. "When a man loses his head over a woman he loses his value to his own employers. First we'll dig the truth out of you, and then we'll attend to Porter."

For the first time the Eurasian girl showed a trace of uneasiness, but she quickly recovered her aplomb. "You mean Porter refuses to cooperate with you."

Adrienne shrugged, and appeared to have been placed on the defensive.

"That means you don't really know anything. You're guessing, and you want me to confirm your guesses."

"You ought to know," Adrienne said, "that in this business we never guess."

"As I said before, I work in show business."

"Will you or will you not tell me the truth about this morning?"

"I'd be glad to make up a story if that would satisfy you," Nancy said, "but I'm afraid it wouldn't. Because I have nothing to tell. You've been reading too many suspense novels. Or perhaps you saw my last film. It was all about spies."

"I'm afraid it may be the very last film you'll ever make, dear," Adrienne said, looking regretful. "It does seem a shame to spoil such a pretty face and marvelous body. I'm not all that unattractive myself, so I know what appearance means to a woman."

Nancy made no reply, but seemed somewhat shaken.

"Perhaps you'd like a last cigarette, and a chance to change your mind." Adrienne lighted a cigarette and held it out to her.

The prisoner started to refuse, realized the gesture would serve no useful purpose and accepted.

Adrienne sat back in her chair, saying nothing and waiting, a faint smile on her lips.

113

Nancy looked around the room for the first time. She saw a single, small window, realized there was only one entrance and knew there had to be armed guards on the far side of the door. Obviously there was little opportunity to escape, and in her present state of undress the task would be made still more difficult, even if she managed to get away.

Adrienne took the butt from her and snuffed it out. "Very well, dear. Will you talk?"

The Eurasian girl remained silent.

Adrienne went to the door, opened it and beckoned.

The Deacon came into the room, wearing a mask. He halted, flexed his left hand and stared at it until the prisoner looked, too. Scars marked the tips of his fingers, where no nails grew.

Nancy shuddered.

"The young lady prefers your company to mine," Adrienne said. "Do try not to maim her too badly."

The Deacon turned toward Nancy, and as he slowly walked forward he continued to flex his mutilated fingers.

"Dinner was splendid, and I'm sorry I couldn't do it justice," the Director said as he and Franklin Richards settled down with their brandy in the industrialist's library. "I'm so sedentary these days that I've cut down on my food. This is the first time in months I've traveled farther than the eleven miles between my office and my house."

His host offered him a cigar, then took one himself. "I must admit I was surprised when your office telephoned to say you were on the way out here and were already in the air."

"Frank, this may be the most delicate mission I've ever undertaken. I had a meeting with the President before I left, and both of us felt this was something I had to do myself."

"I realized at once that Project Neptune faces a new crisis,

Charles," Richards said.

"Not necessarily." The Director looked at the glowing tip of his cigar and sighed. "I've spent my career in the wrong business for this assignment. I'm no diplomat, and I scarcely know how to begin."

"If you're trying to tell me that detente has gone into a higher gear and Neptune is being called off, I've been afraid of it from the beginning."

"No, nothing like that, Frank. We need the results of Neptune to solidify detente and make it work. We're totally committed to the project. In fact, the President was saying just today that after you put out to sea he intends to give the leaders of Congress a secret briefing."

"Good. Then the problem can't be all that serious."

"Frank," the Director said, "you don't need me to tell you that no one has ever questioned your patriotism. Never mind the role you're playing in Neptune. Your past record speaks for itself, and I doubt if any man has ever demonstrated his loyalty more convincingly. That's what makes this situation so distressing."

Richards accepted the compliment graciously, and it was evident he had no idea what was coming.

The Director took a deep breath. "Caesar's wife must be above suspicion, too."

The industrialist was stunned; then, as he began to recover from his initial shock, his eyes hardened. "Are you implying—"

"I imply nothing. To be candid, some of my colleagues have been apprehensive about Marie from the outset. Partly because of her French background. Partly because of her reputation as a hostess, which led them to fear she might be an irresponsible social butterfly. And partly because the activities of any attractive woman not under the direct control of the Corporation make them nervous. Sooner or later everyone in the intelligence community becomes paranoid, I'm afraid. It's a highly communicable occupational disease." The Director spoke soothingly.

But Franklin Richards was not mollified. "This is outrageous. I have every right to resent it, Charles, and I do."

"Of course you do. I just ask you to hear me out. We've put everyone directly or indirectly connected with Project Neptune under a microscope as a precautionary measure. That includes Marie. In the very recent past we've investigated her, and she comes out one hundred percent clean. Not a blemish, not even a shadow of doubt. I'm emphasizing that point."

"So I gather." Richards was still angry.

"This very morning, Frank, there was an incident that upset many of us, including me. It could mean nothing, as I myself am inclined to believe, but so much is riding on Project Neptune that I'm compelled to check it out."

"I'm listening."

"We've been playing a tricky game with a double agent, someone we know to have been on the Russian payroll. This morning the agent was making a drop. That is, passing along supposedly secret information to a messenger. The exchange took place at a shopping center not far from here, and was carried out. Now. The agent went into a snack bar and sat two places from Marie, who happened to be having a cup of coffee there."

Richards' knuckles turned white as he gripped the arms of his chair. "Are you suggesting that this agent was using Marie as a messenger?"

"By no means," the Director said. "There was no communication of any kind between them. All I'm presenting to you is a fact. Marie—of all people—was present at a critical time. When a known foreign agent was passing data to a courier."

"I'll stake my own honor on Marie's integrity!"

"Naturally," the Director said. "Her presence may have been nothing but a coincidence. One of those extraordinary, freakish things that make my job a nightmare. But put yourself in my place, Frank. I needn't tell you the importance of Project Neptune. I'm sure you understand its potential significance far better than I do. Nevertheless, I'm responsible to the President, and through him to the American people, for the security of this operation. I'd be remiss in my duty if I failed to make a new check."

"Shall we call Marie in and put it to her?"

"With all due respect, Frank, that's the very last thing I want to do. I share your conviction that Marie happened to be a totally innocent bystander this morning, and that she had no idea of what was happening just a few feet from her. But the first rule of the intelligence business is that even a conviction doesn't become a hard fact until it has been proved."

Richards' anger began to subside. "I sympathize with your position, Charles, and I even feel a bit sorry for you."

"Anglo-Saxon justice rests on the foundation that one is innocent until proved guilty. The Corporation—of necessity —must assume that every individual is guilty unless conclusive evidence demonstrates his innocence. I live in an upside-down world."

"I know of no way you could possibly prove that Marie knew literally nothing about this agent's activities!"

"I believe there is a way, Frank, and the President joins me in the hope that you'll consent to cooperate with the Corporation in making a simple test. The very suggestion is degrading, and I hope you'll forgive the insult."

"I'll do anything to clear Marie!"

"Thank you." The Director breathed more easily. "Keep in mind that the double agent may know nothing of Project Neptune or your connection with it. The test itself will be simple, but our approach to it must be cautious."

"Just tell me what you want done!"

"I shall, Frank, as soon as I hear from Porter, who is trying to set up the arrangements. With any luck I'll hear from him later tonight or early tomorrow morning. I realize I'm trying your patience, but Neptune is the most important operation of its kind ever undertaken, so every risk must be reduced to a minimum. Sometimes the Corporation is too zealous, but in anything that concerns this project, the end does justify the means."

Porter came into the bare room and snapped on the overhead light.

Nancy Wing lay crumpled in a heap, and did not move.

"I had hell's own time finding you and getting in here," he said as he knelt beside her. "Are you okay?"

She moaned, then made an effort to pull herself together. "That bastard was careful not to break any of my bones. But what a workout he gave me. I'm still not sure if I'm alive or dead."

He went to the door, returning with a bottle of whiskey, a sandwich and her shirt, jeans and shoes.

Nancy took the bottle from him and raised it to her lips, then painfully began to dress.

Porter helped her. "If I'd known, I could have prevented this."

"It was that vindictive woman. She came after me because you prefer me to her."

"She tried to stop me from getting in here." He lifted her to her feet so she could finish dressing, then helped her to a chair and offered her the sandwich.

"I'm starved," she said, "but I'm afraid to eat. I've been promised another torture session tonight, and food will just make me sick."

"If I have anything to say about it," Porter told her, "they'll keep their distance from you. All of them."

"I—I haven't dared hope—"

"I know. Eat this and you'll feel better."

Nancy ate ravenously.

"I'm doing everything I can for you," Porter said. "There's even a chance I can get you out of here. Tonight."

She looked at him, hope and fear in her eyes.

"As you know," he said, "I have my own pipelines to Washington. I've already called headquarters and told them I want you released into my custody."

"Oh, Porter, if you can get me out of the hands of these monsters!"

"I think I can manage. But I'll need your help."

"I'll lose my mind if that bastard works me over again. I couldn't see his face, but I know he was enjoying himself."

"Don't think about him," Porter said. "Let's concentrate on you. First, it's no secret to headquarters, of course, that you worked for the Russians. As that very substantial payment I made to you testifies. Now there's an uproar because you taped a phone conversation of mine and took some photographs."

In spite of her exhaustion she sat upright, and her chin jutted forward.

"You can play this either of two ways," Porter said. "If you're stubborn, I can do nothing for you. They'll keep you here and sweat the truth out of you. Every session will be more vicious than the one before it. Until you break down. You're still a beautiful girl, but you'll be hideous by the time they're done."

"I'm sure," she murmured, "that's what that bitch wants to do to me."

"There's no doubt of it," Porter said. "Your alternative is to cooperate with me. I'll not only have you out of here in a quarter of an hour, but I'll get more money from Washington for you."

Nancy stirred. "How much, do you think?"

His scheme was working, but his expression did not change. "I should think that would depend on the extent of your cooperation. Tell me everything you can, and it will be substantial. Work with me actively from now on, and it'll be a great deal more."

She realized he was offering her future employment as a double agent, but she hesitated. "The Americans aren't the only ones who are vindictive. Not many life insurance companies will sell policies to agents who play both sides of the street."

"If we do this the right way," Porter said, "I'm sure I can get you complete protection, too."

"You'd put your own neck on the chopping block for me?"

"That's what I'm doing."

"Why?"

Porter took her hand. "That should be obvious."

He was speaking a language she understood. She had made enough conquests to accept a man's infatuation with her as a normal, natural tribute.

"You have a clear choice," he said. "But you'll have to make up your mind right now. The people who picked you up at our house today want credit for squeezing the truth out of you. Without it costing anyone a bloody penny."

"My shoulders are sore," Nancy said as she reached inside her shirt and squirmed out of her bathing suit top.

Porter was encouraged. In spite of her weariness and discomfort she was making an effort to utilize her strongest weapon, her sex appeal, so she had no intention of submitting to the ministrations of Adrienne and the Deacon.

"There you have it," he said, and waited.

She took another sip from the whiskey bottle. "You've

kept your word to me, and you aren't angry because I spied on you."

"If you're going to work with me, I advise you not to double-cross me again. I'll be taking a chance by making you my partner, and if I go out on a limb for you, don't saw it off or we'll both crash to the ground."

She flipped back her matted, sweat-soaked hair in a self-confident gesture. "Ask away."

"A courier picked up a tape and film from your dashboard glove compartment. Who is he?"

"I don't really know. I've probably never seen him and never shall."

"KGB?"

She surprised him by giggling. "I think so, but I wouldn't swear to it. They aren't my only employers."

So she was acting as a triple agent. "The Chinese?"

Nancy nodded. "There are so few places in this area for letter drops that both of them told me to use the shopping center parking lot."

"What's their interest in me?" Porter demanded.

"The KGB knows you've been doing security control for a super-submarine being built at the Richards yards. I'm to find out all I can about the submarine."

So the Russians were aware of Project Neptune, but were mistaken about the details. Therefore he could use the girl to feed them false data and further confuse them. "What about the Chinese?"

"Peking knows something mysterious is happening at the shipyard, and they believe the Americans are developing a new weapon. They'll take anything I can get for them."

The Chinese hadn't learned the object of Project Neptune either and were fishing. "What are your pay arrangements?"

"I'm on straight salary. With both of them. It's the only way I work."

"Then we mustn't disappoint them," Porter said.

She knew he meant she would be used to pass along useless and misleading information. "On salary?"

"Not exactly. I'll get you several thousand tomorrow as a retainer fee, and then you'll be paid as you perform. In all, I'd think you can count on another twenty-five thousand. Provided you do as you're told and don't try to make any under-the-table deals."

"What I like about doing business with the Americans is that they pay more than the rest put together. But I like working with you even more. I can rely on you, Porter, in or out of bed."

He grinned at her. "Let's make certain I can rely on you."

"You've saved my skin tonight, and I won't forget it."

"I'll be back to fetch you as soon as I've arranged for your release," Porter said, and left the room.

A group of his subordinates awaited him in the living room.

"I want to see Miss Howard privately," he said dismissing the others, then detaining the Deacon for a moment. "I'm giving you a commendation, my lad. Your softening process did the trick."

Adrienne listened in silence to Porter's account of his interview with the Eurasian girl. "It sounds solid," she said at last, "but how do we know she wasn't telling you what she thinks you want to hear?"

"We don't. I'm inclined to believe it was truth, but we'll find out as we go along. You're going back to the Richardses' house?"

"Unless you have something else for me to do."

"You and the Deacon softened up Nancy Wing for me, and that's quite enough for one day. Bring the Director up to date for me, will you?"

"He'll want to know whether she told you any of her

122

contacts, and whether she knows Marie."

"We've made great progress in one evening. By using her as the bait we'll pick up leads on both the Russian and Chinese networks. If Marie is a pawn, Nancy either wouldn't know it or wouldn't admit it. Just tell the Director I'm ready for the step he and I discussed this afternoon, and if that pans out I have a wild idea that should solve most of our problems."

"Very well." She knew better than to question him about matters he was not yet ready to reveal to her. "Where will you be if the Director wants to reach you tonight?"

"I'm moving straight back into my role as the tender-loving-care chap. I'm taking Nancy back to the house and putting her to bed after her ordeal."

"You know," Adrienne said, "if you can really use the Wing woman as a successful shield for Project Neptune, I won't mind all the nights you've slept with her. Not too much."

In the morning Porter returned to the command post, where he conferred at length with the Director, working out a careful strategy. Shortly before noon he was back at the rented house overlooking the sea.

Nancy, who had slept late and luxuriated in a hot bath, was drying her hair, and switched off the apparatus as he came into the bedroom.

"You're looking better," he said as he kissed her.

"I'm feeling more like myself."

"I have some news for you that will speed your improvement," Porter said, and handed her a certified check for $5,000. "This is a down payment on your new job. You can mail it to the bank in Oakland on our way to the airport."

"Where are we going?"

"I've rented an airplane to take us to Seattle for twenty-

123

four hours of shopping, recuperating and celebrating. This is one day you can dress up and wear your *cheongsam.*"

She needed an hour to dress and make up, and a small aircraft awaited them when they reached the local airport. Porter refrained from mentioning that pilot and airplane were being provided by the Corporation. The short flight to Seattle was uneventful, and the driver of the taxi that took them into the city was a Corporation employee, too. Nancy was a stalking horse, and would be guarded far more thoroughly than she knew.

The couple spent the afternoon shopping, and Nancy celebrated the turn in her fortunes by splurging on an extensive new wardrobe. In one shop a $500 silver bracelet caught her fancy, too, so Porter, still playing the role of the infatuated lover, bought it for her. When they returned to their hotel suite she was radiant.

"There's just time for you to change," Porter told her. "There's a private club here in the hotel that's supposed to be the nicest place in town, and I have a temporary membership, so I've made us a reservation for dinner."

"You're too nice to be a boss," Nancy said, "and far too sweet to be in our rotten business. Which of my new outfits shall I wear for you?"

"Surprise me," he said, "but just for the fun of it wear your wig."

"I thought I'd go Oriental tonight."

"Let's not push our luck. I don't think we've been followed, but I prefer to take no chances."

He read the newspapers while she prepared for the evening, and when she rejoined him she was wearing a low-cut white dress, with Western makeup that matched her blonde wig. She was lovely, and Porter told himself she was undoubtedly the most beautiful triple agent in the intelligence community.

Others thought she was attractive, too, and she created a stir as they were conducted down the length of the oak-paneled dining room to their table. Their cocktails were served, and Porter raised his glass. "To you and me, partner."

"To us," Nancy said, and they drank.

Another couple were led to the adjacent table, and the men feigned surprise. "Join us," Franklin Richards said.

Two waiters and a wine steward stood nearby, watching the reactions of the women as Porter said, "Mrs. Richards, Miss Wing."

Marie was her usual bland, cheerful self. She knew, of course, that Porter and Adrienne were not really married, so she undoubtedly concluded that this woman had a truly personal relationship with him.

Nancy appeared to be somewhat impressed.

Neither indicated any previous meeting by as much as a flicker, and unless they were superb actresses they were unacquainted.

As they were sipping their drinks and making small talk, however, Marie suddenly interrupted the conversation. "Don't I know you from somewhere?" she asked the younger woman.

Franklin Richards stiffened.

Porter sat very still.

Nancy shook her head. "I don't think so. I've never forgotten any celebrities I've ever met."

The moment passed, the conversation became general again, and when their second drinks were served Richards, following instructions, asked casually, "Where are you staying these days, Porter?"

"Oh, Nancy and I have rented a vacation house on the Strait of Juan de Fuca. We're spending most of our time doing nothing but work on our suntans."

"Well," Richards said, "we have a house up that way. You'll have to come over. And perhaps Miss Wing would like a tour of our shipyard."

The maneuver, Porter thought, was one of the most delicate he had ever attempted.

"I'd love it," Nancy said.

Porter was certain she was sincere.

"I know!" Marie exclaimed.

Her husband gripped the arms of his chair.

"When you said you're staying on the strait I remembered. You visited the new shopping center the other morning, Miss Wing. I'm sure you did."

Nancy didn't know what to reply, and Porter was no help, so she decided truth was the best defense. "I believe I did attend to some errands at a shopping center one day this week."

"Indeed you did, and you stopped in at a little snack bar. I was having coffee there at the same time."

"Now that you mention it, I did go into a little place for a cup of tea."

"I knew it!" Marie was triumphant. "I have a photographic memory for attractive people. Don't I, Frank?"

"Indeed she does," Richards said.

So the coincidence was explained. Or was it? If Marie was as innocent as she seemed, the appearance of the two women in the shopping center snack bar had no significance. And, on the surface, only someone innocent of wrongdoing would mention the matter in front of a man who, she knew, held a position of importance in the Corporation. On the other hand, if she was guilty, only a diabolically clever woman would try to confuse an experienced intelligence officer by mentioning the trivial incident.

Franklin Richards was beaming, and it was obvious he

126

believed his wife's inadvertent explanation had cleared the air.

Porter was content to let him think the subject was closed. The Corporation could keep Marie under close surveillance without interference, and what her husband didn't know might not hurt him. More evidence had to be accumulated before a final verdict could be rendered.

After a leisurely dinner the two couples separated, with Porter and Nancy returning to their suite. She accepted a nightcap from him, placed it on the coffee table in front of her and momentarily forgot it.

"Did Franklin Richards really invite me to tour his shipyard, or was he just being polite?" she asked.

"I'm sure it was a genuine invitation."

"How could he?"

"I don't see why not," Porter said. "It's his shipyard, so he can do as he pleases."

"Suppose the KGB is right, and he's building a super-submarine there for the American Navy. Mind you, I haven't asked you whether the report is true or false. After the way you've treated me I don't want to cause problems for you. But assume there is such a super-submarine. How can Richards allow a stranger to wander through his shipyard?"

"He knows where I work, so he must believe that anyone associated with me is safe."

There was a wicked gleam in her eyes as she smiled. "How I'd love to notify Moscow that I've had the invitation from him! Even Andropov himself will become excited."

"When we return to the strait," Porter said, "I suggest you send off such a message."

"You wouldn't object?"

He shrugged. "When I'm assigned to a case, I have responsibilities. If Richards elects to expose a project he's handling under a government contract, that's his problem. Until I'm told to protect that submarine—if there is one—Richards can take his own risks."

"Will he actually let me tour the place?"

Porter grinned. "Sure. I think they'll ask us to their house in the next few days, and if he doesn't mention the shipyard to you, there's no law that prevents you from jogging his memory."

"I was sure you'd step in and stop the whole thing!"

"You improved my rating with my bosses when you sacrificed the Russian observation team in Hong Kong. You've done it again by telling me the Chinese are fishing for information. So I know of no reason to cut you off when you can do yourself good in Moscow. We're partners, after all. What's more, you're my girl."

Nancy rose, came to him and slid her arms around his neck. "I am, more than you know. But you'll find out, beginning right now."

As he followed her into the bedroom he congratulated himself for having conducted a successful maneuver. Nancy was shrewd in protecting her own interests, but she had been catapulted into a situation beyond her depth as an intelligence agent, and was hampered by her ingenuousness and her narcissism. He would bring off the trickiest caper of his career provided that he continued to convince her he was so infatuated with her that she could use him for her own purposes.

EIGHT

When they returned from Seattle to the rented house, Nancy happily busied herself unpacking her new belongings, which filled several suitcases. While she was occupied Porter wandered off to the kitchen for a word with the housekeeper.

"What's new, Mrs. Stevens?"

"Miss Howard has called twice from the shipyard. She wants to see you as soon as it can be arranged."

"I think I know what's troubling Miss Howard," he said with a smile. "I'll drop out there right now."

Explaining to Nancy that he wanted to contact his superiors with regard to their next cash payment to her, Porter first drove to the command post. There, as he anticipated, he found Blackman awaiting orders.

"Tomorrow morning our little lady will be going to the shopping center again to make another drop. I want a heavy tail placed on that courier. We've got to learn the next step in the chain of communication so we can trace it to its source."

"We'll follow him," Blackman said. "I won't bungle again. It seems to me the courier will probably head for some point on the shore and go over to Vancouver Island by launch or helicopter. The natural transmittal center hereabouts is Victoria, and by crossing an international border into British Columbia he can make surveillance more difficult."

"That's what I'd do if I were wearing the courier's boots," Porter said.

"With your permission I'll call Colonel Redfern of the Royal Mounted intelligence and alert him. Then he'll be prepared to take over if the courier shows up in Victoria."

"Do it," Porter said, "and keep in touch with him by shortwave throughout the operation. The Canadians are tired of being used as an espionage base by Moscow and Peking, and they're bloody efficient, so I'm sure they'll work with us."

His arrangements completed, he drove rapidly to the shipyard, where he found Adrienne in an office bearing the legend *Deputy Personnel Director*.

She wasted no time. "Porter," she said, "either you've really flipped over the Wing woman or the part you're playing has destroyed your perspective. Frank Richards has just told me she's going to pay a visit to the yard—at your suggestion. Do you realize the risk we'll be taking with someone who is still working against us? I think you've gone mad!"

He placed a hand on her shoulder, halting her angry diatribe. "Come with me," he said, "and then you'll understand."

They walked in silence to his car, which was parked behind the main administration building, and drove about a mile and a half to the far end of the shipyard.

"You're going the wrong way," Adrienne said. "The *Neptune*'s dock is at the far side of the yard."

"Keep that in mind," Porter said. "We're making a little preview tour of what Nancy Wing is going to see."

They left the car and walked a short distance to an inner fence of electrified steel, topped by barbed wire. A sign adjacent to a small gate announced: RESTRICTED AREA. AU-

Armed guards were on patrol inside and outside the fence, just as they were at the *Neptune*'s drydock, and a cluster of guards stood at the gate itself.

"Hello, Bryan," Porter said to one of his own men, who was in charge of the group. "I'm taking Miss Howard on a little sightseeing tour."

Adrienne had to sign in, as did Porter. It was obvious that she was annoyed, but she waited until she and Porter were alone again inside the gate. "I thought I was in charge at the Richards yard. How does it happen that Bryan is on duty here without my knowledge?"

"Bryan and a great many others," Porter said, "are on direct assignment by the Director. This operation is my private baby, strictly outside your jurisdiction."

They came to a high board fence, and had to be passed through an inner gate. Beyond it stood a drydock, where about one hundred men were at work, many of them using pneumatic drills as they bolted sections of metal together.

Porter led Adrienne up a steep flight of rough, wooden stairs, and at last they came to a scaffolding platform. From the heights they looked down at a huge ship under construction.

Adrienne was puzzled. "It looks like a submarine."

"It is," Porter answered. "The largest submarine ever constructed. It has an overall length of three eighths of a mile, and fully loaded should have a gross weight of more than twenty-three thousand tons."

"My Lord. I thought there were no submarines afloat with a gross tonnage of more than nine thousand, absolute maximum."

"You're right," Porter said. "The *Neptune* is going to be unique. Observe the construction of her sail. Looks a bit like a whale's mouth, doesn't it? Big enough to open and gobble up almost anything, even a smaller submarine."

Adrienne glanced at him, but made no comment.

"The construction of the aft deck is unique, too. Her silhouette is unlike that of any other submarine ever built in this country or Great Britain. Or Russia, for that matter."

"You say she's being called the *Neptune*."

"Right. Her name and serial numbers will appear on her prow in the next day or two. Along with her periscope, atomic projectile emission plates and other paraphernalia."

"I'm afraid I don't understand."

"Neither will Nancy Wing," Porter said. "One of the many facets of Franklin Richards' genius is his ability to build ships in sections, completing the job in a small fraction of the time that any other yard would require." He couldn't help grinning as he added, "Richards designed her himself. In almost no time. And construction has been under way for only forty-eight hours."

"But that's impossible!"

"Richards knows it, the Director knows it and so do the workmen assigned to the job. Every last one of them is a trusted Richards employee with years of seniority. The project should be nearing completion by the early part of next week."

"This makes no sense," Adrienne said. "And why call the submarine the *Neptune?*"

"I neglected to mention one other aspect of her construction that makes her extraordinary." Porter leaned on the platform's wooden railing. "Her hull is made of aluminum, blended with certain alloys. An incredibly lightweight metal, so malleable that it can be molded by hand."

"If I didn't actually see that monstrous vessel down there, I'd swear you were joking."

"This," Porter said, "will be the only ship in the world that's all hull. No interior of any kind."

132

Adrienne stared at him for a moment, then burst into laughter.

"At last you've guessed."

"This is just a dummy," she said. "A mock-up."

"Correct. It isn't actually a ship. Nancy gave me the tipoff for it when she said that the Russians want information on our new super-submarine. This means—at least I hope it does—that they know nothing whatever as yet about the real *Neptune*. They've caught wind of something going on here, and they've assumed we're building a mammoth submarine either to find their sunken *Zolóto* or to raise it to the surface."

"So you're obliging them by building this fantastic shell!"

"The largest red herring on earth," Porter said. "The Director saw the potential the moment I mentioned the idea to him, and so did Richards, who stayed up all night to design the hull. Some of the men who are working down there at this moment aren't welders. They're sculptors."

"Do you mean that literally?"

"I do. Flown in from Corporation headquarters. A couple of them have never worked in metal before, but they're shaping up nicely. Pun intended."

She looked down at the hull. "What a marvelous decoy. If the scheme works."

"It should. We'll give it every opportunity. In the next day or so Nancy and I will be invited to the Richardses' house for dinner. By the way, it will be wise if you spend that evening elsewhere. I doubt if Nancy has fond memories of you."

"I prefer not to watch you two holding hands," Adrienne said, her voice tart.

He deemed it wise not to comment. "Richards will ask her to come to the yard for a tour. She won't be taken anywhere near the real *Neptune*, of course. He'll bring her here, and they'll climb up to this platform. Just the two of them. Then Richards will be called below on a supposed emergency. He'll go off to confer with somebody, and Nancy will be alone up here. For about five minutes."

"I hope she'll be carrying her trusty minicamera, and that she has a lot of film," Adrienne said.

"Two rolls. One for Moscow and one for Peking."

"You're smart, Porter. I disliked the whole plan of using the Wing woman this way, but you've established a perfect pipeline to the KGB. And presumably to the Chinese, too."

"The Russians will be certain to see the *Zolóto* connection," Porter said. "I'm guessing the Chinese know nothing about the lost Russian submarine, so they'll simply believe we're building this oversized whale for its own sake. That'll give their naval intelligence people something to stew about."

"Do you see any bugs in your scheme?"

"Several," he said. "An expert in submersibles might not be fooled by this decoy, but I'm assuming Nancy doesn't know all that much about ships."

"I was graduated from her level a long time ago," Adrienne said, "and I was taken in by it. Completely."

"The Red Navy analysts will need time to study the photographs, of course. Eventually they'll want more, particularly data on the power plants, blueprints of the unusual sail—and so forth. By that time the real *Neptune* will have dredged up the *Zolóto* submarine. If our luck holds. A gigantic hoax like this is either one hundred percent successful or a total failure, with no in between."

"I like it."

"The other weakness is something I can't measure. Marie Richards."

"I'm convinced Marie is legitimate," Adrienne said.

"Maybe so." He told her in detail about the meeting with

134

Marie and Franklin Richards in Seattle.

"That sounds like her. I'm willing to bet my own career on her innocence."

"You have no proof."

"Only my feminine intuition. Which also tells me that the Wing woman is going to cause us some more problems before we're done with her."

Her dislike of Nancy was flattering, but he continued to avoid such discussions. "The reason I'm still apprehensive over Marie Richards," he said, "is because she's the one person in this entire project whom we can't control. She may be blameless, as you believe. If she isn't, though, then God help us."

"You're going to keep her under surveillance?"

"Until the *Neptune* puts out to sea, and even then we'll monitor her cables. On second thought, I believe the expedition should maintain radio silence except for emergencies."

They looked again at the decoy, then descended the stairs to the ground.

"So far," Porter said, "we're doing okay. But as we get closer to sailing time, double your precautions against sabotage."

Nancy Wing followed the shore road to the Richards shipyard, and was delighted by the way things were working out. Porter had expressed no interest in accompanying her, saying he was interested only in the defense projects to which he was assigned. His docility was a help, too, and it was no problem keeping him satisfied—and compliant.

She halted the convertible at the entrance gate, telling the chief guard on duty that Franklin Richards was expecting her.

He made a telephone call, then assigned a guard to ride with her and guide her to the administration building.

Richards greeted her in his handsome office, its walls lined with photographs of ships he had built. "You took my advice and wore pants," he said. "Good. We'll be climbing some tricky scaffolding. Would you like a drink before we go, Nancy?"

"No, thank you. I'll need to be sober if I'm going to climb ladders."

They drove to the decoy site in Richards' Aston Martin, went through the formalities at both security gates, then climbed to the platform above the dummy ship, the workmen swarming below paying no attention to them.

"You're one of the first outsiders to see the *Neptune*," Richards said when they reached the makeshift observation platform. "The Navy will make an announcement about her construction in three months, when she's scheduled to be launched."

"A very impressive ship," Nancy murmured as she stared down at the dummy.

"There isn't another in the world like her," Richards said. "I'm afraid I'm not allowed to discuss her dimensions, speed or the size of her crew. The U.S. Navy is very sensitive about such statistics. But when she goes to sea you can tell all your friends you saw her on the ways here." He played the part of the proud shipbuilder to perfection.

"Will she be used as a transport for passengers? She's so large." Nancy's ingenuousness was equally clever.

"The Navy will do what it pleases, but she's the first multipurpose submarine ever made," he replied. "A launching platform for atomic projectiles. A transport for Marines. Or," he added, pausing for an instant, "she'll also be capable of performing certain underwater research functions."

He plunged a hand into a jacket pocket, which was a signal to a Corporation agent below.

The man promptly hailed him, shouting that he had to see

136

him on a matter of the utmost importance.

Richards excused himself. "Come below with me if you're uncomfortable up here," he said. "If not, I'll be right back."

"I'd love to stay a bit longer," she said.

"Of course." He disappeared down the stairs.

The opportunity, Nancy told herself, was an agent's dream come true. The workmen were ignoring her, Richards went to a corner of the lot to talk to the man who had summoned him, and no one within sight seemed aware of her existence.

She took a ballpoint pen from her shoulder bag, steadied it against the rough wooden rail and clicked it repeatedly. Then, after dropping it into her bag, she removed an ordinary-looking lipstick and repeated the process.

When Franklin Richards returned to the platform she was applying a coating of lipstick to her mouth. "This has been a thrilling experience," she said. "I don't know how I can ever thank you for it."

"Your pleasure," he said, "has already repaid me."

They returned to his office, where she accepted a cup of tea, but she stayed for no more than a quarter of an hour, saying she was already late for an appointment.

Richards made a brief telephone call when she left.

A Corporation employee followed her out of the parking lot, and another picked her up at the gate. Blackman had established a network that operated smoothly, and every few miles, as Nancy headed up the shore road in the direction of the rented house she shared with Porter, another car took over.

The surveillance was routine, but finally the man covering her at that moment broke radio silence. "She's just turned onto Spruce Lane," he said. "Take over at the other end."

A one-story wooden building, badly in need of paint, stood at the end of the lane, and over the door was a weatherbeaten sign:

COUNTRY STORE

Canned Goods   Groceries

Tobacco   Hardware

Drinks   Bait & Tackle

C. Agropolis, Proprietor

When Nancy entered, a man with curly hair and a handle-bar moustache lounged behind the counter, smoking a cigar and listening to a baseball game on a transistor radio.

There was one other customer in the place, a burly man in a flannel shirt and nondescript trousers, who was selecting soups and baked beans from a sparsely stocked shelf. He was intent on his labors, and ignored the girl.

"I have a little problem," Nancy said, "and I hope you can help me. Do you carry cartridges for ballpoint pens?"

"That depends on the make," the man behind the counter said, speaking with a heavy Greek accent.

"I'm not sure. Let me show you." She fished in her shoulder bag, and finally produced her pen.

The proprietor turned it over in his hand. "I'm not sure, lady," he said. "I look in the back." He disappeared into an inner room, taking the pen with him.

The male customer moved from the grocery shelf to another, where he studied a row of pipe tobacco tins.

The proprietor reappeared. "Sorry, lady," he said. "I got none that will fit this pen."

Nancy took the pen from him. "Oh, dear. I don't suppose you have cosmetics here?"

"A few things. What you want?"

"I need a new lipstick of this shade." She handed him the lipstick she had used to good effect at the shipyard.

He removed the top and stared at the contents. "Maybe I got it, maybe I don't," he said, and vanished again.

Nancy lighted a cigarette while she waited.

The other customer took a tin of tobacco and went to a

refrigerator with a glass door, where he peered at six-packs of beer.

Again the proprietor returned. "This is the closest I got," he said, handing her the old lipstick and another with a dust-covered case.

Nancy dropped her lipstick into her bag, opened the new one and placed a tiny smear on the back of her hand. "This isn't exactly what I want, but it will do. How much do I owe you?"

"Two dollar anna quarter, lady."

While she was producing the right amount, the other customer moved to the counter with his purchases. "Gonna rain tonight, Chris?"

"Sure. All the time we get rain."

Nancy thanked the proprietor and departed.

A few moments later the other customer left, too, climbed into his dilapidated pickup truck and snapped on his short-wave radio.

Porter manned the telephone line in the command post himself, speaking to Corporation headquarters, while Blackman paced the length of the room. "This is a red flag, urgent. Give me a rundown on Chris Agropolis. Runs a country store on Spruce Lane, about twelve miles east of Port Angeles. Hell no, you will not call me back. I'll hold the line, and if you don't get back to me in no more than five minutes, you'll explain the delay to the Director. In writing." He sat back in his chair and rolled a cigarette with his free hand.

Blackman stopped pacing. "We know there's a camera in that ballpoint pen. Mrs. Stevens will check as soon as she has the chance after the girl gets back to the house, but it's safe to assume there's a camera in the lipstick, too."

"Seems that way," Porter said. "Mac's report sounds like a classic letter-drop."

"Franklin Richards doesn't know if she took any pictures of the decoy submarine?"

"He couldn't tell, and neither could Vic, who was watching her through binoculars. She fiddled around with her shoulder bag, and all he saw for certain was that she used a lipstick just before Richards returned to the scaffolding. So the whole thing fits."

Blackman smiled, but remained tense.

"You're sure you have enough people covering this Agropolis?"

"A small army."

"Just so they understand they're to keep under cover, and under no circumstances are they to pick him up. Ditto for any contact he makes. If Nancy delivered film to him, we want it to have clear, unimpeded sailing to its destination."

"The boys understand, Porter. There won't be any slips. What I don't understand, though, is why the girl used a new courier drop instead of waiting until tomorrow morning and going through the shopping center routine."

"Because I know about the shopping center, and she wants to pass along the film behind my back. Probably she had instructions to use Agropolis in an emergency. Either that or he was being saved for vital drops."

"We could send a team to question his neighbors about him," Blackman said, "but I don't want to do anything that will either tip him off or scare him away."

"No neighbors," Porter said, and turned back to the telephone.

"Yes, Porter here. . . . Oh, splendid! Tell Brian Davidson he's made my day. . . . Fire away. . . . Right. . . . Right. . . . Lovely. . . . I can't remember the last time headquarters came through for the poor wretches in the field. We bless you for this, all of us." He replaced the instrument in its cradle and, enjoying the suspense he was creating, carefully rolled another cigarette.

"Well, Porter?" Blackman demanded.

"A noble name. Aristotle Christopher Agropolis. Aged sixty-one. An ignoble background. Spent World War Two in Russia. Surfaced in Athens when the Communist party became legal, but went underground again during the Papadopoulis dictatorship. Migrated to this country in early sixty-nine. Spent a year in Seattle, moved to Olympia, Washington, and about three months ago bought the little store near the Strait of Juan de Fuca he now operates. No immediate family in the United States and has few known friends. Lives quietly, minds his own business and stays out of trouble. No interest in politics. Headquarters will dig up more on him if we want it, but this is enough."

"Plenty," Blackman said.

Porter allowed himself the luxury of a dry chuckle. "Our Chris has KGB written all over him. We still don't know how Nancy gets in touch with the Chinese or what she tells them. For that matter, we aren't really certain she works for them. But there can't be any question now that she's reporting on the sly to Moscow."

"Congratulations," Blackman said. "This is your most effective caper in a long time."

"We won't flap our wings and crow just yet," Porter said. "We know the bait is being offered to Andropov on a silver platter, but it remains to be seen whether he swallows it."

"There's not much we can do to speed his digestive process," Blackman said.

"You're wrong, old boy. But I want him to see the bait and taste it before I shove it gently down his throat." Porter stood, yawned and stretched. "Nancy must be home by now, so I'll go make all the appropriate noises to her." He walked

141

to the door, then turned. "That reminds me. Add three men to the detail keeping watch over her. That girl is worth her weight in diamonds to us, and I want her to stay healthy."

He drove the short distance to the house, where Mrs. Stevens awaited him.

"Her ladyship went down to the beach," the housekeeper said, "so I checked her bag. That lipstick is a camera." She looked grim.

"Cheer up. If she runs out of film I'll buy her more." He sauntered off to the beach.

Mrs. Stevens, who knew nothing about what had transpired, could only gape at him.

Nancy had changed into a bikini and was sunning herself. She had a right to look pleased with herself, Porter thought.

She smiled up at him. "I wish you'd come with me. Frank Richards showed me the huge submarine he's building, and it was an incredible sight."

"I want no part of it, thanks." He removed and folded his jacket, loosened his necktie and lowered himself to her blanket. "Ready to earn the next share of your fee?"

"Always." She sat up, clasped her hands around one knee and leaned back.

"Headquarters," Porter said, "is ready to pay you another five thousand if you'll tell me your Chinese contact."

Nancy hesitated.

"I told them it was no go if they picked him up. You don't want Peking gunning for you, and neither do I."

She pushed back a lock of her long hair and frowned. "If they don't intend to pick him up, why do they want to know?"

Porter shrugged. "I assume they want to trace the network." It was well worth $5,000 to learn the nature and extent of the work she was supposedly doing for the Chinese.

"All right, then. I've already told you once. The shopping center pickup."

"I see." He saw a great deal. Not only would the Corporation and the Canadian Mounties be saved many days of hard labor, keeping large numbers of operatives tied up, but he understood the order of her allegiances. She was feeding questionable material to Peking, but Moscow remained her primary employer.

Consequently he would continue to bear down in dealings with the KGB, and could relegate the Chinese to a secondary place. His own priorities were settled at last.

"I hope your headquarters will keep their word to you," she said. "I'll be under suspicion if the courier disappears."

"Never fear," He said, leaning toward her and kissing her. "I'm protecting you." For once, he thought, he was telling her the truth.

"What arrangements shall we make?"

"I've prepared some photostats of various charts you can pass along. They're sufficiently valid that Peking won't think you're turning in useless rubbish. Make your shopping center drop on Friday, and I'll have the five thousand for you that same day."

"Why Friday?"

The question was shrewd, but he couldn't explain he wanted her kept busy that morning because he had to attend to something of primary importance himself. "Headquarters doesn't take me into its confidence, you know, but I suppose the chaps who'll be tailing him are off duty for the next couple of days."

"You know so much about these things," she said, and laughed.

"Too much." This was the opportune moment to plant the seed that would become the core of his deceptive caper. "I'm thinking of getting out."

143

"What will you do?"

"What will we do, you mean. I'll retire. Provided I can stash away one large bundle of cash first. Then you and I can go off somewhere and forget this rotten business."

Nancy was too surprised to reply.

Porter gave no indication that he knew what she was thinking. She was accumulating her own nest egg, and had no intention of spending years in retirement with a grizzled former agent who was fifteen years her senior. Once she disentangled herself from the intelligence community she would return to her theatrical career with a vengeance.

"I don't know what to say," she murmured. "It never crossed my mind you'd want to retire. Of course," she added hastily, "there's nothing I'd love more than to go off with you somewhere."

Porter put his arms around her and, staring out at the sea over her shoulder, told himself that every cog in his master plan was meshing. If anything, things were going too well.

Nothing in the schedule for the *Neptune* followed traditional routines. Other ships were launched, went out for sea trials and, when they returned to port, simultaneously underwent adjustments and received finishing touches. Other ships were launched at elaborate ceremonies, with celebrities in attendance while a prominent lady went through the christening ritual.

The interior of the *Neptune* was in final shape: furniture was in place, gear was stowed away, flour and sugar and potatoes and canned goods were stored in the hold directly below the galley. Only the electronic gear that would be flown to her at sea, along with the submersible football field, was still missing.

The entire crew was on board, every member having passed the scrutiny of Adrienne Howard and her associates

144

following a thorough investigation by the FBI. The passengers—scientists, underwater experts and electronic specialists—would be flown to the ship at sea in another ten to fourteen days. Until then their cabins stood empty.

Not even the genius of Franklin Richards would enable the *Neptune* to sail on her mission across the Pacific until she had undergone at least the minimum trials, so an entire new procedure had been devised. She would spend a week and a half in the protected waters of the shipyard harbor, where various operations would be simulated. Most adjustments would be made in the harbor, and only if necessary would she be taken back into drydock.

The day of the launching was overcast, and not even the workmen who had built the 42,000-ton ship were on hand, their absence breaking another tradition. No bands played, and only a small group of people gathered on the platform built at her prow. The only woman, Marie Richards, was unobtrusively dressed. Three admirals were present in civilian attire, and even their aides had been excluded. The Director of the Corporation had wanted to come from Washington, but had been dissuaded by Porter, who had pointed out that he might be recognized and that his presence would be regarded as significant.

Franklin Richards remained in his office until the last possible moment, attending to routine business, but a quarter of an hour before he was due to join his wife and the admirals he received a telephone call from the President of the United States. The call came in on a private line rather than through the shipyard switchboard, but the conversation was guarded.

"I just called to wish you and your ship Godspeed, Frank," the President said. "I hope you find enough coal deposits and oil fields in the sea to help us break the back of this energy crisis."

"We'll try our best, Mr. President," Richards said.

145

"Do I understand correctly that the *Neptune* won't slide down ways?"

"That's right, sir. We carry our own generator and cranes for underwater coal exploration purposes, and we don't want any of our equipment jarred out of place if the ship smashes into the side of the ways. So we're using a special system I've devised. We'll force seawater into the drydock, and the *Neptune* will float out by herself."

"Very clever. Good luck to you, Frank."

"I hope to be in Washington for a day or two before our expedition sails, Mr. President."

"Good! Give me advance notice, and bring your charming wife with you. We'd be delighted to see both of you before you take off."

"Thank you, Mr. President, I'll let you know." Richards rang off, and as it was time to leave, he went to the parking lot and drove alone to the launching area.

Most of the roads in the vicinity were closed, and Corporation agents were strategically stationed on the heights to insure that no tourists or other unwanted visitors might witness the event by accident. Or otherwise.

Porter and Adrienne surveyed the scene from the bridge of the *Neptune*. Their subordinates were everywhere in the yard, in the surrounding neighborhood and in several harmless-looking fishing boats in the harbor, so the launching was as private as security precautions could make it. Unknown to anyone else, including the ship's officers, a dozen members of the crew were actually Corporation undercover agents. No one would pry today, either deliberately or inadvertently, and there would be no leaks of information.

But the task that faced Captain Humphries and his staff was overwhelming, and the atmosphere was tense. Most ships, even those built in wartime, were tested at sea in trials that lasted anywhere from a week to a month. Because of her extraordinary mission the *Neptune* would be denied that privilege, and any errors in construction would have to be unearthed by unorthodox means, any tuneups she needed would have to be discerned by subtle methods.

The bridge was automated, with a dial-filled console showing the duty officer all he needed to know to aid navigation. Sensitive needles told him the wind pressure, the running of the sea, his precise location and the direction in which the vessel was moving. Two radarscopes indicated the presence of other ships within a radius of ten miles, and a third, a sophisticated over-the-horizon radar, alerted him to the approach by sea or air of an object as far as forty miles away. Nearby, too, was a master board, a duplicate of the instruments used in the chief engineer's office below, that told at a glance the second by second performance of the engines.

The *Neptune* was even equipped with two sets of Denny-Brown stabilizers, fins that could be extended in foul weather and retracted in fair weather. They were intended to hold the ship steady, reducing both her rolling and pitching when the seas were rough, and customarily were employed only on luxury passenger liners. So much of the *Neptune*'s unique equipment required special handling, however, that Franklin Richards had taken the precaution of installing the stabilizers to protect her.

The wheel could be operated manually, to be sure, but it was automated, too, so the ship's course could be preset by push-button controls, with a minicomputer making compensations for variations in the wind and strength of the sea. The five petty officers who served as helmsmen had taken courses at a computer school to prepare them for their present task.

In spite of the tensions the bridge was quiet. Captain Humphries stood at the control panel, and looked out through the plate-glass windows that gave him a more than 180° view. The executive officer, a Navy commander on

147

leave, was stationed beside the engineering instrument board, and the first lieutenant took up his post at the radar screens.

A junior officer was on duty at the telephone switchboard, and when a light set in the bulkhead in front of him turned red, he became active. "The chief engineer's compliments, sir. All preparations below are completed."

"Very good, Mr. Blake," Captain Humphries said. "Instruct the engineering division to stand by."

"Aye aye, sir." The young officer repeated the orders.

Through the windows those on the bridge could see Franklin Richards join the group on the platform.

Porter and Adrienne moved into the open on the starboard "flying wing," an extension of the bridge, so they could hear the proceedings.

Richards pulled a switch that slowly raised the metal plates at either side of the drydock, and the sea rushed in, the water level rising swiftly as the panels ascended to a height of about ten feet.

Within moments, or so it seemed, the twin screw propellers were covered by the surging, foaming water.

Captain Humphries picked up a red telephone that connected him with the chief engineer. "You may commence operations," he said.

The power was turned on, the bridge began to vibrate slightly, and the *Neptune* came to life.

The captain smiled. "You may notify the sponsor."

A lieutenant went to the port flying bridge and signaled to a small group of officers and men behind him. The task could have been performed by telephone, but at this solemn moment the old traditions were being observed.

The American flag began to ascend the mainmast, with a blue and white Richards pennant below it.

The water continued to rise, and soon the ship would be afloat.

Marie Richards took hold of a bottle of champagne attached to a long ribbon. "I christen you *Neptune,*" she said in a clear voice that carried to the flying wings. "May Almighty God protect you and your crew, and may you succeed in your work."

She released the bottle, which descended in an arc and smashed against the prow.

The executive officer gave an order, and everyone on the bridge saluted.

The timing was perfect, and a moment later the *Neptune* was afloat. No longer a mass of metals and machinery, a container for equipment and gear and supplies, she became an entity in her own right, a living inheritor of the traditions and customs men had observed since they had first gone to sea.

The group on the platform stood at attention, too. Then Marie hugged her husband, and Porter could see that she was weeping.

"Stand alert, helmsman," Captain Humphries said. "Position neutral."

"Aye aye, sir."

Again the master picked up the red telephone. "Reverse," he said. "You may proceed at low speed, eleven-dash five."

The *Neptune* crawled out of her berth, backing gently into the harbor. The great adventure on which so much planning and effort, so much time and money had been lavished was at last under way.

NINE

The planning and execution of the *Neptune*'s construction had been so precise that, after a week of limited trials, it was determined that only minor adjustments needed to be made. Her departure on her mission was scheduled for two weeks later, by which time the changes would be made, and additional supplies and gear would be taken on board.

Immediately prior to Franklin Richards' presailing trip to Washington he conferred at length with Porter behind closed doors in the Corporation command post, and the next day Porter paid a visit to the engineering and naval architecture divisions of the shipyard. His business there completed, he went to Adrienne's office.

Her subordinates continued to keep watch on the *Neptune* ashore and at sea, but the major part of her immediate task was finished, and her mood was ebullient. "I'm going to soak up the sun in a deck chair every day, courtesy of the Corporation," she said. "We're on the last lap ashore."

"You are," Porter said.

Adrienne's broad smile faded. "On second thought, if a typhoon hits us I'll probably get seasick."

"Just suppose, and I'm cursed with a vivid imagination, that the KGB is lying in wait for us. We raise the *Zolóto* and start home with our prize. Oh, the U.S. Navy and Air Force are protecting us, but the Russians send a powerful squadron to intercept us and reclaim their property. Will we send them packing—and risk World War Three? Or will we surrender their submarine, its secrets and their dead to them? Without a murmur and without publicity, of course, which would make it far easier to keep face."

"I don't know," she said. "I can't think of a more terrible dilemma. It would have to be settled by the President and the National Security Council."

"The problem has kept me awake nights," Porter said. "And so has the possibility that the Russians might try to sink the *Neptune* while she's sailing to the South China Sea. I haven't been troubled by insomnia for years, so I'm doing something to get rid of it. I'm eligible for a pension, so I'm resigning from the Corporation."

Adrienne was horrified. "Now? When Project Neptune is reaching the make-or-break stage?"

"I've dealt with one crisis after another for more years than I care to remember," Porter said. "I'm sick of the business, and God knows that's the truth. I'm also a lovesick lunatic who wants to go off somewhere with his girl. Preferably a private island for two, provided I can raise the money to buy the place."

"I see." She stared at him for a long time. "No, Porter. You're the best in the business, but this is too much. The KGB won't buy it."

"Even Andropov has read Pushkin," he said. "Tolstoy. Dostoevsky. Not to mention the forbidden moderns like Boris Pasternak. *Weltschmerz* and love are an irresistibly powerful combination. Every good Russian knows that."

"No, Porter!" There was panic in Adrienne's voice. "You're pushing your luck too far."

"You're just jealous," he said, "because I'm taking some-

151

body else to that private island."

"It so happens I am jealous, but that's beside the point. You're assuming that Andropov and his staff are cretins."

"All bureaucrats are cretins. Don't take my word for it. Just spend a full day with Brian Davidson."

"You've lost your sense of humor along with your intelligence," Adrienne said.

"You're very short-sighted. People who develop a taste for red herring lose their appetites for ordinary food. So I'm thinking of opening a posh restaurant on that private island."

She was crestfallen. "Nothing I might say will dissuade you?"

"If I'd wanted a lingering death," he said, "I'd have applied, long ago, for a desk job at Corporation headquarters. Atrophy would have set in immediately."

"When do you take off for your brave new world?"

"Today. Blackman will attend to routines, under your supervision. I'm formally handing over the command to you, as of right now."

"The last time I shed tears over a male I was fourteen," Adrienne said. "He had acne and wore braces on his teeth."

"It was his omniscience and razor wit that enslaved you, I presume?"

"It was his stupidity, actually. He was congenitally incapable of realizing he might be defeated."

"But he had charm?"

"In my naive, girlish way I found him overwhelming," Adrienne said, and embraced him.

Porter kissed her, and as they clung to each other he told himself to put her out of his mind. A man in his position could not afford attachments that might weaken his resolve.

She broke away from him and dabbed at her eyes. "Look what you've made me do," she said. "I hope you're satisfied."

152

"I'll do my best to conform. Before we meet again I'll visit an orthodontist and a dermatologist." Porter turned away quickly and left the room.

The names of the nightclubs changed frequently on Rush Street, adjacent to the Chicago Gold Coast, but the atmosphere remained the same. The lighting was dim, the prices outrageous, the sophistication synthetic and the aura as sleazy as it was shabby. The overweight blonde singer in the tight-fitting black sequin dress had gone off to her dressing room, the trio who played jazz of the 1920's were refueling at the bar, and the customers from Indianapolis, Fort Worth and Des Moines outshouted one another as they ordered fresh rounds of drinks from the tired waitresses in tiny miniskirts. Their boisterousness was almost as forced as the attempts of the proprietors to give the place a patina of elegance.

Porter sat at a table in the corner farthest from the band, one arm around the shoulders of Nancy Wing, who looked ravishing in a new auburn wig. Few who knew her would have recognized her, but she was not inconspicuous in a long sheath of green velvet. She was drinking tea, he confined himself to ginger ale, and only the man they knew as Mr. Wallace had liquor in his glass.

Mr. Wallace, who spoke with the vowel-flattening twang of Iowa or Nebraska, wore a necktie of shiny satin, a jacket with too-broad lapels and cufflinks the size of silver dollars. He looked at home in a Rush Street dive, and the waitresses called him by name.

Only his unblinking, hard eyes indicated that he might be other than a drygoods salesman enjoying a spree in the big city. "What's your present status, pal?"

"I collected my last paycheck," Porter said, "and I sent a

letter of resignation to the Director."

Mr. Wallace raised an eyebrow. "Before making a deal with my friends?"

"I was fed up, and if I must I'll buy a cottage on the Cornwall coast and settle down there. I'd like the extra money, of course. I have a special use for it." He patted Nancy on the thigh, then let his hand rest there.

"You can deliver?" Mr. Wallace's eyes bored into him.

"Naturally. Do you take me for an amateur, old boy? Full blueprints of the hull, engines, armaments and special equipment."

"No kidding?"

"I have sample material that proves the authenticity of what I'm offering."

"I'll take it."

"After we set the deal," Porter said.

"Does your material include blueprints of special devices that might be used for the—ah—recovery of undersea treasures?"

"I never discuss details until I know what I'm getting in return," Porter said.

Mr. Wallace stared hard at him. "What's your price?"

"One hundred thousand dollars in cash, deposited in a Swiss bank account already opened."

"That's damn high."

Porter shrugged. "If your friends won't pay it there are others who will." He kissed Nancy on the neck, and she snuggled closer to him.

Mr. Wallace turned to her. "Can you verify that he'll deliver what he says?"

"He always keeps his word," she said. "If he didn't, I wouldn't be here."

"I can't okay that big a payment on my own," Mr. Wal-

154

lace said. "I'll have to apply for authorization through channels."

Porter remained complacent. "How long will that take?"

"A couple of days."

"I'll give you forty-eight hours, Mr. Wallace. After that the price will go up."

"You drive a hard bargain."

"I'm enjoying a buyer's market." Porter stroked Nancy's thigh.

"You'll take your material to my company's headquarters, I assume."

Porter laughed. "You may tell Andropov for me that I haven't yet taken complete leave of my senses. I bring him my merchandise, and then I vanish forever into Lubyanka. The only one who knows or cares is Nancy, and if she gets talkative the same will happen to her. Try again."

"You must have something in mind," Mr. Wallace countered.

"I do. It's only a matter of time before my ex-boss learns I was handy with a photocopier, and then his lads will be gunning for me. I've got to pull my own disappearing act before that happens. Nancy and I have our future together to protect." Porter's arm tightened around her shoulders.

"Sounds reasonable to me," Mr. Wallace said.

Nancy entered the conversation, and said, "Porter is always reasonable."

He gazed at her with infatuated eyes, then turned back to the KGB intermediary. "We're prepared to hole up in Chicago until the day after tomorrow. Meet us here with a flat acceptance or rejection."

"Then what?"

"If we have a deal, have a private airplane waiting for us at O'Hare Airport, and fly us to Havana. We'll want a long-range aircraft waiting for us there, and we'll go on. Arrange the refueling stops wherever you please."

"What's your destination?"

"Singapore."

Mr. Wallace was incredulous. "Singapore?"

"I know the town, and I have connections there. I have an obvious reason for wanting to live sitting beside me, and liquidation isn't too easy to arrange in Singapore these days. Particularly as your company's employees are none too popular with the government there." Porter's smile was amiable.

Mr. Wallace pondered for a time. "You won't be carrying your merchandise on your person, of course."

"I've been in the business long enough to take basic precautions. Let's just say I'll hand over the merchandise, which any expert will know at once is authentic, in return for positive proof that the cash deposit has been made as I directed."

"Then you've already sent your blueprints on to someone in Singapore."

"Have I, Mr. Wallace? As we said when I was a schoolboy, the fascination of cricket is the many ways a ball can be bowled."

Wallace smiled. "You live up to your reputation, pal."

"That's comforting." Again Porter kissed Nancy's neck. "The wear and tear are debilitating, of course, so I want to retire while I'm still young enough to have some fun."

"Any other conditions, Mr. Porter?"

"Just one. A minor point to safeguard your interest as well as mine. The representative of your company who meets me in Singapore must be someone with whom I'm already acquainted."

"Smart. That will prevent an impostor from horning into the act."

"My former employers have been known to play such

156

dirty tricks," Porter said. "And we'll also need to be wary of people from other companies that have shown a lively interest in the merchandise."

"I'll get back to you right here in forty-eight hours," Mr. Wallace said, and signaled the waitress for the bill. "Boy, I've got to hand it to you. When it comes to guts, you've got them. You're taking on the whole damn world single-handed, but it doesn't throw you."

Porter rose, held Nancy's chair for her and put both arms around her when she stood. "It was John Dryden, I seem to recall, who said that none but the brave deserve the fair. My reward is worth whatever risks I may be taking."

A heavy fog rolled in from the Pacific soon after dark, blanketing the shipyard harbor and complicating the task of the Corporation lookouts stationed at strategic places in the area. They solved the problem, at least in part, by putting up highway detour signs on the coastal roads and halting all traffic, both motorized and pedestrian.

The foul weather made it possible for the fishing boats and pleasure craft in the harbor to begin their operation earlier than they had originally planned. Using infrared searchlights that enabled their crews to see without being seen, they made their way across the water to the *Neptune,* where supplies, gear and a number of highly sensitive instruments were taken on board.

At 11:00 P.M. Franklin and Marie Richards bade good-night to a group of dinner guests, and soon thereafter, still wearing evening clothes, they strolled to a car parked near the rear gate of their estate. By midnight they were on board the *Neptune.*

Corporation representatives took further advantage of the fog by rounding up some of the scientists and technical experts who were in the area, and they, too, reached the ship by 2:00 A.M. This fortuitous circumstance would make it necessary to fly no more than about thirty of the passengers to the *Neptune* after she passed out of sight of land.

The last to board were members of a Corporation security detachment, led by Adrienne Howard. Their launch glided up to the ship at 4:49 A.M., and as soon as they had climbed the ladder Captain Humphries gave the order to weigh anchor.

Few people saw the great ship put out to sea. A small flotilla of launches escorted her, four of them fanning out ahead of her to clear small craft from her path. Soon after sunrise she sailed out of the Strait of Juan de Fuca into the open Pacific.

The few passengers who were still awake could see virtually nothing out of their cabin portholes because of the fog, which had not yet dispelled. So none of them realized that two attack submarines of the United States Navy, both atomic-powered, moved into their assigned positions about a quarter of a mile from the *Neptune*, one on the port side and the other starboard. They rode on the surface, but both were prepared to submerge when other shipping appeared on their radar screens.

An Air Force reconnaissance jet screamed overhead at an altitude of 3,000 feet, and a break in the haze made it possible for those on the bridge to see the aircraft dip her wings in salute. In the weeks ahead the frequent appearance of Air Force sentinels would be taken for granted.

The first lieutenant appeared almost as soon as he was summoned to the bridge.

"You may relieve me, Mister," Captain Humphries said. "I'm turning in, but don't hesitate to call me if there's trouble. There's a small fleet of Russian fishing trawlers about ten leagues north-northeast of our present position, according to the Air Force, but we'll outrun them and they can't identify us on their radar, so we should be okay."

"Very good, sir." The lieutenant saluted and took the watch.

Captain Humphries yawned and walked to his quarters directly aft of the bridge, nothing in his manner suggesting that this was anything but a routine voyage of an ordinary vessel.

The bikini-clad Eurasian girl and her companion in swimming briefs stretched out on deck chairs beside the pool of what had been the Havana Hilton, and other guests lounging nearby assumed they were a honeymoon couple. They were in almost constant physical contact, with the man either stroking the girl's arm or holding her hand.

Members of a Czechoslovakian cultural mission, stocky and glum, ignored the pair, as they did everyone else. Three Polish university professors attending an educational conference bowed when they passed the deck chairs, but did not speak. Only the captain and mate of a Bulgarian freighter were gauche enough to stare openly.

Porter and Nancy spoke to each other only in Mandarin after he had decided it might prevent complications. His American-flavored English was identifiable, and he preferred anonymity. All the same, two Cuban security officers in sports shirts and slacks loitered nearby, trying in vain to appear inconspicuous.

Three Russians wearing rust-colored suits, black shoes and neckties appeared at the pool and, sitting under a beach umbrella, opened bulging briefcases. Launching into an animated discussion of trade figures involving sugar and tobacco, they were so aggressive they dominated the poolside. When a waiter appeared they ordered *kvass*, taking it for granted that the Russian brew was available here, and their faith soon was justified.

159

Porter kept his eyes closed, giving no indication that he understood Russian.

"How much longer must we wait?" Nancy asked him in Mandarin.

He opened his eyes and glanced at his watch. "Our contact is two hours late now," he said in the same tongue, "but time means very little here. Relax, why don't you? This is very pleasant."

"I'm trying, but I keep wondering if anything has gone wrong."

"Impossible," he said, and refrained from mentioning that he had been wondering the same thing.

The Russians became aware of the language they were speaking, noted that the girl was part-Chinese and glared at the couple.

Porter's expression was bland as he gazed off into space. The cold war was being waged everywhere, on all levels, and he knew the KGB had been spurred to greater alacrity because he had hinted that China was interested, too, in his blueprints of the super-submarine under construction at the Richards shipyard.

By this time, he reflected, the *Neptune* was somewhere in the Pacific, sailing toward her rendezvous with the sunken *Zolóto*. Meanwhile his own project was developing without a discernible hitch.

So far so good.

A slender Cuban in smartly tailored sports shirt and slacks emerged from the hotel and headed straight for the reclining couple. "I am informed you speak Spanish," he said to Porter as he extended his hand. "I am Ramon Silvero, Deputy Minister of Security."

"I am honored, *señor*," Porter said, bowing and shaking hands. "We regret that the lady doesn't understand Spanish."

160

Nancy's dazzling smile spoke for itself.

"I regret the delay in the arrangements for your transportation," Silvero said. "I hope you are not too much inconvenienced."

"We hope we can return here after we conclude our business in the East, *señor.*" Porter refused to be outdone in courtesy.

The official pulled up a somewhat battered metal chair in need of paint and spread a handkerchief on it before he sat. "The delay could not be avoided. We were asked to provide you with an airplane, and we assumed you would travel with Aeroflot. But our mutual friends in Moscow telephoned in great excitement last night. They believe you would be too conspicuous at refueling stops in a Russian airplane."

"Of course." Andropov, Porter thought, was taking no chances, knowing the Corporation would miss no possible opportunity to destroy the fugitive former agent.

"After a small measure of trouble," Silvero said, "we managed to obtain a privately owned airplane with neutral markings that happened to be in Belize."

The Russian interest in Central America made it unlikely that the presence of an available airplane in Belize was accidental. "What make is it, Señor Silvero?"

"A Boeing seven-oh-seven, I believe. It will be ready for you to board in about an hour and a half, unless you wish to stay for lunch. I shall send a car and driver to take you to the airport."

"That's very kind of you." Porter was puzzled by the informality of the departure schedule. "How many other passengers will be on board, Señor Silvero?"

"Why, none. Only you and the lady. Together with the flight crew and cabin attendants."

Porter needed all of the self-control he had acquired through long years in the intelligence community to conceal

161

his elation. There was no question that the Soviet Union attached the utmost importance to his mission and had been taken in by the photographs of the decoy super-submarine. Moscow was paying a fortune to transport him and Nancy to Singapore; never had he known any agent to be accorded such red-carpet treatment by any government.

There were drawbacks to the situation, of course, and he recognized them immediately. He had been isolated, cut off from any possible source of help. Certainly he could not rely for assistance on Nancy Wing, who would not hesitate to betray him in a crisis for her own benefit or salvation. He was completely alone, not for the first time but possibly for the last.

His predicament became even clearer after he and Nancy changed and checked out of the hotel, where their bill had already been paid. A Cuban Ministry of Security car and chauffeur took them to the airport, where they were driven straight to the far end of the field. There the huge silver aircraft awaited them, with a crew of three in the cockpit and four attendants in the cabin, three of them men and one a woman.

Seven KGB representatives had been assigned to take him and Nancy to the rendezvous, and they not only were instructed to deliver the passengers safely, but undoubtedly would prevent them from making contact with anyone along the way. The original red herring ploy had been so effective that Andropov was taking no chances.

As Porter climbed the steps into the spacious cabin and the heavy door closed behind him he entered the world of the KGB from which there was no escape. In the light of his present situation his scheme seemed even more hare-brained than it had when he had outlined it to a horrified and disbelieving Adrienne.

*   *   *

162

The logistics had been easy enough to plan, but difficult to execute. The *Neptune,* avoiding the major sea lanes, sailed across the central Pacific, then made a dogleg to Hawaii, the largest and southernmost island in the chain that composed the state of the same name. After staying out of sight of land it moved closer, finally casting anchor in the roads outside the port of Hilo, a sleepy provincial city of about 25,000 population.

From the deck of the ship the towering volcanoes of the island were plainly visible, smoke rising from several of them. The volcanoes were a major tourist attraction, but all flights in small aircraft from Honolulu had been cancelled for the day, a variety of excuses having been made to disgruntled customers.

Meanwhile a group of thirty-two technical experts, computer operators, scientists and underwater salvage authorities who had traveled separately to the Presidio, the old U.S. Army base in San Francisco, had been flown in a military aircraft to Honolulu, from where they had been taken directly to the Navy base at Pearl Harbor.

There another, smaller airplane awaited them, this one a seaplane, and they transferred to it without delay. The trickiest aspect of the operation was its timing, and constant radio contact was maintained between Pearl Harbor and the *Neptune.* There were no breakdowns in the communications, and no snags developed.

Minutes before the ship dropped anchor the seaplane took off, and a short time later it came down in the water a few hundred feet from the *Neptune,* casting up a spray before it taxied to the starboard side of the vessel, where a metal ladder had already been lowered.

Franklin Richards stood at the head of the gangway to welcome his associates on board.

The seaplane took off again, the *Neptune* weighed anchor,

then sailed out of sight of land as she headed south around Hawaii before turning westward again. The entire operation in the Hilo roads had taken less than an hour.

Adrienne Howard stood on the aft passenger deck overlooking the cavernous, tarpaulin-covered container compartment and gazed out at the wake as the ship steadily increased its speed. Beside her was the Deacon, who had accompanied the seaplane party.

"We had no problems," he said. "We were clean all the way. I checked all the surveillance reports myself before we left the Presidio, and nobody except our own people tailed any member of the group."

"So far so good, then." Adrienne was silent for a moment. "We're pretty much cut off from the world, you know, with no one on board permitted to send or receive messages. Have you heard any news about Porter?"

"Not a word. He's vanished from the face of the earth, and so has the Wing girl. A very neat disappearing act."

"I felt sure he'd handle it." She tried not to show her concern. "The word was leaked that Porter resigned from the Corporation, I suppose?"

"Oh, yes. At least a dozen guys came to me with the story, so I'm sure the Russians picked it up. Was that the intention?"

Adrienne made no reply.

"Look," the Deacon said. "I've been in this business long enough not to stick my nose into places it doesn't belong. But I can't buy some cockamamie fairy tale that Porter has quit the Corporation. Not in the middle of Project Neptune. He isn't the sort who'd walk out."

"I just hope," Adrienne said, "that the KGB believes the story. For Project Neptune's sake. For mine. And for Porter's."

TEN

The caviar was great, if one happened to like caviar, but Porter didn't. And the Russian version of champagne was so gaseous that he belched for a couple of hours after drinking only two glasses, so he didn't try that experiment again. He asked the barrel-chested steward and the equally husky stewardess to bring him whatever they ate. Thereafter he subsisted on *borscht* laden with raw onions, a pungent salami and black bread, which he washed down with *kvass*, a beverage similar to beer with a slightly sour flavor all its own.

Nancy winced whenever he leaned close to say something to her, and he couldn't blame her. The odors of garlic and onions must have made his breath repellant, but at least his need to simulate the role of an adoring lover was eased somewhat, and that was all to the good. Porter realized that Nancy was beginning to rub his nerves raw, and small wonder.

Familiarity was dulling the fine edge of his pleasure in their sexual relationship, and they had little else in common. She was a two-faced bitch who wouldn't hesitate to serve up his head on a platter, complete with an apple stuffed in his mouth, if it would serve her own interests. So he was still worried about her primary loyalties, other than to herself.

She was still in the employ of the Russians, of course; that much was clear. But he had no idea where she stood with the Chinese, and that worried him. If Peking got wind of his defection to the KGB, he felt certain, immediate steps would be taken to prevent the consummation of that marriage. The Chinese might have reasons to dislike the Corporation, but their hatred of the Russians verged on the pathological, and they could be nasty—more vindictive than any other people he had ever known in the business.

The trouble, he reflected as the aircraft flew high over the Pacific Ocean cloud cover, was that he was growing too damned old and tired for this kind of work. His luck had held out for a long time, largely because of his own vigilance, but his joints ached after sitting for hours in the cramped seat, and that was a signal telling him to pack it in.

Nancy was dozing in the seat beside him, and as he glanced at her it occurred to him that her makeup was almost never smudged. She wore it like a mask, and he wondered what might be behind it. Nothing, probably, except the narcissism and greed that enabled her to sell her services, her body and what there was of her soul to the highest bidder of the moment. There had been a time when he would have felt mildly sorry for her, but that day was long past. Pity was an emotion that a field agent didn't dare feel, and the mere fact that he allowed himself to think in such terms was an indication that he was far over the hill.

Porter wished he could believe, with Voltaire's Pangloss, that this was the best of all possible worlds. In that case he'd go off somewhere with Adrienne Howard. Not to a rose-covered cottage, which would make a sophisticated couple ill. Oh, they could go the Cornwall coast for a few weeks of fishing occasionally; she'd sit still for that. Basically, however, they'd do best in an apartment hotel some place in the sun, an establishment where all services were provided. He

166

couldn't imagine himself mowing a lawn, drying dishes or repairing a leak in a washbasin. His life hadn't prepared him for such an existence, nor was Adrienne the domestic type. He wasn't ready to admit that he was in love with her. That was going a bit too far. But the only kind of person with whom he could settle down in relative peace was one who took murder, mayhem and chicanery as normal, everyday occurrences. The same was true of her, and they could share their nightmares. Ordinary people simply wouldn't understand what made a field agent tick. Not that he or Adrienne knew, either, but at least they would be bound together by mutual sympathy, and it was far better than trying to live alone. A few retired agents had tried it, and tranquility had so undone them that they had climbed back into harness. No agent really retired until they closed the lid of his coffin.

If he was clever, though, he could live well. Should this present caper pay off, in spite of the odds, he knew of no reason he couldn't keep the $100,000 the Russians would be paying him for the blueprints and specifications of a nonexistent new submarine. Brian Davidson would scream, naturally, and would insist that the money be deposited in the Corporation treasury, but it would be pleasant to tell Davidson exactly where to go and precisely how to get there. The prospect improved Porter's spirits slightly. With the better part of a billion dollars being squandered on Project Neptune, the Corporation wouldn't miss such a paltry sum.

He and Adrienne could buy a little condominium for only a fraction of the loot. In the mountains behind the French Riviera, perhaps, or on the west coast of Florida. He had no way of knowing whether the idea would appeal to her, or whether she'd accept, but he'd lose nothing by asking. At least he wouldn't have to propose marriage—or would he? Adrienne was as tough and resilient as they came, but even a totally liberated woman might be inclined to balk

167

at too informal a partnership.

The mere contemplation of such a wild scheme was absurd, Porter told himself. But it did keep his mind off the hazards that awaited him in Singapore, and he wished he hadn't dreamed up this caper. He tried to comfort himself with the thought that it was going smoothly, perhaps a little too smoothly for his peace of mind.

Perhaps it was the inaction of the moment that was weighing him down and making him itchy. One of his favorite theories was that a field agent was at his most vulnerable when he sat on his arse and tried to use his mind. He'd been sitting for so long that the pattern of the Russian upholstery of his seat was permanently imprinted on his rear.

He unbuckled his seat belt, stretched and walked forward to the bathroom, aware of the intent scrutiny of the KGB stewardess. He could imagine the orders Andropov had given the crew: "Don't let the man or the girl out of your sight, and permit them to communicate with no one. Make just one mistake and you'll spend the rest of your shortened life in a Siberian labor camp."

Emerging from the bathroom, Porter came face to face with the burly steward, who was just leaving the cockpit. "What's the good word, Comrade? Are we holding to our schedule?"

"Of course," the man said. "But there are minor complications that could not be avoided."

Porter felt a twinge of apprehension, but continued to smile. "What sort of complications?"

"Our representative who has been assigned to hold a rendezvous with you has been delayed."

"Why is that?"

The steward became contemptuous. "Perhaps the Corporation reveals such things in wireless messages, even when they are coded. But we do not. The pilot's instructions made no mention of the cause of the delay."

"Fair enough." Porter shrugged, as though such things were of no consequence to him.

"Therefore we will not fly direct to Singapore. We will make an intermediary landing and await orders to proceed."

"Sounds great," Porter said. "Any idea where we're going instead of Singapore?"

The man's eyelids blinked twice. "I will inquire of the captain whether I am permitted to tell you, but I already know the answer. I saw the wireless message myself, and there was no mention in it of telling the passengers our temporary destination."

The KGB, Porter had to concede as he returned to his seat, played their cards very close to their collective chest.

Now he had a real cause for worry. Had the KGB discovered his ruse? If so, a bullet would find its way into the back of his head soon after they landed. Unless Moscow still hadn't learned the reason for his deception, and Moscow was inclined to be exceptionally curious, so they would sweat the truth out of him. He'd hold out, of course, but he didn't know how long he could manage these days. Every experience with a torturer made a man break down faster the next time because his imagination worked overtime and he knew what was coming. Porter was afraid he lacked the stoicism of the Deacon, but knew this was not the opportune moment to change professions.

Nancy was awake when he returned to his seat, and he held his breath as he bent down to kiss her. A small gesture of consideration was the least he could do for her, since she, too, well might be called upon to pay with her life for his sins.

The breadth of the Pacific Ocean was deceptive. People who flew from California to the Orient over the world's largest sea in a day and a half often were unaware of its size,

169

but it was impossible to fool those who sailed her surface, even in a ship that maintained speeds equal to those of the *Queen Elizabeth II*.

The *Neptune* plowed steadily westward through tranquil seas, the sky overhead a bright blue, the sun warm and the winds gentle. Only the roar of U.S. Air Force jets, repeated hourly, was a reminder that this was no ordinary cruise.

Members of the crew appreciated the calm and the weather, but the civilian members of the expedition were too busy to notice. Every morning after an early breakfast they assembled in the Operations Center, and there, for the next ten hours, they rehearsed the roles they would play when the attempt was made to raise the *Zolóto* from its resting place more than three miles beneath the surface of the South China Sea.

Each morning Adrienne Howard stopped in to watch for a time, and was struck by the quiet of the session. Nearly one hundred men and about twenty women were gathered in the salon, and all were intent on their own work. There was no unnecessary conversation, no jokes were exchanged and each participant concentrated exclusively on his assigned task. These people were experts in undersea salvage, sonar and computer operations, and none needed instructions.

The majority wore earphones, plugged into a console resembling an electric organ that sat on a dais at one end of the huge cabin. Seated before it and resembling a schoolmaster supervising a class was Franklin Richards, and on either side of him was a computer readout specialist who kept watch on scores of dials and, under his supervision, coordinated the activities of the others. Occasionally he punched a switchboard button and spoke a few words through a microphone to one of the experts, but his pace was always unhurried and he never raised his voice. Not even Sir Thomas Beecham conducting a symphony rehearsal had ever appeared more tranquil, more in control of himself.

Only the observers who manned the underwater television sets would have nothing to contribute until the *Neptune* reached her target area. They amused themselves by watching marine life, and played a game in which they gave themselves points that depended on the nature of the species they spotted. Barracuda, tuna and sailfish kept their interest alive, but one afternoon they saw a school of grayfin sharks, and were so fascinated by the ugly creatures that thereafter they could not duplicate the excitement they had felt earlier.

The complexities of the functions performed by the computers was astonishing. Gyroscopes first built for undersea use in atomic-powered submarines and adapted for surface use revealed the precise location of the *Neptune* from one split second to the next, and a recently perfected sonar device attached to a small computer of its own instantly calculated the distance from the underside of the *Neptune*'s hull to any underwater object located up to six and five-sixteenths miles from the vessel. The device was accurate to an amazing degree, and was never more than three millimeters off target.

The salvage operators rehearsed their jobs endlessly, repeating them under the direction of a smiling but alert Franklin Richards until every move, every gesture was done automatically and without hesitation. In effect these experts were scientific assembly-line workers, and the ultimate success or failure of Project Neptune would depend on their ability to work swiftly and surely, never pausing to wonder if they had erred.

Meanwhile, on the bridge, Captain Humphries kept his own vigil. Out of sight of the *Neptune* but visible on her radarscopes were her escorts: a heavy cruiser to port side, a light cruiser to starboard and an aircraft carrier trailing behind her. Had a hostile airplane managed to penetrate her defense perimeters its observers would not have guessed that the four ships were sailing in concert, that the slightest change in the *Neptune*'s course was reflected without delay in the changes made by the warships.

No stray airplanes appeared, to be sure, and Adrienne had nothing to occupy her time other than to stretch out on a fantail deck chair for several hours each day to improve her tan. No security problems arose, no crises erupted, and she found herself worrying more and more about Porter.

Again and again she reflected that she was concerning herself unnecessarily. No man who had ever worked for the Corporation was better able to look after himself, and he had demonstrated over the years that he was more than a match for the KGB's best. No one was indestructible, certainly, but he still belonged in a special category.

Had he been working alone she might have relaxed, but what made her apprehensive was his close, continuing association with the Wing woman. Porter was wise to her, and so far had found it easy enough to outmaneuver her at every turn. All the same, he was sleeping with her, and intimacy that continued over a protracted period could cause even the most meticulous of field agents to become careless. Adrienne had trapped two senior KGB operatives in just that way, so she knew her fears were solidly grounded. What annoyed her was that she couldn't understand why she was stewing over Porter. Even if he survived intact, with his calm unruffled, they would separate after this mission ended and might never again be assigned to work together. At best she could hope they would go to bed a few more times, but she had good reason to know how fleeting such pleasures could be.

All the same, she wanted to see him again. He was the one man she had known—in more years than she cared to recall —with whom she believed she could form an enduring relationship. Not, God forbid, that she would care to marry him; that would be too much. Yet it would be comforting to awaken in the morning and know he was beside her.

The very idea was ridiculous. Porter would never allow himself to be domesticated. And if he did reappear, intact, she was willing to bet that damned Eurasian broad would be clinging to his arm. Yes, and he'd have a valid, sound reason to be playing her along, one that the Director himself would approve.

Adrienne realized she was jealous for the first time since she had been an adolescent, but she didn't care. She was just sorry she hadn't turned the Deacon loose the night he had given the Wing woman a scrubbing. Accidents had been known to happen. Often. And no field supervisor had ever been fired from the Corporation for overzealousness.

She had to admit, grudgingly, that even if Nancy Wing did show up with him she'd be so relieved she wouldn't mind. Well, not all that much. Maybe.

What irritated her beyond measure was the knowledge that Porter had deliberately placed himself in an untenable, exposed position. There might have been a dozen ways to neutralize KGB interest in Project Neptune and to direct the Chinese fishing expedition into harmless waters. Oh, no. He had to be a big hero, even though he knew there were no heroes in this business.

She didn't even know how he intended to extricate himself from the Singapore mess he had created. Blackman had quietly vanished just before the *Neptune* had sailed, so she assumed he was involved, but she didn't share Porter's faith in Blackman. If only he'd confided in her instead, she would have been in a position to help him squeeze through what would be one of the tightest nets drawn in years.

Damn male obstinacy. Damn male pride. Damn male vanity. And while she was at it, damn the male sex drive. She still suspected that Porter was more deeply involved with the Wing woman than he had told her, and it was possible he had devised a way to include her in this silly, dangerous caper because he still had a yen for her. So damn Nancy Wing, and above all, damn Project Neptune for interfering in what might have developed into a genuine, abiding relationship.

A deep voice crackling on a loudspeaker over the intercom aroused Adrienne from her reverie. "Miss Howard," the man boomed. "Captain Humphries' compliments, and please report to the bridge without delay."

This was the first time Adrienne had been summoned, and she hastily gathered her belongings and donned her short beach robe over her bikini before hurrying forward to the bridge. Her attire wasn't suitable, but there had been a note of urgency in the message, so to hell with propriety.

The master of the *Neptune* was seated in the overstuffed leather chair that naval custom reserved exclusively for his use, and was engrossed in a study of charts, but he rose to his feet as Adrienne approached.

She perched her sunglasses on top of her head, aware of the scrutiny of two junior officers and the helmsman. As a matter of principle, however, she refrained from apologizing for the informality of her dress.

Humphries grinned at her. "Are you as healthy as you look, Miss Howard?"

"I believe so." She knew he hadn't summoned her to compliment her on her suntan.

His smile faded. "I assume I'd have been notified if you had relaxed your ban on the sending or receipt of wireless messages by passengers."

"Of course, but there's been no relaxation of the rule. We made it very clear before we sailed that no messages would be sent and none received, even in personal emergencies. Russian tracking equipment is every bit as sophisticated as ours, and you know as well as I do that they have disguised fishing trawlers scattered all over the Pacific. As long as I'm

174

in charge of security on board, I won't change that rule without a written order, personally signed by you!"

"I have no intention of signing anything, Miss Howard. And rest assured I'll back you up if necessary. I prefer not to become involved in a confrontation unless I'm forced to intervene, that's all."

"What's the problem?" Adrienne had changed from a relaxed girl into a woman with a steel spine.

"You'll need your strength. Marie Richards wants to send a message to New York, and her husband is supporting her."

"Marie!" She frowned, then shook her head.

"I just thought I'd warn you. Frank Richards is waiting for you in the communications office, and he's in a pretty frightening mood."

"I'll take care of him."

"Let me know if you need my help," Humphries said.

"I won't." Adrienne left the bridge and walked down the corridor to the communications center.

She found Franklin Richards pacing the private office of the signals officer, a lieutenant commander who eased himself out when she appeared.

"Well, Adrienne!" Richards wasted no words. "I know no private messages are permitted, and I appreciate the reasons for the rule. But this situation is different!"

"We can make no exceptions, Frank," she said. "I'm sorry."

"Look here, this is very embarrassing. Marie suddenly remembered she hadn't cancelled a dinner engagement for next week with my managing director for United Kingdom operations and his wife. They'll think we're terribly rude."

"I'm sure they'll forgive you in due time. When you're able to explain." Adrienne perched on the edge of the lieutenant commander's desk.

"I realize Marie was under a cloud some weeks ago,"

Richards said, trying to curb his anger. "So I'm not asking that you send the message as she worded it. Reword it yourself, and put it in code if you wish. I don't care if you send it through the Corporation and ask them to notify my New York office. Handle it any way you please, just so the wireless is sent!"

"I'm sorry," Adrienne said. "But the rules can't be broken. I can't permit exceptions."

"I'm just requesting you to bend them a little."

"Impossible."

"Have you forgotten my contributions to Project Neptune?" His temper was soaring.

"Indeed I haven't, Frank. You *are* Project Neptune, and that's what makes this so difficult. I'm not doubting the authenticity of Marie's message. I'm not even hinting it might be other than what it is. I still can't permit it to be sent. The KGB not only could pick it up, but could get an immediate fix on the location of the *Neptune*. If they know anything about what we're doing, they'll put every tracking vessel they own on our trail, and they'll find us."

He wasn't accustomed to being denied, and his face was fiery. "In principle I'm forced to agree with you, Adrienne. But I don't see how one harmless message could cause trouble."

"I do, Frank, and that's why I'm here. I didn't come along for the joyride. Have me fired and put off the ship the minute we hit Hawaii on our way home, if that will salvage your pride. Until then—no private messages!"

Richards stared at her for a long moment, turned on his heel and stalked out.

Adrienne sat still for a time before fishing in her shoulder bag for a cigarette and matches. It was a rule of thumb that problems often arose on a job when they were least expected, and she just wished Marie Richards hadn't been involved.

176

She had expressed her own certainty that Marie wasn't in touch with any foreign government, and she still found it hard to believe that the wife of the man responsible for Project Neptune could be disloyal to him, much less to her adopted country. All the same, Adrienne was shaken.

The lieutenant commander looked in. "All clear?"

"The rules still stand," she said. "Only you, Captain Humphries and the executive officer are permitted to send wireless messages, and you're restricted to such official business as the Captain deems vital for the safety of his ship and the success of his mission. There will be no exceptions!" She left the cabin without waiting for a reply.

The lieutenant commander watched her as she made her way through the outer office, and all of his staff members were looking at her. Corporation employees were a strange breed. This one was exceptionally attractive, marvelously feminine, but the lieutenant commander didn't believe she even thought of herself as a woman.

Papua New Guinea, one of the newer nations on earth, occupied about half of the world's second largest island, the other portion belonging to Indonesia. Although only one hundred miles separated New Guinea from the Australian mainland, Papua was still in the Stone Age. And Port Moresby, its capital, was the hellhole of creation.

Porter stood on the balcony of the hotel suite he and Nancy occupied and, clad only in his shorts, looked out across the roofs of the thatched huts of the town at the jungle, which stretched as far as he could see. Even on the outskirts of Port Moresby it looked like a dense, impenetrable green sea.

The equatorial heat was almost unbearable. The humidity made it seem even worse and the ceiling fan that turned lazily overhead did nothing but blow a gentle stream of searing air at his back. Even the smell of rotting vegetation that was so common in the tropics was overwhelming here. Air conditioning was still unknown in this primitive land, and the hotel, supposedly one of Port Moresby's best, was so decrepit it looked as though a typhoon wind would destroy it. By some miracle of balance unique in the South Pacific, it continued to stand.

There was mold on the bathroom tiles, what was left of the paint on the walls was flaking, and a lizard with a flicking tail, slowly making its way from floor to ceiling, did not bother to change its color as it climbed. Porter absently brushed away a fly intent on investigating his ear, and reminded himself that, heat or no heat, it would be necessary to close the jalousies before turning on electric lights after nightfall. There were no screens in the hotel, presumably none anywhere in town, and swarms of mosquitos would be attracted by lights, as would the invisible gnats that moved into the city from the jungles in huge droves.

One of the advantages of being on the second floor was the absence of snakes in the suite, and for that much Porter was grateful. On his one previous visit to the island he had seen several species, all of them poisonous.

The ever-present heat and humidity were the least of his concerns, and as he stood on the balcony he wondered, as he had been doing for hours, why the KGB had elected to break his journey for an indefinite period of time. Perhaps submarine experts who had been studying the photographs of the dummy *Neptune* suspected that a ship of that size was not feasible. On the other hand, it had just been announced recently that the United States intended to build a Trident atomic-powered submarine for use in the 1980's that had a gross weight of 18,000 tons, and as the dummy supposedly would weigh only 5,000 tons more, he thought it unlikely that Moscow would catch on to the deception.

So many things could have gone wrong with his scheme and there were so many angles to be considered that Porter told himself to put the whole matter out of his mind. Experience had taught him to deal with the realities of such problems as they arose.

If the KGB had decided to dispose of him, his escorts would wait until they resumed the flight, and it would be no trick to put a bullet through his head while flying at a high altitude, then weight his body and drop the evidence into the Pacific. If they killed him he imagined they would murder Nancy, too.

What became of him was primarily of interest to him. He had to believe his ruse had been successful so far, and each day he remained alive Project Neptune was shielded that much longer. If and when the Russians discovered he had tricked them, they would find it difficult to locate the real *Neptune* in the vast Pacific, even though they maintained a whole fleet of ships loaded with listening devices and other detection gear. They wouldn't be impelled to conduct a massive search unless and until they discovered the purpose of the *Neptune*'s extraordinary voyage, and he felt reasonably confident that, so far, the secret had been kept.

Only once before in history had leaks been prevented in a hush-hush enterprise of this magnitude. No outsider had ever learned the purpose of the Manhattan Project, the original development of the atomic bomb during World War II. Wartime conditions had made it far easier to impose censorship, exclude unauthorized personnel and trace possible leaks in those days.

If he and Adrienne succeeded in their present task, they'd have cause to congratulate themselves. Provided he remained alive long enough to receive his commendation from the Director. If not, Adrienne could bury it with him.

What he couldn't quite understand was why he was risking his life in so spectacular and reckless a manner when all he could possibly receive in return was another mealy-mouthed letter of commendation. He had enough of them already to paper the walls of a large room, for whatever good that would do him. The Corporation didn't believe in handing cash rewards to its own senior operatives.

It would be absurd to tell himself he was taking outlandish risks out of patriotism. He was a naturalized citizen of the United States, to be sure, but that was no more than the legal requisite necessary for him to hold a job on his level. He was fond of America, just as he was still equally fond of Great Britain, but he had no desire to die for either country.

He might claim, of course, that he was taking chances because of a burning desire to preserve the personal liberties that free men everywhere regarded as their natural heritage. Three cheers for the Magna Carta, Parliament's 1689 Bill of Rights and the first ten amendments to the American Constitution drawn up precisely one hundred years later. But it would be ridiculous for someone in his position to wave the flag for personal liberties and civil rights. A man who had worked for the Corporation for a number of years had violated every last one of them. Frequently.

He would like that $100,000 for himself of course.

Trying to face the truth squarely in what might become the greatest crisis of his life, Porter had to admit he had no idea why he was willingly taking such great risks. Perhaps it was a desire to outthink, outplan and outact the brains of the KGB. Perhaps he wanted to show off, principally for his own benefit, in order to prove that someone who would be a misfit in a society of normal, law-abiding people had a valid claim to existence. It was even possible he was behaving rashly because he was so bored he had nothing else to occupy his time and thoughts. Other than Adrienne, and he would not allow himself to think about her.

The door opened, and Porter reached for his Lilliput, but relaxed when Nancy came into the room.

She was wearing a shawl of some thin material draped in a saronglike effect over her swimming attire, her hair was piled on top of her head and she looked fetching, as usual, but she was distinctly out of sorts. "I just got out of the pool," she said, "but I'm as wet as I'd be if I'd stayed in the water. I've never minded the heat in Hong Kong or Macao. Or even Singapore. But this place is too much."

"I have no intention of bringing you back to Papua New Guinea to live happily ever after," he assured her.

Suddenly she smiled. "Our bodyguards are unbelievable. The assistant steward was on duty while I was swimming. Making certain I didn't drown, run away or something. And would you believe he was wearing a jacket and necktie while trying to make himself inconspicuous?"

"I suppose the KGB regulations require it."

"Just so he and the others are unobtrusive when they follow us tonight. Where shall we dine?"

"One place is as bad as another," Porter said. "We can wander up the road—all three blocks of it—and see what we can find."

"Then I won't dress up particularly. I may wear a *cheongsam.*"

"Don't," he said. "You'll be better appreciated as an Occidental in Port Moresby. There's always been a strong feeling against Chinese here, largely because they own the most prosperous shops and businesses in town."

"One of the things I like best about you," Nancy said as she went off to the bedroom, "is that you're a one-man Baedeker."

Porter helped himself to a beer from a wheezing refrigerator that nevertheless was in running order, and decided not to dress until Nancy was ready. One wore clothes in Papua

181

New Guinea only when necessary.

She surprised him by taking very little time preparing for the evening, and she returned in a short time, her makeup and bare-armed dress Western, as he had suggested.

"Just give me a couple of minutes," he said, hurrying to the bedroom. "The only breeze is out on the little balcony. It isn't much, but it's better than nothing."

"This is the first time I've ever been in a place where even breathing requires an effort," she said.

Porter quickly donned trousers, a sports shirt and socks, and was slipping on a pair of loafers when a chilling scream from the other room snapped him erect.

He snatched his Magnum and raced into the living room.

Nancy was standing on the balcony, immobilized by terror, and extending from the wooden wall only two inches from her head was the hilt of a still-quivering knife.

Porter instantly pulled her into the room, shoved her to one side, out of range of a possible assassin, and then peered out. In the growing dusk he could see no one in the tangled hotel garden below, and he advanced cautiously, the safety catch removed from his Magnum. A thorough inspection revealed that no one was in the garden.

Returning to the living room he guided the girl to a chair, then poured her a stiff drink. While she recovered he removed the knife from the wall and examined it. The handle was of bone, the blade double-edged, and there was no way of determining whether it had been made in Papua New Guinea or imported. It looked like knives fashioned in many parts of the world, and all he knew as he weighed it in the palm of his hand was that it had perfect balance. Obviously it had been made for throwing.

Still holding the knife, he turned to Nancy.

She had recovered sufficiently to have regained her powers of speech. "I saw no one down there," she said. "I was

182

actually looking at the garden, too, and wondering how they manage to keep the jungle from creeping up the walls. There wasn't a soul down there, I could almost swear it."

"There was at least one person in the garden," Porter said. "An expert thrower, too. You weren't an easy target in the half-light, and he had to throw on a rise, which is far more difficult than on a level plane. And he didn't miss you by much."

"Just enough," she said, and shuddered.

"He was no amateur, that's certain." Porter closed the jalousies before turning on the electric lights, and he, too, took care to avoid the balcony.

"I think we'll have dinner right here in the hotel, no matter how frightful it is."

He absently tossed the knife up and down, saw that the gesture disturbed her and placed it under his belt at the small of his back. "Nobody could have mistaken you for me," he said. "The specific target was Nancy Wing, and the method was direct. Who wants you dead?"

"I don't know." Her fright was genuine.

But Porter still had no way of determining whether she was withholding information from him. "Why would anyone want to kill you?" he persisted.

"I honestly don't know."

Obviously he could not analyze her situation or assess his own vulnerability unless he was supplied with facts. "I think we can rule out the KGB. They could dispose of either of us —or both of us—without sweat—on board the airplane."

Nancy nodded, and it was apparent the same thought had occurred to her.

"We can rule out personal enemies for the simple reason they'd have no way of knowing you were in Port Moresby. It's also unlikely that the motive was robbery. You aren't wearing any expensive jewelry that would attract a thief, the

183

wall from the ground up to the balcony isn't easy to climb, and a robber very possibly would have known that you weren't alone here."

She glanced at him, then looked away.

Instinct told him she wasn't revealing her own deductions, but he continued his breakdown. "What's more, a knife really isn't a local weapon. In the interior they sometimes use clumsy spears like the ones used by your ancestors and mine thousands of years ago, but their knives, which they use for skinning animals, are made out of heavy stone and aren't fit for throwing. The people of New Guinea much prefer firearms, even hopelessly old-fashioned rifles and pistols."

"I don't believe a robber would have taken the risk of killing me in return for what he could have taken from me."

"By a process of elimination," Porter said, "we come to Chinese intelligence."

Nancy was silent, and seemed to stiffen.

"They're the logical candidates. But why would they want you out of the way?"

"I have no idea." She had regained her composure.

"Even more important, I don't see how they could have known we'd come to Port Moresby when we didn't know it ourselves until we landed."

"They might have intercepted and decoded the wireless message from Moscow to the pilot."

"That could be," Porter said, and thought of another possibility. Nancy might have found some way to notify the Chinese of her whereabouts, perhaps through some prearranged method. But if he was correct, Peking could have decided she was untrustworthy, had let them down or knew too much to be left at large. Any one of these reasons would be enough to seal her death warrant.

"I can't help you if you're concealing something from me," he said.

"I'm not!" Her eyes were wide, her tone emphatic.

Porter had his reservations, and made up his mind to tell their KGB guards what had happened. The Russians would go to great lengths to protect them from Chinese intelligence until they reached Singapore, if that was indeed their destination, and for the moment they would be safe. Each hour's grace was a free gift, and espionage operations made strange bedfellows, both literally and figuratively.

ELEVEN

U-shaped Umatac Bay on the island of Guam had seen the ships of many nations since Magellan had first landed there in 1521, bringing the dubious benefits of Western civilization to the native Chamorros, a people of mixed Tagalog, Melanesian and Indonesian stock. Over the centuries the natives of this southernmost of the Mariana Islands had known so many conquerors and seen so many warships they had learned that the best way to stay healthy was to mind their own business. So few paid much attention to the huge vessel anchored just inside the mouth of the harbor.

Armed forces of the United States made certain that the curiosity of residents and visitors alike was restrained. The Army maintained an observation post at the peak of Mt. Balanos, a 1,200-foot hill directly behind the harbor. Air Force fighter planes kept the skies overhead clear, and a squadron of Navy patrol boats kept outrigger canoes and other small craft at a respectful distance. Official barges bearing supplies of fresh meat, fruit and vegetables to the ship carried complements of Marine guards who prevented verbal or physical contact between the food handlers and those on board.

Only Captain Humphries and Adrienne Howard were allowed to go ashore, and a Coast Guard cutter took them to the Navy base, where sheafs of messages awaited them and they had the opportunity to get in direct touch with Washington. The passengers, officers and crew of the *Neptune* were directed to remain on board, and once they had glimpsed the clusters of small buildings, the jungle and the relatively few acres under cultivation, they drifted away from the railing.

Many of the passengers elected to stretch out in deck chairs because, in spite of the restrictions on their movements, the weather was perfect. The sun was hot, but the humidity was low and the trade winds, dry and cooling, blew steadily. Other islands portrayed themselves as paradise, but Guam, just building its hotels, restaurants and recreational facilities, actually deserved the title. Within a few years it would be overrun by tourists, who would soon take it for granted as they already did Tahiti, Fiji and other remote places almost inaccessible before the days of the jumbo jets.

In midafternoon Captain Humphries and Adrienne returned to the *Neptune,* the latter depressed because she had learned from Corporation headquarters that Porter had vanished after he and Nancy Wing had flown from Havana to an unknown destination. Late in the afternoon a giant cargo plane with Air Force markings circled Guam, then came in for a landing, and there was a burst of activity. Within the hour tarpaulin-covered barges, all manned exclusively by Marines, made their way across the harbor to the *Neptune.*

The barges were transporting a number of wrapping-shrouded packages, many of them thirty feet long, ten feet wide and flat. Franklin Richards, aided by a corps of assistants, carefully inspected the contents of each package in the open aft hold of the *Neptune* before allowing the next to be hoisted on board.

The task, performed with meticulous attention to detail,

lasted for several hours, and shortly after it was completed the sun sank with the abruptness typical in the tropics, with the brief twilight giving way to a star-studded night. A three-quarters moon was rising by the time the *Neptune* weighed anchor and sailed.

Richards was so eager to assemble the submersible float that he and his associates postponed dinner. The ungainly craft that resembled a football field was joined together, section and by section, the metal fused in the special process that had been developed and perfected in the Richards shipyard. After the last portion was melded into the whole a derrick was used to turn the submersible upside down and the more delicate operation of attaching the gasoline compression chamber was undertaken.

It was midnight before this work was done, and finally the men went off to eat. They volunteered to return to the hold, but Richards preferred to curb their enthusiasm. They were tired and he wanted no mistakes made that might be caused by fatigue, so he suspended operations until morning.

After an early breakfast the experts returned to their labors, installing the sonar and closed-circuit television systems that would provide the submersible with its eyes and ears. The success of the entire project would depend upon the accuracy of these instruments, so Richards took his time, and each step in the procedure was checked thoroughly before the next was undertaken.

That phase required two days of work, and was followed by the equally complicated task of installing the electromagnetic system which would provide the submersible with its muscle. All that remained to be done thereafter would be to fill the hollow lip of the craft with the iron shot that would be released at the bottom of the sea to permit the barge to rise again. This operation could not be performed until the last possible moment, however, as the iron would have to be treated in order to render it antimagnetic.

The *Neptune* sailed due west from Guam, and ultimately would circle north around Luzon, at the top of the Philippine archipelago, as it headed into the South China Sea. Even this route had been selected with great deliberation, and although it was longer by several hundred miles than a voyage farther south, numerous small islands would be avoided and the exact location of the ship at any one time would be more difficult for potential spotters to determine.

Richards was anxious to drop the submersible into the water and tow it behind the *Neptune,* but Adrienne vetoed the idea and was supported by Captain Humphries. There would be ample opportunity to correct imbalances in the craft's performance after they reached the South China Sea itself, she said, and the less time the submersible was actually afloat, the less opportunity there would be for outsiders to photograph it from the air and guess its mission.

In spite of this temporary setback, Richards and his associates knew that the climax of their many months of planning and labor was approaching. They were drawing nearer to their goal, and within a few days they would learn whether they would succeed in a bizarre venture that no men before them had ever attempted.

Obviously the Russians were not responsible for the attempt to murder Nancy Wing. The members of the airplane's cabin crew were augmented by a half-dozen other men, who appeared out of nowhere, and during the four days the party remained at Port Moresby the KGB "guests" were given the protection worthy of a chief of state.

Agents were stationed around the clock in the garden beneath the windows of their suite, another stood guard in the hotel corridor, and whenever they left the hotel, they were surrounded by a cordon that accompanied them to local restaurants or on brief shopping expeditions.

Porter could form only one firm conclusion: the KGB, whatever it had in store for him, wanted to insure that he and the girl reached their destination safely. The cabin steward, who appeared to be in charge, was awaiting instructions from Moscow, and he shared Porter's lack of appreciation of whatever pleasures Papua New Guinea offered visitors. Porter could only guess that the man's superiors were telling him little more than he was passing along to the passengers he was transporting.

The ordeal ended suddenly after four days of marking time. Porter and Nancy were killing the morning at the swimming pool, where they remained in the shade in a vain attempt to keep cool, when the steward came to them.

"We leave at once!" he announced, and escorted them to their suite so they could change.

"Are we permitted to ask where you're flying us?" Porter wanted to know.

The KGB man looked surprised. "Singapore, of course. That was our agreement!"

Porter concealed his relief. So far, so good. The Russians had not discovered his deception, and he was not being flown to Vladivostok for intensive interrogation prior to liquidation. There was still a chance he might survive.

A quarter of an hour later the KGB continued to display intensive security precautions. A half-dozen agents surrounded Porter and Nancy as they left the hotel, and a small caravan of three automobiles awaited the party. Other guards were waiting at the airport, where sleepy Papua New Guinea customs and immigration authorities scarcely bothered to look at passports before granting the necessary exit permits.

A strong escort walked with Porter and Nancy across the field to their waiting aircraft, and even after they climbed on board, the KGB men who stayed behind continued to stand guard outside.

These elaborate arrangements were enough to convince Porter that Moscow was still taken in by his ruse. But he knew better than to rejoice; as the airplane rose, circled the field and headed westward, he knew that each passing minute brought him closer to the ultimate showdown that, while protecting Project Neptune, made his own situation more dangerous.

The task of lowering the submersible into the water was accomplished with dispatch, and Franklin Richards lost no time inaugurating tests of the craft's sensitive equipment. The *Neptune* spent a full morning creeping at a speed of only five knots per hour so the football field could be submerged, and Richards was satisfied when she reached a depth of six hundred feet without incident. Her sonar needed tuning and minor adjustments had to be made in the clarity of the undersea television pictures she sent back to the mother ship, but these were expected technical problems, and the experts dealt with them at their leisure.

The atmosphere on board ship changed abruptly, however, when the voice of Captain Humphries boomed over the loudspeaker system: "Attention all hands and passengers! We are now approaching the target area. All sound navigation and ranging personnel please report to your duty stations without delay."

Adrienne Howard remained on deck for a time and watched as ultrasensitive microphones attached to long lines of hair-thin metal alloys were unreeled with painstaking care so they would not foul the propellers. She was no authority on sonar, but found its basic principles easy enough to understand. Underwater vision was limited, but sound traveled farther than it did on the surface, and the microphones, when lowered to a depth of up to three miles, were remarkably accurate in detecting objects below.

The process of feeding out the lines took several hours, with the *Neptune* cruising at a cautious speed of ten knots. The better part of a year had passed since the last bathyscaphe test had been made, pinpointing the location of the sunken Russian submarine, and it was taken for granted that the vessel's position might have shifted during that time.

At noon Adrienne paid a brief visit to the bridge, where Captain Humphries, with charts spread out before him, was directing the navigation of the ship. The automatic pilot and other devices had been switched off, and the helmsman at the wheel was in direct charge of the ship's movements.

The captain glanced at Adrienne. "We're threading the needle," he said, "and I prefer my own judgment to that of machines."

She realized her presence might be a distraction, so she went amidships to the control chamber, where four sonar operators, each wearing a set of earphones, sat before consoles whose needles would show the presence of objects below.

Franklin Richards had stationed himself on a platform behind the quartet, and from his vantage point he could monitor all four of the consoles. The needles stood at "0" as she approached, and he smiled when he saw her.

"The microphones are just hitting the two-mile level," he said, "so there won't be much excitement for another hour or two."

Scarcely had he spoken when a bell rang, and one of the console needles leaped from "0" to "7"—which was three points below maximum.

"Strike seven!" the operator said.

Everyone in the chamber stiffened, and Adrienne felt her pulse throb.

But Richards remained calm. "The microphone is dropping through a school of fairly large fish, I suspect. Nothing more serious than that."

"How do you know that the Russians don't have a submarine down there, waiting to disrupt our operation?"

"I don't. But all four of the sonar devices would pick it up fast enough, and in no time we'd have a 'ten' rating on every last one of them."

"How soon do you estimate we'll be on target?"

He shrugged. "Hitting the bull's-eye at sea isn't the same as pinpointing a target on land. The *Neptune* will crisscross an area of about forty-eight square miles, and the *Zolóto* could be sitting on the bottom anywhere within that zone. With luck we could find her at any time, but we might have to spend a day or two making our search."

"Strike four!" another of the operators called.

"One large fish, probably," Richards said. "There are a lot of grayfin sharks in this part of the South China Sea."

"Could they interfere?"

Richards became grim. "We'll allow nothing to interfere," he said.

A young ensign approached. "Miss Howard, Mr. Richards," he said, speaking in a low tone, "Captain Humphries' compliments. He'll appreciate it if you'll join him on the bridge."

Something in the officer's voice made Adrienne uneasy, and she could see that Richards looked a trifle disturbed, too. Neither commented, however, as they walked forward.

Captain Humphries was frowning at a report typed on a yellow flimsy. "We're in for possible trouble," he said. "Our meteorologists say there's a gale blowing about two hundred and fifty miles south by southwest of us. She may reach typhoon strength, and she's heading in this general direction."

193

"This isn't the season for typhoons," Adrienne said.

"Not the normal season, I'll grant you," the captain said, "but they're always a danger in these waters. This is the beginning of the little rainy spell, so anything can happen. Frank, if we're going to be in the path of a typhoon you'll have to haul your submersible out of the sea and stow her in the hold."

"How much advance notice can you give me, Charlie? Shave it as thin as you can so we won't lose time hauling her in and refloating her again."

Captain Humphries' voice was dry. "Even a storm of gale force will make a hash of your operations, as you well know. We'll take no risks with your equipment, Frank."

Both men were silent, and Adrienne stepped in. "What are the chances of the storm hitting us, Captain?"

He raised an eyebrow. "If I knew that, Miss Howard, I'd be able to work miracles. I've asked Clark Field in the Philippines to send out a weather plane to check for us, so we may have a clearer picture after the pilot flies in and out of the storm. And here's the answer to the question neither of you has asked. If a typhoon does develop and head this way, we may have to sail as much as two to three hundred miles off course."

Richards was alarmed. "That could delay Project Neptune by as long as a week."

Adrienne felt a sinking sensation in the pit of her stomach. The *Neptune* looked like no other vessel afloat in the world, and if she remained in the area for as long as a week to ten days, the Russians and Chinese would be certain to guess she wasn't searching for undersea coal deposits this far from home.

Captain Humphries sighed. "A lot of obstacles have been overcome since you and your friends in Washington first dreamed up Project Neptune, Frank. You've invented and

194

built some remarkable machinery and gear, and this ship is a marvel. But not even the Corporation has the skill and ingenuity to fight the forces of Nature. If a typhoon is going to make us its target, we'll just have to batten down, ride out the storm and pick up where we left off when it's all over."

Richards looked out at the sun shining in a cloud-free sky. "Until the worst happens," he said, "we'll keep hoping for the best."

"In twenty minutes," the chief steward said, "we will land in Singapore."

"There are no changes in my original arrangements, I trust," Porter said.

"Only a small detail or two," the steward replied. "Some friends will have a car awaiting you, and will take you to your rendezvous with our representative."

"Sorry, chum." Porter had anticipated just such a shift, and remained calm. "The lady and I are going to a hotel, where a room is being held for us. I have some private matters to set up before I go to the meeting. Matters that will guarantee our safety if and when I've made a deal with your people."

"But my instructions—"

"To hell with your instructions." Porter did not raise his voice. "My original conditions were specific, and Moscow accepted them. For reasons of my own I have no intention of allowing them to be altered. Even the meeting place has been arranged, and I'll be there four hours to the minute after the wheels of this airplane touch the ground. No sooner and no later."

The man was startled by his resolve, and became nasty. "An Anglo-Saxon trait that always mystifies me," he said, "is how you refuse to recognize long odds."

"We've had a great deal of practice," Porter said cheer-

195

fully. "We've been fighting odds for centuries."

"You realize we can compel you—"

"I realize you can kill Miss Wing and me before we ever hit the ground," Porter said. "I also realize that Comrade Andropov will never get his hands on certain documents that I've traveled halfway around the world to deliver to one of his associates. It may be an old Slavic custom to change rules while a game is in progress, but I don't happen to play that way. Take it or leave it."

The man walked forward to the cockpit, muttering to himself.

"That was dangerous," Nancy said.

"Everything we've done since I've gone underground has been dangerous."

"Were you serious when you said Andropov wouldn't get the documents you agreed to supply?"

"The KGB will have to meet my terms," Porter said.

She hesitated for an instant. "I've assumed you've actually been carrying them, perhaps on microfilm."

"You've assumed wrong." Porter had no intention of telling her the precautionary arrangements he had made to safeguard the blueprints and other documents concerning the dummy jumbo submarine. "For your own sake you'll have to trust me."

"Wouldn't it be safer if I know, too? I mean, suppose something happens to you—"

"Nothing will happen to me," Porter said, "as long as I'm the only one who knows the specifications."

The wheels touched down on the runway, and the girl fell silent.

Porter felt almost certain she had been assigned by the Chinese to obtain the documents from him, and if he was right she would make another attempt before he went off to meet the KGB representative from Moscow. Perhaps the knife thrown at her in Port Moresby had been intended as a warning, and time was running short.

One way and another, the next few hours would be the most crucial of his life.

"Strike 'ten,' " the sonar operator called.

His colleagues echoed his cry. All four console dials showed a maximum intensity.

Franklin Richards snapped a switch, and a deep, humming sound came out of a loudspeaker unit on the deck beside him. The noise rose and fell, rose and fell.

Adrienne was reminded of waves.

The speed of the *Neptune* was cut abruptly, and she gradually drew to a halt after drifting for another mile or two, then went into reverse and began to inch backward.

"Attention all hands and passengers," Captain Humphries said from the bridge. "We are on target."

Richards was wasting no time, and picked up a telephone. "Demagnetize the ballast," he said. "Yes, turn on your machines right now, and I'll join you shortly." He glanced at his watch and smiled. "We'll be ready to roll before dawn," he said. "Just twelve more hours of waiting."

Adrienne was in a hurry, too, and went to the communications center, where she gave the signals officer a message that had been prepared before she had left the United States. It was addressed to a "Mrs. William Smith, care of Commanding General, Clark Field," and the message itself was innocuous: "LOVELY CROSSING. BEAUTIFUL WEATHER. DIDN'T GET SEASICK ONCE. SEE YOU SOON. LOVE, MARY."

The Corporation coordinator at Clark Field, the largest U.S. Air Force base on earth located on other than American soil, would know what she meant. The *Neptune* had located the sunken Russian submarine far below the surface of the sea, and frantic preparations were under way for its recovery.

197

The actual operation would begin in twelve hours, as soon as the shot that would be stored in the submersible was demagnetized.

Adrienne went forward to the bridge to congratulate Captain Humphries. Modern navigation, combined with sonar, had enabled him to find the needlelike lost submarine in the vast undersea haystack of the South China Sea.

The master of the *Neptune* nodded absently as she expressed admiration for his feat. "I've just had a report from that weather plane," he said. "The gale is standing still, gathering strength, and sure as hell is unholy she's turning into a full-fledged typhoon. There's still no way of telling whether she's going to come toward us, but I hope Frank Richards' gadgets do what they're supposed to do. And without delays."

A carload of Russian agents followed the taxi from the airport into downtown Singapore, and for all Porter knew or cared, his driver worked for the KGB, too. He had anticipated just such a move, and had made his preparations accordingly.

Nancy was silent in her corner, and appeared to be brooding.

Porter hadn't visited Singapore for more than a year, and was impressed anew by the remarkable prosperity of the city-state. Her economy in ruins when she had been retaken from her Japanese captors at the end of World War II, Singapore had broken away from the new nation, Malaysia, determined to go it alone. The odds against her had been overwhelming, but she had succeeded in spite of them, and was the miracle of the Orient.

Her people, a mixture of Malaysians, Chinese, Indians and Occidentals, had banded together under a stable government and, in spite of the city's location close to the equator, had devoted themselves to unremitting hard labor. The results were to be seen everywhere, and the taxi passed scores of new, automated factories and mills, then rolled through streets lined with skyscraper office buildings, banks and hotels. There were virtually no beggars in Singapore now; shantytown slums had given way to comfortable high-rise dwellings, and the pedestrians of every race who dodged in and out of the long lines of automobiles, lorries, pickup trucks and other vehicles looked more prosperous and better fed than the residents of any other community in the East.

Night was falling, but there was no diminution of traffic, and in spite of the almost suffocating heat the residents of Singapore emulated the brisk walk of a Londoner or New Yorker. No one strolled. The city-state was a tightly knit little nation in a hurry. There was none of the drabness of Peking here, none of the poverty of Calcutta or the smug complacency of Hong Kong.

Porter and Nancy checked into their hotel, and he saw that only two and one-half hours remained before his scheduled meeting with the KGB representative, so he headed straight for the shower. Returning to the bedroom, clad only in his shorts, he found Nancy systematically searching his wallet and his suitcase.

There was a hint of sadness in her smile. "Forgive me, darling, but you left me no choice. I need the specifications for the large submarine, and I must have them immediately."

He took a single step forward, but halted when he found himself looking into the muzzle of her tiny Kolibri. Too late he realized that his own weapons rested on a dressing table behind her.

"Believe me," she said, "after all you've done for me I didn't want it to happen this way."

Porter ignored her pointed pistol, and picking up a clean shirt from the floor, where she had thrown it while emptying

199

his luggage, he began to dress.

"I'll do whatever is necessary to get those documents from you," she said. "Anything at all."

He continued to dress.

"Don't force my hand," Nancy said.

Porter simulated a yawn. "In the first place," he said, "I have no documents here. Surely you don't think I'd be stupid enough to carry them on my person when we've been the guests of the Russians all these weeks!"

"You must have them! I've seen microfilms the size of a tiny pinhead, so I know—"

"In a situation such as the one we've been in," Porter said, buckling his belt, knotting his necktie and reaching for his jacket, "I prefer human ingenuity to such wonders of our age as microfilm dots. Now, as I was saying, you could shoot me, and you're welcome to try. If you kill me, however, you'll never get the documents, will you?"

Nancy glared at him and bit her lower lip.

"I've had every intention of sharing a very large sum of money with you so we could ride off into the sunset together," he said. "Whatever became of that lovely dream?"

"I'm under obligations to get those documents and give them to certain people. If I fail, I won't live long enough to ride off into any sunset."

"More's the pity." Porter reached out swiftly, slapped her hand aside and, catching hold of her wrist, forced her to drop her tiny pistol.

She cursed him.

Paying no attention, he strapped on his Magnum and slipped his Lilliput into his jacket pocket. "My dear," he said, kicking her pistol under the bed, "I urge you to have greater faith in me. I'll come back here for you as soon as I've finished my meeting—"

"I don't believe you," Nancy cried. "You've been planning

all along to desert me! You're no more in love with me than I am with you."

Porter had to concede that she was a somewhat better actress than he had imagined. "Oh, well. Let's say I'm fond of you, so I'm willing to meet you after my conference."

Her eyes filled with angry tears. "You'll trick me, as you've done all along."

"The same to you," he said, and grinned.

"You've used me as window dressing. I still don't know why, and I suppose it doesn't much matter that you've been working on one of those complicated schemes the Americans love."

Porter's shrug was eloquent.

"If I don't deliver those blueprints," Nancy said, "I'm in trouble."

"Too bad your friends didn't come straight to me and offer a cash deal. I'd have done for them what I'm doing for the KGB."

"How much do you want?"

"I'm afraid it's a bit late now for that sort of thing," Porter said. "The Russians are keeping me under the closest possible surveillance, and you know it as well as I do. They'd be distinctly unhappy if I sold a set of specifications to someone else. Besides, I don't happen to carry a duplicating machine with me. Give my compliments to my friends in Peking, and tell them that next time I hope they'll take advantage of their opportunities more quickly."

Nancy's hands fell to her sides. "You don't care what becomes of me."

If she gave as good a performance in her films, he thought, she would become a star. "Do you know the Chung Lai restaurant on Harbour Road?"

A flicker of hope appeared in her eyes. "Of course."

"Meet me there at eight this evening. I'll either come for

201

you myself or send word where you're to go. If you're being followed—and I assume you will be—you may have to shake off the tail."

"I'll try," she said, but sounded dubious.

Porter raised a hand in salute, then left the room. Not giving the girl another thought, he was relieved to see that no one awaited him in the corridor, but he didn't fool himself. KGB agents would be stationed at every entrance to the hotel, and would follow him wherever he went.

A sudden thought occurred to him as he walked down the hall, and he checked both of his guns. As he suspected, Nancy had removed the ammunition from both while he had taken a shower. He had been negligent, and now he had to return to the room to load the weapons. Rarely had he been this careless, and he was annoyed with himself as he doubled back.

He unlocked the door, stepped into the room and stopped short.

Nancy Wing was crumpled on the floor. Her neck had been broken, and her sightless eyes stared up at the ceiling.

No one else was in the room, the bathroom or the clothes closets.

The contents of Porter's luggage were still scattered on the bed and floor. Nothing else in the room had been touched.

He had been absent from the room for no more than three or four minutes, so it was obvious someone had been lying in wait for Nancy, had entered as soon as he had departed and had killed her when she had revealed that she had been unable to obtain the documents from him. Later, perhaps, he could feel pity for the girl who had immersed herself beyond her depth in a profession where no quarter was given and none was expected.

Right now there were other things to be done, and no time to be lost. Certainly he couldn't afford to linger here until the

Singapore authorities found her body.

Digging into a corner pocket of his suitcase, he removed two clips of ammunition for his Magnum, loading the automatic with one and dropping the other into his pocket. Then he loaded his Lilliput and took an extra handful of bullets with him. He hadn't planned to return for his belongings, but now it would be impossible for him to come back here.

As a final gesture he turned Nancy's luggage upside down, scattering cosmetics and clothing. The room was in a shambles, and the police would believe that robbery had been the murderer's motive. Only when he failed to return would he be under suspicion.

For an instant Porter looked for the last time at the body of Nancy Wing. Then he left the room again and went on to meet his own destiny.

TWELVE

The sonar devices guided the *Neptune* to a place on the surface of the South China Sea directly above the sunken Russian submarine, and there she dropped her anchor. Additional sonar equipment was lowered to a depth of more than three miles, and the pinpointing on charts that followed soon revealed that the *Zolóto* had shifted its position on the bottom slightly during the preceding year, moving about twenty feet.

Preparations for the following day's attempt to raise the vessel continued through the night. The demagnetizing of the submersible's ballast in a special compression chamber was the most important of these activities, and all of the special generators made for the mission were functioning, storing energy for the work ahead.

The submersible, attached to the mother ship by a towline, bobbed gently in the calm water. After dinner a team went on board and, under Franklin Richards' direct supervision, filled her special underside compartment with 8,652 gallons of high-octane aviation gasoline that would be used to send her to the bottom and back to the surface again as the petrol compressed and decompressed.

Three of Adrienne Howard's Corporation agents, all

armed with submachine guns, were stationed on board the submersible through the night, prepared to repel any invaders who might try to intervene. In these last hours before the critical phase of Project Neptune began, it was no longer possible to maintain complete secrecy, and the U.S. Navy cruiser, flagship of the rear admiral in charge of the escort, anchored less than a mile away. Its three launches were lowered and their heavily armed crews sailed continuously around the *Neptune* and the ungainly float. Five squadrons of fighter planes from Clark Field also took part in the protection of the project, and no fewer than three were in the air at any given time, keeping the skies overhead clear.

The scientists and technical experts who had been practicing for days ate an early dinner, but few were hungry, and most of them went to play bridge or backgammon, but could not concentrate on their games. Some went off to bed, but few could sleep, and the entire company would be awakened at 5:00 A.M. for the start of the final phase of the operation.

Franklin Richards made no attempt to rest, and personally tested every instrument, every piece of equipment that would be used the following morning. Endowed with greater drive and more inner resources of energy than most men, he was inexhaustible. No detail was too small to capture his attention, and thanks to his zeal a small leak was discovered in a gasoline compression valve. At his insistence the entire valve was replaced, even though it would have been easy to repair the malfunctioning part.

Technicians inspected all of the consoles that would be used, and experts who had spent a full year in training for their highly specialized task tested the twin gyroscopes and the highly sensitive computer they directed. These devices would be used to keep the football field horizontal as it submerged and, of far greater importance, prevent it from tipping when it rose to the surface again with the sunken

Russian submarine on board. The release of the iron shot used as ballast on the submersible would be controlled by the computer, which would send electrical impulses to the lip of the float. Compartments in that lip would be opened or kept closed according to the directions of the computer because mere men could not calculate the degree of list and then correct it as rapidly as might be necessary, particularly when unseen and unmeasured underwater currents struck the huge barge.

Adrienne made no attempt to sleep, and roamed the *Neptune* after eating a small sandwich and a bowl of soup. In a sense, she thought, her task was finished, and she would become active again only in the event of an emergency. The communications center on the operations deck was in constant wireless touch with the Navy escort and the Air Force squadrons, attempts to maintain silence having been abandoned in this crucial stage. The two warships that made up part of the escort were equipped with sonar devices of their own, and were on watch for a possible intrusion by a Russian nuclear submarine, in case a last-minute attempt was made to disrupt Project Neptune by force.

The bridge players, Adrienne saw, were making stupid bids and forgetting what cards had been played; the backgammon players moved their counters in defiance of the odds. The library appeared deserted, but she caught a glimpse of someone sitting in a high-backed chair, then saw Marie Richards holding an opened book in her lap.

"This is the worst part," Marie said. "The planning was fun, the building was exciting, but now I only feel dread."

"That's what upsets me," she said. "Suppose we fail. All the money and effort and time lost forever. Frank has thought of nothing else for months and months. Neither have I, really." She turned back to her book, but it was apparent she had no idea what she was reading.

If something went wrong tomorrow, Franklin Richards would suffer far more than would anyone else involved. A failure to recover the *Zolóto* would be a blow to the United States, but the pride of a genius would be devastated.

"Miss Howard," the loudspeaker blared, "the captain would like to see you in his quarters."

Adrienne climbed a flight of stairs and went to the suite directly behind the bridge.

Captain Humphries was in his combination living cabin—office, and looked pale beneath his tan as he stood at a porthole. "This," he said, thrusting a yellow flimsy at her, "is the latest from the meteorologists."

She scanned the report: "STORM HAS DEVELOPED INTO FULL-SCALE TYPHOON PACKING WINDS OF UP TO 115 MPH AND STILL INCREASING. PRESENTLY ON DIRECT COLLISION COURSE WITH NEPTUNE, ALTHOUGH CHANGE IN DIRECTION COULD OCCUR AT ANY TIME. IF NOT, FORCE 6 WINDS SHOULD BE ANTICIPATED BY 1700 HOURS TOMORROW."

Adrienne raised an inquiring eyebrow.

"Unless the typhoon shifts," the captain said, "gale-strength winds will start hitting us around five in the afternoon."

"Even if everything goes according to schedule," she said, "the operation won't end before seven or eight tomorrow night."

"That's why I'm telling this to no one except you right now," Captain Humphries said. "I won't say anything to Frank Richards until later tonight, after we see what the storm is doing. The Russian sub down at the bottom may be important to a lot of people, but I'm responsible for the lives of everyone on board the *Neptune*. And if a crunch comes, I'll pull out, even if it means losing the sub."

Two Russian agents, screamingly obvious in a Singapore crowd in spite of their efforts to remain inconspicuous, followed Porter through the streets. He had planned his moves with care, including their timing, and a glance at his watch told him he was on schedule. First he went to the general post office, where he showed his passport and picked up a bulky registered letter awaiting him there. Then he headed directly across the street to a bank, where he took out a safe deposit box.

Using a small piece of carbon paper and a blank sheet of paper he had brought with him for the purpose, he placed them under the signature card, and in a bold, easy to forge hand he wrote the name, *Leo Tolstoy*. The KGB, totally lacking in a sense of humor, would not appreciate his little joke.

He was given a safe deposit box, placed the envelope in it, and pocketing the key, he left the bank only minutes before it closed its doors for the day.

As he moved to the curb to hail a taxi he saw two Russians in a waiting automobile, and was tempted to ask them for a ride since they would be going to the same place. But this was not the moment to create complications.

After a short ride he was deposited at the front entrance of the Raffles Hotel, long one of Singapore's landmarks and for many decades prior to World War II the glory of the British raj. Its landscaped lawns and gardens were vast, and its front porch, where the cream of British colonial society had sat in rockers, consumed gin slings and gossiped, was said to be the longest in the world. Only an American resort hotel in northern Michigan disputed that claim.

Newer hotels, resplendent in chrome, glass and steel that made them resemble their counterparts all over the globe, had reduced the stature of the Raffles. Most of her guests were German, Japanese and American tourists traveling in groups, who entered and left en masse, cameras slung over the shoulders of their multicolored sports shirts, their footsore, souvenir-laden wives trailing behind them. The hotel was in need of paint and the floorboards of the porch creaked under Porter's weight, but he had known the Raffles in her days of grandeur, and what remained of her magic was not lost on him.

He strolled past Americans drinking bourbon, Japanese sipping warm sake and Germans downing steins of beer, until, at the far end of the porch, he spotted a bulky figure behind an open, three-day-old copy of the London *Daily Telegraph*. The man was alone.

"Georgi," Porter said, "you're a proverbial sight for the proverbial sore eyes. I haven't seen you since our little chat at the Corporation safe house in Virginia. I wondered if Andropov would have the good sense to send you."

Georgi Verschek lowered his newspaper, folded it with care and placed it on a vacant rocker beside him. He was wearing the KGB uniform, a dark, loose-fitting suit, white shirt and narrow necktie, and by no stretch of the imagination would he have passed as an Englishman. He smiled slightly, but neither rose nor extended his hand. "You are on time, as always," he said. "I must grant you that much."

"I could have been here days ago." Porter lowered himself into the adjacent rocker, moving the newspaper. "I didn't appreciate the steam bath in Port Moresby, I can tell you. Why the delay?"

"Andropov refused to believe you were truly defecting, and the entire Council agreed with him. But we obtained certain proof that the large submarine the Americans are building at the Richards shipyard is genuine, so we decided to go through with our deal."

"I'm always truthful with Andropov, Georgi. And with you." Porter summoned a white-coated waiter, ordered two pink gins and turned back to the Russian. "This will be your treat, Georgi."

"You're very free with my money."

"The Kremlin's money. You're still on an expense account, but I'm not."

Verschek shrugged, bit off the end of a cigar and lighted it. "Some of the confusion," he said, "arose because your recent activities make little sense. We have known each other for a long time, Porter, and you are guilty of bad form."

Porter rolled a cigarette.

"I refuse to believe you are in love with that Wing harlot, or that you're chucking your career because of her."

Porter laughed. "I've never known anyone with greater sexual appetites."

"At our age," Verschek said reprovingly, "sex no longer matters all that much."

Porter tried not to think of the dead girl in the hotel room.

"You knew she was working for us."

"Of course."

"You also knew she was on the payroll of the Chinese."

"That's what made her dangerous," Porter said. "I preferred to bring her with me, so I could keep an eye on her."

Verschek slapped the arm of his chair. "That is precisely what I told Andropov!"

The waiter arrived with their drinks.

The Russian grudgingly counted out change and added a small tip that sent the Malaysian waiter off in a huff. "She cannot be trusted by anyone."

"So the Chinese thought. She had a close call in Port Moresby."

The KGB man shrugged. "If Peking is on her trail she is as good as dead. But that is no matter to you and me. These unreliable amateurs cause clutter in our business."

"To professionalism," Porter said, and sipped his drink.

Verschek emptied his glass in a single gulp, as though he were drinking vodka. "You are prepared to conclude our deal?"

"That's why I'm here. That's why I risked leaving America as I did, and why I placed myself at the tender mercies of your gorillas."

"You have the blueprints and specifications of the new submarine with you?"

"Better than that. They're in a place where only one person has access to them, and you can be that person, Georgi. May I see the color of your money?"

The Russian took a bulky envelope from his pocket, handed it to him and watched him. "Cash," he said, "not in a Swiss account."

Porter counted 100 banknotes, each of $1,000 denomination. "Very nice," he said.

Verschek caught hold of his arm before he could place the envelope in his pocket. "Please, first the documents."

Porter handed him the key to the safe deposit box and the carbon copy of the signature he had written. "You or one of your people will have no trouble duplicating this signature. Go into the bank tomorrow morning, and you'll find the papers waiting for you."

"Explain!"

"It was a simple procedure," Porter said. "I mailed myself the documents, care of the general post office here. Registered, so no one else could claim the letter. Then I took it to the bank just before coming here to meet you."

Verschek studied the signature and grinned. "Andropov will wonder why you used the name of Count Tolstoy. Ah, well. When I have seen the documents you will be paid the money."

"I'll take the money now," Porter said, "or you won't collect the papers. If I had carried them on my person your people could have jumped me, you know. I couldn't afford to take the chance."

"How do I know the specifications are to be found in the safe deposit box? How do I know you aren't cheating me?"

"You have the word of one professional to another."

Verschek snorted.

"Besides, Georgi, your organization is too efficient for me to play games with you. If I tried to fool you the KGB would follow me to the ends of the earth, and either do me in or turn me over to the Corporation for disposal. I'm not sure which would be the worse fate."

"Nor am I. You give me little choice, Porter. And I know why you wanted to meet me at the end of the business day, after the banks are closed."

"You're right. I have no intention of hanging about in Singapore waiting for your thugs to recover the one hundred thousand dollars. Andropov is as big a skinflint as Brian Davidson, and he'd promote you to deputy chairman of the KGB on the spot if you returned the money to him." Acting with great deliberation, Porter pocketed the envelope.

Verschek laughed, displaying a gold tooth. "You are wise to retire," he said. "When a man has nothing more to learn in his profession, it becomes boring to him." He stood and retrieved his newspaper. "All the same, I dare say we shall meet again."

"I sincerely hope not."

The Russian's smile was bloodless. "Good luck," he said,

and sauntered down the long porch in the direction of the hotel entrance.

The crisis was at hand. Two heavy-set Russian agents were sitting about fifty feet down the porch, and Porter knew they intended to rob him of the money as soon as their superior disappeared from sight and could disclaim any knowledge of the incident.

He was equally certain they planned to murder him. If he survived and passed the word to the world intelligence community that the Russians no longer kept a bargain, it would be very difficult for the KGB to hire the informers who were the lifeblood of every secret service. Besides, he had performed a vital function and now was of no further use to Moscow, and it was Andropov's way to dispose of someone in that position.

He had selected this very place on the porch because he had known how the Russians would react, and he had less than a minute to put his own carefully made plan into effect. The moment Georgi Verschek disappeared from the porch his men would act.

It was growing dark, and the lights that illuminated the garden and lawns had not yet been turned on. Porter turned away from the KGB pair so they couldn't see what he was doing. Taking his Magnum from his shoulder holster he released the safety catch, made sure the silencer was securely in place, and then poised for a leap.

Suddenly he bolted over the waist-high railing and, crouching low, raced for the temporary security of a clump of palms about ten yards to his left.

A bullet landed in the trunk of a tree scant inches from Porter's head. The Russians were using silencers on their weapons, too.

He threw himself to the ground to make them think he had been hit, rolled forward and sprang to his feet again behind

the cover of the thick palm trunks. Other KGB agents undoubtedly were on the grounds, too, but he first had to make
a stand against this pair in order to win a brief breathing
spell.

They separated and advanced cautiously.

The half-light of dusk was deceptive, and Porter realized
they would make better targets if he allowed them to advance
closer, but he couldn't afford the luxury of waiting. He aimed
at the man on the left, squeezed the trigger and then fired at
the second agent.

One dropped to the ground, and as his companion turned
to him Porter sprinted across the lawn toward the fence that
surrounded the hotel property.

He ran past the swimming pool, where several bathers
stared at him.

As he reached the five-foot-high steel fence the floodlights
were turned on. Jamming his Magnum into its holster he
climbed over the fence.

It had been his intention to hail a taxi, but a more attractive alternative suddenly presented itself. A number of local
residents, most of them presumably men and women who
worked the day shift at the hotel, were standing in a queue
and boarding one of the old double-decker buses that had
been imported when Singapore had still been a British colony.

The last two men were climbing on board when Porter
joined them, hauled himself onto the bus and lost himself in
the crowd as the vehicle started to move.

It gained speed, but before it turned a corner he caught a
glimpse of three men with blond hair climbing the hotel fence
and dropping into the street outside. For the moment, at
least, he had lost them, and he concentrated on paying his
fare. In spite of his intimate knowledge of Singapore, this was
the first time he had ever taken a bus in the city, and to the

214

amusement of his fellow passengers, he didn't know how much to pay.

He stayed on the bus until it reached the crowded Chinese district, and there he transferred to another that was headed in the direction of the waterfront. When he left it at the end of its run he saw he was about a mile from his destination, but there were no taxis here, so he had to make the last stage of his escape journey on foot.

The Singapore harbor, a vast jungle of ships and cranes and modern machinery, was responsible for the city-state's prosperity, and was active twenty-four hours a day. Freighters and tankers were unloading and taking on cargo at their berths, a dozen passenger vessels rode at anchor, and there were even more sampans and junks, some of them diesel-powered, than could be seen in Hong Kong.

A sea of oil storage tanks stretched inland, and beyond it were huge warehouses. There were factories everywhere, too, some manufacturing products of Malaysia's tin and rubber, others making biscuits and tomato sauce and scores of other processed foods for Singapore's own millions.

Along the street that faced the water were the cheap bars, hotels and brothels found in any great port, and merchant seamen went from one tavern to another until they had spent all of their money. Prostitutes of many nationalities were on hand, too, and a number accosted Porter, but quietly shrugged off his indifference. Singapore was a gentle city, her people having taught themselves the self-discipline of living together in harmony, and it was said that only rarely was a drunken sailor robbed.

For the moment Porter felt in no danger, but he took the precaution of looking back over his shoulder repeatedly, and several times he stepped into a doorway and paused to make sure he wasn't being followed.

At last he saw what he was seeking, a concrete wharf that

stretched about three hundred feet into the water. Bobbing up and down in the water beside it was a large helicopter resting on pontoons. On the wharf, visible in the light of a street lamp, was a sign:

SEE SINGAPORE AND THE STRAITS
FROM THE AIR!
30 to 60 Minute Trips
Special Fares for Groups

Only the discerning might have noticed that this powerful aircraft was too large and modern for its advertised purpose. No lights were burning on board, and the operators of the venture appeared to have taken themselves elsewhere. Few tourists came into the area, but the pedestrians wandering past the wharf did not think the presence of the helicopter strange, and paid little attention to it. Merchant seamen in search of a drink or a girl had other matters on their minds.

A pistol shot sounded, and a bullet chipped cement from the wall of a warehouse behind Porter.

He reacted instantly, dropping to a squatting position and extinguishing the street light with a single shot. The whole area was thrown into darkness.

A pair of tarts making their way up the street ducked for cover into the nearest bar, and several meandering seamen scattered. In almost no time the immediate neighborhood was virtually deserted.

Porter crept forward along the base of the warehouse, and in the gloom he could see three figures near the wharf, blocking his access to it. He sent a rain of fire at the trio, then ran across an open space to the wall of the next building, the entrance to a dilapidated brothel.

One of the trio was sprawled on the ground, but the others remained vertical, and peered through the darkness as they searched for him. One down, he thought, and two to go.

Porter squeezed the trigger again, sending a spray of fire back and forth as he crisscrossed the target area. A second of his foes fell, and the third took refuge behind a pylon.

It would be difficult for the enemy to miss if Porter stepped into the open, so his situation required the use of cunning. He had emptied the Magnum in this last burst, so he slipped in a new cartridge. Then he took careful aim with the empty casing, and heaving it as he would a hand grenade, he threw it so it landed on the wharf to the side of the surviving member of the trio.

The man shifted his position, and as he moved Porter dashed forward, firing as he ran.

His enemy returned the fire.

Porter had the advantage, however, and paying no attention to a savage jolt in his left shoulder, he emptied his chamber a second time. The man pitched forward, his automatic pistol clattering on the cement wharf.

Safety beckoned at the end of the pier, and Porter ran with all his might toward the helicopter.

The aircraft was not deserted after all. Someone on board shouted, "Watch out behind you!"

Porter instinctively swerved, ducked and spun around as a heavy-set man appeared from behind another pylon. It was impossible to determine what arms he was carrying, and Porter did not wait to find out, but kicked him viciously in the groin.

The man doubled over, dropping an automatic pistol.

Porter leaped forward, intending to hit him over the head with the butt of his empty Magnum, but the man straightened, and they grappled.

"This is a surprise, Georgi," Porter said. "But you did mention meeting again."

Georgi Verschek cursed him in Russian as they crashed to

217

the wharf together and rolled over and over.

Both tried to gain the upper hand, and the KGB agent managed to grasp Porter's throat with both hands.

Unaccountably, Porter felt dizzy and realized his strength was ebbing, so he knew he had to react quickly. He drove his right fist into the pit of the Russian's stomach, and as Verschek relaxed his grip a trifle he smashed his left into the man's face.

An excruciating pain traveled the length of Porter's arm, and for an instant he thought he would lost consciousness.

But his blow snapped Verschek's head back, and Porter had the chance he had been seeking. He drew his Lilliput from his pocket, simultaneously removing the safety catch, and emptied all six chambers into the KGB agent's body.

Verschek made no sound as he died.

Porter managed to haul himself to his feet. "Shame on you, Georgi," he muttered. "All that fuss for the sake of a little money."

Police sirens sounded in the distance.

The helicopter came to life, its jets roaring, its lights turned on.

Blackman materialized beside Porter, and supported him as they ran to the helicopter. "You were so tangled up together I couldn't shoot him. That was a near thing."

They threw themselves into the aircraft, and as they closed the door behind them the pilot began to taxi into the harbor, his speed increasing.

The helicopter began to rise, its engines blotting out the sound of the sirens.

Porter looked out of the window and saw several police cars, their roof lights blinking furiously, pull to a halt at the base of the wharf.

The helicopter, ascending swiftly, headed out to sea under full power.

"How badly were you hit?" Blackman asked.

Porter didn't know what he meant.

His assistant pointed to his shoulder.

His shirt and jacket were soaked with blood, but he laughed. "Thanks for calling it to my attention, old chap. A small price for a red herring to pay, don't you agree?"

Because of the possible approach of the typhoon, Franklin Richards advanced the start of the salvage operation to 3:30 A.M., preferring to begin in the dark to avoid a possible curtailment of his activities at the climax. The loading of demagnetized iron shot into the lip of the submersible was under way more than an hour earlier, with cranes lowering more than 7,000 tons of the metal pellets to the float. The entire task was automated, making it unnecessary for the men who watched in the glare of floodlights to do anything other than supervise and be ready to intervene only if something went amiss.

Nothing untoward happened, however. The technicians had rehearsed every move so many times they knew what was expected of them, and as they watched the lights and gauges on their control boards they knew what was expected in each step of the procedure. Nothing was left to chance, and there was no guesswork.

Adrienne was not on hand for the loading of the ballast. A long day stretched ahead, and experience had taught her that at least a little rest would be necessary for her to face it, so she changed her mind about sleeping, and at midnight retired to her cabin for a few hours. She lay on her bed fully dressed, secure in the knowledge that the Deacon was on duty and would call her in the event that she was needed. The Navy and Air Force were taking responsibility for the security of the present phase of the operation, and only if and when the *Zolóto* was recovered would she be required to return to work in earnest.

In spite of her belief that she wasn't tired, she drifted into a deep sleep. A heavy pounding at the door of her cabin awakened her, and a glance at the clock told her it was 2:45 A.M.

The Deacon stood in the passage. "The captain wants you in the communications center," he said. "Pronto."

She combed her hair while climbing the stairs.

The captain and the signals officer were awaiting her. "There's an aircraft that's trying to penetrate the security zone," he said.

"What kind of an aircraft?"

"No national markings. Beta squadron is keeping it under surveillance. It's a seagoing helicopter, and the pilot identifies himself as Y-twenty-six."

"Never heard of him," Adrienne said.

"He keeps insisting he wants to talk to you, so I've told Beta squadron to hold off until you give the word."

Adrienne shrugged.

The signals officer picked up a microphone. "This is *Neptune* calling Y-twenty-six. Come in, please."

"Y-twenty-six calling *Neptune,*" a high-pitched voice said over static. "These fighter planes are making us nervous. We wish you'd get Miss Howard."

"I'm here," Adrienne said.

A deeper, equally metallic voice came over the wireless. "I wish you'd call off your fly-boys, my love. If they swoop down on us just once more I may not be able to keep my breakfast date with you."

Adrienne's temples began to pound. "Identify yourself, Y-twenty-six."

"If I tried to pick you up at a bar," the metallic voice said, "I hope you wouldn't smash my knuckles with an ashtray."

Tears came to her eyes, and her voice trembled as she said,

220

"Neptune to Beta squadron. Please escort the helicopter to us. Safely. Make sure nothing happens to anyone on board!"

The commander of the Air Force squadron acknowledged the order.

Captain Humphries and the signals officer looked at Adrienne, waiting for an explanation.

She offered none, and for the first time since they had known her she seemed flustered. "I've got to put on makeup and change my clothes before he gets here," she said, and fled to her cabin.

THIRTEEN

The months of planning and building, preparation and practice came to an end at 3:30 A.M. The air was muggy, indicating that a change in the weather was due, but the star-filled sky was clear, and a full moon provided far better illumination than did the floodlights that shone on the submersible from the *Neptune*.

The last of the demagnetized ballast had been stored in place; a final check revealed that all instruments were operable and that all plugs were secure. The technicians making the inspection climbed a ladder to the deck of the *Neptune*, and were followed by Franklin Richards, who went straight to the operations center.

He hurried to the master control panel, where three project supervisors were monitoring the many needles, gauges and lights. His wife was waiting for him, too, and for an instant he put an arm around her shoulders.

"All systems are go, sir," the chief supervisor said.

Marie Richards smiled at her husband, stepped forward and pulled the switch turning on the delicate mechanism that began the decompression of the gasoline stored in the chamber beneath the huge float.

"Cut all lines to the submersible," Richards said.

"Very good, sir." An assistant supervisor punched a button, and four automated knives cut the heavy lines.

Almost one hundred experts and technicians were on duty in the operations center, but no one moved, no one spoke, no one as much as lighted a cigarette. After three minutes the tension was almost unbearable, and one minute later the huge football field barge sank beneath the surface of the South China Sea.

Cigarettes, pipes and cigars appeared, and stewards began to push carts laden with coffee and sweet rolls from console to monitoring board.

Franklin Richards looked as unconcerned as he did lounging beside a swimming pool. "Activate television cameras," he said.

One by one the four cameras attached to the submersible were turned on, the images they portrayed reflected on a score of receiving sets throughout the center, as well as projected onto a screen that occupied all of one bulkhead.

The float required ten minutes to sink 100 feet, and thereafter descended at an ever-increasing rate.

"Do you want the sonar switched on, Mr. Richards?" the chief supervisor asked.

"Test it every fifteen minutes, as scheduled, but don't leave it on until the field has gone down two and a half miles. We don't want to interfere with the sonar devices on the destroyers that are keeping watch for hostile submarines." Richards picked up a telephone and dialed the captain. "We're under way, Charlie. What's the latest on the weather?"

"The typhoon is turning nastier, with winds up to one hundred and twenty-five miles per hour."

"Still headed toward us?"

"I'm sorry to say we're still directly in her path, but you understand she can shift her course at any time."

"Suppose she doesn't change. What's my deadline?"

"With luck, you may have an hour or two longer than we thought. The wind and seas will begin strengthening by late afternoon, and we'll face gale conditions by about seven tonight."

"I hope that's all the time I'll need. Keep me informed."

Adrienne, who had been watching from a vantage point near the master console, saw the Deacon signal to her, and went without delay to the bridge.

"Your helicopter is coming in," Captain Humphries said. "We'll be seeing her lights in another sixty to ninety seconds."

"Tell him, please, to come in off our port bow and dock portside. All the electric, sonar and television lines are clustered aft, with the emergency lines on the starboard side."

The captain laughed. "Any time you want to leave the Corporation for a job in the Navy, let me know. The helicopter has already been given strict instructions."

The twinkling lights of the aircraft came into view off the port bow at a height of about 1,500 feet, and began to sink lower.

A searchlight picked up the helicopter in its beam and followed it.

"Turn off your damn flashlight," the irate pilot said over his intercom. "You're blinding me!"

The searchlight was snapped off, and the helicopter made a soft landing one hundred yards from the *Neptune,* then began to taxi toward the ship.

Adrienne hurried down to the main deck, accompanied by the Deacon, and ran forward to the bow. Most of the Corporation personnel had already gathered there, but everyone else concerned with Project Neptune was too busy elsewhere.

Two seamen lowered a steel ladder that unfolded in sections, and the pilot made fast to a line that was thrown down to him.

The searchlight was turned on again, the door opened and Porter appeared, shielding his eyes from the glare. He mounted the ladder slowly, using only his right hand, with Blackman close behind, helping him.

The Deacon steadied him as he came onto the deck.

"What happened to your shoulder?" Adrienne demanded.

"I regard that as an inadequate expression of greeting," Porter said, and drew her to him with his sound arm.

They kissed at length, ignoring the presence of their embarrassed subordinates. Senior agents were not expected to show their emotions, even under extenuating circumstances.

Adrienne took charge. "Come with me to the sick bay."

Porter held back. "I gather from the messages we've been exchanging that the show is under way. I don't want to miss it."

"First you'll have the bullet in your shoulder removed and your wound dressed. The show will last all day, so you'll have ample time to see Project Neptune."

Porter astonished the Corporation operatives, particularly those who had worked with him for years. "Yes, ma'am," he said meekly, and allowed Adrienne to lead him below.

Porter went to bed in the ship's hospital after the surgeon was finished with him, and slept soundly for several hours. One of the Corporation agents, who was keeping watch, immediately notified Adrienne when he awakened, and she came below for breakfast with him.

His first concern was for the helicopter pilot, who, she told him, had gone off to land on the deck of the Navy cruiser and would remain on board.

As they ate breakfast Porter related his story.

"One of Verschek's people will recover the phony submarine specifications in the morning and take them to Moscow," Adrienne said. "By the time they learn there is no such ship we should be back on the American mainland. You're mad, but you've pulled off the biggest caper ever. Congratulations."

"I've had more fun doing other things."

She hesitated for an instant. "It's none of my business, but what did you really think of the Wing woman?"

"She should have followed her acting career and married a film producer who would have made her a star. It was her only chance for happiness. She wasn't cut out for our kind of work."

"I'm not sure anyone is," she said. "What happened to the money Verschek gave you?"

"I forgot all about it." He laughed and pointed to his soiled clothes, which a hospital orderly had folded and placed on a chair. "Inside jacket pocket, right-hand side."

Adrienne removed the money and counted it. "One hundred thousand. Lovely."

"My official report to Davidson," Porter declared, "will say I lost it during the fight on the Singapore wharf. Put it away. You and I will think of ways to spend it. Later. Right now I want to see what's happening to Project Neptune."

"You should stay in bed and rest."

"I'm as healthy as I've ever been," Porter said, "and this is the biggest day in the history of intelligence operations. If I must, I'll go up to the deck stark naked."

Adrienne knew he would make good the threat, so she went off to find him clean clothes, brought them back and helped him dress.

The early morning sun was streaming through the plate-glass windows of the operations center when they entered. Franklin Richards was pleased to see Porter, but by mutual consent they postponed a discussion of anything other than the pressing business at hand.

"The submersible has descended a little more than a mile,"

226

Richards said, speaking over the steady hum of the electric generator, "and there are no hitches."

"When do you expect to reach the target?" Porter wanted to know.

"By noon, if all continues to go well. We must. This freak storm promises to be one of the worst in years. All aircraft will be grounded, and even our escort will have to scatter. I've got to have the *Zolóto* on board by sundown, at the latest." Richards turned back to his instrument panel.

Porter made the rounds of the center with Adrienne, and was struck by the quiet. A few of the expedition's scientists and technicians chatted in low tones, their voices drowned by the steady drone of the generator. Men smoked and drank coffee, and some were eating a second breakfast at their duty stations. All appeared relaxed, but the calm was deceptive. Everyone present knew he was taking part in an enterprise that was unique, and many pairs of eyes maintained a watch on every quivering needle and gauge.

Suddenly an alarm bell broke the silence, and a dark mass appeared on a radar screen.

"A Russian submarine!" Adrienne exclaimed. "It slipped through our net!"

Porter shook his head. "Impossible. The escort ships would have picked it up on their sonar long before this."

Richards apparently felt the same way, and they followed him onto the deck, hurrying aft as the alarm bell continued to sound.

Porter caught a glimpse of a silver-gray flash off the starboard side. "Shark!"

"I'm afraid you're right," Richards said. "A whole school of grayfins." There was no need for him to mention that if the sharks cut any of the vital lines to the submersible, Project Neptune would be ruined.

Plans had been made for even this contingency, and several men ran below, returning quickly with cylinders that looked like hand-operated fire extinguishers. Hurrying aft on the starboard side they aimed these at the sharks, at least a dozen of which were circling the lines directly below the surface. Thin streams of a colorless liquid squirted out, and began to boil and foam as they hit the sea.

The sharks thrashed wildly, and dark shapes darted away. Within minutes the crisis seemed to have been averted.

As the foam subsided, however, one huge creature, at least twenty-five feet long, remained near the electric cables, its powerful tail breaking the surface repeatedly.

It appeared to be staying in one place.

"My God!" Richards was pale beneath his tan. "The creature is caught on the lines!"

Even as he spoke, three divers were hastily donning their scuba gear. Every member of the Project Neptune team had been drilled so thoroughly that it was unnecessary to give orders.

The three divers were joined by a fourth.

Adrienne looked at the slender figure. "Marie! You can't allow her to do this, Frank! That's a killer shark!"

Richards shook his head. "Marie is more agile and can handle herself in the water with greater ease than anyone I know." He raced aft for a word with his wife before she climbed down a rope ladder into the water.

"I don't like this," Adrienne said, "but I don't know how we can stop her."

Porter shook his head. "To think I didn't trust her," he murmured.

Marie was the first in the water, and approached the shark warily.

The creature became aware of her proximity, and thrashed more violently.

The other divers hit the water and spread out in a semicircle, swimming slowly.

Marie approached the imprisoned shark from the left, two others drew nearer on the right, and one diver, acting as a decoy, remained several yards from the creature's snout.

"Now!" Marie called, disappearing below the surface with a long knife in her hand.

Almost simultaneously the divers on the shark's right went under the water, and only the decoy stayed on the surface.

It was difficult for those on the deck to see what was happening. The sea foamed almost as heavily as it had when the repellant had been poured in, and it was evident that the shark was straining to break loose.

A thin trickle of blood that spread on the surface to the shark's left indicated that Marie had been the first to attack.

The maddened shark made a supreme effort and broke free of the cables.

Marie was its obvious target, but she faced it valiantly, not retreating, and struck at it repeatedly with her knife.

The others divers came to her aid, and all three of the men slashed and stabbed at the grayfin until their arms were weary.

The boiling sea grew even more agitated, and Adrienne, who could look into the muzzle of a gun without fear, leaned against Porter, afraid she would be sick.

All at once the sea grew calm, and the divers hastily swam to the ladders. Marie was the first to ascend. There was a long rip in her rubber diving suit, but she appeared to be unharmed.

Even as the divers left the water, other members of the expedition harpooned the dying shark and hauled it on board the *Neptune* before its still-spreading blood attracted the rest of the pack and it became necessary to use more repellant.

Marie embraced her husband. Then, finally sheathing her

knife, she looked at the ugly foe she had killed. Reverting to her role of the giddy society hostess, she spoke lightly. "I've always wanted a pair of genuine shark's tooth earrings," she said, and went off to the master suite to change her attire.

Shortly before noon the sonar system was activated, and an intermittent buzzing sound indicated that the submersible was on target. The volume of the sound increased, its duration lengthening, and when the float's rate of descent picked up speed as it reached a depth approaching three miles, the atmosphere in the operations center crackled with suspense.

The underwater television cameras still revealed little other than an occasional fish, but the monitors assigned to these units peered more intently at their screens. The sonar operators fine-tuned their listening devices, adjusting and readjusting the knobs on their auditing sets. The electric generator, working at full capacity, hummed loudly, and no one spoke.

High clouds appeared overhead, moving from south to north, and gradually they thickened until, at about 1:00 P.M., the sun vanished behind a thick, gray blanket. Adrienne noticed the ominous change, and silently called it to Porter's attention. If Franklin Richards was aware of the approaching storm he gave no indication, and concentrated his full attention on the control panel.

Stewards brought sandwiches and cold meats, coffee and soft drinks to those who wanted to eat, but few were interested. The hour of climax was at hand, and food would have to wait.

At 1:22 P.M. the buzzing of the sonar became constant and filled the operations center, obliterating the equally steady hum of the generator.

"Submersible is approaching target," Richards said over an intercom, and his voice was less than calm.

The television screens continued to reveal nothing of consequence.

At 1:24 P.M. Richards announced, "Submersible has touched bottom. Switch to manual controls."

Two of the operators pulled large levers. No one else moved.

Richards pushed forward on a metal stick resembling a gearshift on an automobile, and the huge float crept along the ocean floor.

It was astonishing, Porter thought, that a man sitting on the surface of the sea could manipulate a bulky object located almost eighteen thousand feet beneath him.

The buzzing of the sonar stopped for a moment.

Richards instantly reversed the movement of the submersible. Beads of sweat appeared on his forehead, and Marie, who stood beside him, wiped his face with a towel she had brought to the center for the purpose.

The sound of the sonar rose again.

"There's the sub!" one of the supervisors shouted.

Gradually the sunken *Zolóto* came into view on the television screens, her cigar shape increasingly visible. Observers with good eyesight could even make out the numbers on her rust-streaked gray hull: *14–2967.*

Someone cheered, but suddenly fell silent. The task of raising the vessel had not yet started.

Franklin Richards stared hard at the screen, then maneuvered the float until it stood close to the submarine, lying parallel to it. The move appeared to be made in slow-motion and lasted for an eternity, but it was completed at 1:48 P.M.

No one needed to be told that the *Zolóto* was resting in several feet of mud, and as the submersible continued to press forward it seemed that nothing would induce the submarine to budge.

"Release five hundred tons of ballast on the outer edge,"

Richards directed. "Gently, now."

Viewers could see iron shot rising from the lip of the float farthest from the sunken vessel, and soon that side of the submersible began to tip upward, rising until it reached a 30° angle.

This enabled the near side of the great barge to dig under the *Zolóto*.

Adrienne caught her breath when the submarine started to roll away from her captor.

Richards had anticipated such a development, however, and increased the speed of the maneuver to its maximum.

Nothing whatever happened, however, and several men groaned involuntarily.

The float continued to dig, relentlessly pushing forward.

For a breathtaking moment the submarine hesitated, and looked as though it would fall away again. Instead it began to slide onto the surface of the barge.

At 2:03 P.M. the *Zolóto* rested on the float.

"Release seven hundred tons of ballast on the near side," Richards said. "Not too fast. No, a bit faster. Good!"

The submarine gradually inched toward the center as the float righted itself.

The supreme crisis was at hand. "Attach full magnetic pressure to target!" Richards ordered, and there was a ring of command in his voice.

The sound of the generator rose to a scream.

"Turn off sonar!"

The buzzing ceased, the sonar operation no longer being needed.

The submarine was firmly attached to the submersible now, but the arduous task of raising her to the surface was just beginning.

"Release one thousand tons of ballast from all vents. On count. Five. Four. Three. Two. One. Release!"

The tension in the operations center was unbearable. All four sides of the lip opened simultaneously, and small, dark shapes could be seen rising from them.

The wait was interminable. Then, shuddering slightly, the submersible seemed to drift upward from the ocean bed.

"Release all ballast instantly!"

The television screens turned a solid black, the viewers unable to see anything for some minutes as the rest of the iron shot was expelled from the submersible. The operation was concluded at 2:31 P.M.

As the screens cleared it was plain that the float was rising, electromagnetic power holding it on a horizontal level, with the *Zolóto* unmoving in its center.

Franklin Richards changed his shirt.

A buzz of conversation filled the operations center, and suddenly there was a call for the services of the stewards. Men who had been unable to eat were ravenous.

Richards voice cut through the bedlam. "It's too soon for congratulations! Eat, if you wish, but continue to man all posts! We're not out of the woods yet!"

As the float continued to rise the fuel stored in the chamber decompressed at an ever-increasing rate, reversing the process that had taken place when it had gone to the bottom. The meters attached to it indicated, at 3:24 P.M., that it had ascended more than three quarters of a mile.

Richards took a few moments to notify the bridge of what was taking place, and Captain Humphries immediately sent a wireless message to the admiral on board the cruiser: *"Aunt Martha is doing as well as can be expected."*

Common sense told Richards and the supervisors they would be wise to eat. Nature had taken charge of the operation, and their only task now was to prevent the float from tipping so far to one side or the other that the electromagnetic hold on the *Zoloto* would be broken and she would sink to the bottom of the sea again.

Adrienne and Porter helped themselves to sandwiches, too. He wanted a beer, but no one else was drinking anything alcoholic, so he decided to wait.

Shortly after 4:00 P.M. a grinding sound alarmed everyone in the operations center.

The voice of Captain Humphries came over the intercom. "Ladies and gentlemen, we're in for a blow, so I'm extending our Denny-Brown stabilizers."

Four finlike devices, two on each side of the *Neptune,* moved out to a distance of about thirty feet. A glance out of the windows indicated that the sea was becoming choppy, and the clouds, now a deeper, darker gray, were scudding across the sky more rapidly.

A short time later the captain came to the operations center, pausing just long enough to look at the rising float on the television screens. "Frank," he said as he joined Richards, "it looks now as though the eye of the typhoon will pass about one hundred to one hundred and fifty miles to our east, but it's still going to be one vicious storm. The winds are down to one fifteen miles per hour, but that isn't much of a consolation."

Richards went to the nearest television screen and pointed to the dark hulk of the *Zolóto.*

"I know," Humphries said. "I've been watching on my own set on the bridge."

"All I'm trying to emphasize," Richards said, "is that I can't call off the operation now, storm or no storm."

"I know." The captain clasped his hands behind his back and frowned.

"When will it hit?"

"From now on," the captain said, "the weather will grow steadily worse. The Navy escort will stand by with us as long as possible, but eventually they'll have to weigh anchors and ride out the blow. I expect aircraft will be grounded in another two or three hours. At least we know that the whole Russian Navy couldn't attack us tonight, even if they knew we had succeeded in snagging their submarine."

"It's now four-thirty," Richards said, "and the submersible has risen about a mile and quarter. One and three quarters still to go." He fed the figures into a small computer, then studied the response printed on a slip of paper. "She should hit the surface around seven-forty this evening."

"More or less simultaneously with gale winds of up to force six. Which will grow worse through the night. Ultimately I anticipate we'll get hurricane winds of up to force nine or ten."

"Once the submersible reaches the surface," Richards said grimly, "it will take the better part of an hour—under normal weather conditions—to haul the submarine on board. God knows how long it will take under typhoon conditions."

"I'll do my best to hold the *Neptune* steady for you as long as I can," Humphries said, "but I've been a sailor long enough to know I can't compete with the sea, and neither can you."

"Not even the sea," Richards said, "is going to take that submarine away from me."

By 6:47 P.M. the submersible and her cargo were only three eighths of a mile beneath the surface, and continued to rise to the surface more rapidly than had been calculated. But the sea became rougher, too, as the winds increased, and although a full hour remained before sunset, the sky was as dark as though night had already fallen. The stabilizers checked the movements of the *Neptune* somewhat, but her roll was already noticeable, and she was beginning to pitch, too, which was an even more serious development. Under other circumstances she would have weighed anchor and headed into the storm, but Captain Humphries, in spite of his grave misgivings, continued to ride in place.

The minute-by-minute ascension of the barge no longer mesmerized the members of the Project Neptune staff, but the operations center remained crowded, and no one left. The race against the storm had become the most important element in the drama still to be played.

There was little that men could do other than wait and watch. Two of Franklin Richards' lieutenants went to the open aft hold to make certain its sliding metal cover would function properly after the *Zolóto* was made secure in her niche. At 7:05 P.M. Captain Humphries conferred by telephone with Richards, and the latter then ordered the raising of the hydraulically operated, electromagnetized cranes.

The roll of the *Neptune* immediately became more pronounced, and she began to pitch erratically. Waves were beginning to break over her bow, and occasionally one that was as powerful as it was unpredictable slapped against her side, causing the whole vessel to shudder.

The rain, which had been gentle, was falling in a sheet now, and the wind blew it almost horizontally, causing a drumming sound as it beat against the thick glass of the operations center. The daylight continued to fade prematurely, and at 7:18 P.M. the captain ordered all floodlights turned on.

A thin, white line showed around Franklin Richards' mouth, but he betrayed no other signs of nervousness, and the staff took courage from his seeming calm.

At 7:23 an unseen underwater current struck one end of the submersible, tipping it, and the *Zolóto* rolled to one side.

There was nothing the men on the *Neptune* could do to correct the condition. They breathed more easily as the float righted itself. The electromagnets continued to hold the submarine in place, even though it was off center, but everyone knew that another current might cause it to fall overboard and sink to the bottom again.

Finally, at 7:31 P.M., Richards gave the order that had been awaited since the start of the operation. "Lower your claw-cranes," he said.

The balance of the *Neptune* was disturbed as the cranes dipped down into the sea off the fantail, and the ship pitched even more violently. Although the floodlight beams were the most powerful man could devise, it was impossible to see clearly through the pelting rain.

The magnetized cranes needed no human help, however, and finding their target beneath the surface, they closed around it.

Richards waited until he was certain the grip was secure. "Jettison submersible's gasoline," he directed.

The float, growing lighter by the second as her fuel drained into the sea, rose more rapidly to the surface, giving the cranes assistance.

"Cut off electromagnetic lines to the submersible," Richards ordered.

Only the cranes held on to the submarine now.

"Bring your cargo on board!"

The cranes rose into the air, cradling the *Zolóto* of more than 6,000 tons gross weight.

The typhoon mocked the efforts of mere men, and winds of force nine velocity struck in repeated gusts, causing the *Neptune* to roll and pitch perilously.

But the cranes did not release their cargo, even though the bow rose high out of the water, then plunged abruptly until it was almost completely submerged. The automated equipment performed flawlessly, and the submarine was lowered into the open hold.

"Close your hatch cover!" There was hoarse triumph in Richards' voice.

237

The *Zolóto 14–2967* was safely on board, the cranes were retracted, and the closing cover made the prize secure.

But the battle was not yet ended. Franklin Richards wanted to salvage his football field, which was still attached to the mother ship by a number of lines and cables.

The storm was not to be denied at least one victim, however, and one by one the lines were torn loose in the shrieking gale.

The voice of Captain Humphries came over the intercom. "Frank," he said, "your submersible is breaking up. There's no way to save it."

Richards merely shrugged as the storm smashed the float, reducing a marvel of ingenious human design to bits of metal and wire, cloth and wood that were scattered in the South China Sea.

The rescue of the sunken submarine was completed against odds that no man could have imagined, but there was no elation. Franklin Richards hurried off to his suite, where he was violently seasick, and many of the others, including Adrienne, followed his example.

Porter was one of the few who remained in the operations center, and clinked champagne glasses with Marie Richards. But even those who remained on their feet were too bone-weary to celebrate.

The storm did not begin to abate until midmorning, and a weary Captain Humphries notified his Navy escort of his position. They sailed at full speed to rejoin him, and as the clouds began to dissipate, the Air Force squadrons once again appeared overhead.

Adrienne was still in bed, recovering from the effects of her illness, so Porter took complete charge of the security operation. Corporation representatives were stationed in the aft hold and on the deck above it, all of them armed with submachine guns and under orders to halt the approach of anyone other than authorized personnel.

Two distinguished nuclear physicists, accompanied by a senior scientist on the staff of the Atomic Energy Commission, went into the hold, remaining for several hours. Thereafter they maintained complete silence regarding their findings, and neither then nor later did anyone, including Franklin Richards and others who had participated in Project Neptune, learn whether a Russian atomic bomb had been recovered.

The trio had scarcely emerged when two of America's top code experts went below. They stayed for the better part of the afternoon, by which time the sun was shining again in a serene sky. Like their nuclear energy colleagues, they too said nothing, and it was impossible for anyone to discover whether they had come across the Russian naval code that the President and National Security Council had regarded as being easily as vital as the salvaging of an atomic device.

Not until early in the evening did a team of undertakers and their assistants go to the hold, carrying stacks of coffins. They were also under orders not to talk, and nothing was said regarding the number of the *Zolóto*'s dead crew they prepared for burial at sea.

The Corporation guard was maintained without a break on the uneventful voyage to Honolulu. Additional Navy ships joined the escort, and the flotilla arrived at the Pearl Harbor Navy base without fanfare. There the dismantled submarine and its contents were returned to the mainland by Air Force cargo planes.

Many of the civilians left the *Neptune* at Pearl Harbor, among them the entire Corporation contingent. Franklin and Marie Richards gave a quiet party for the entire company before it dispersed, but no speeches were made, and the gaiety was a trifle forced. Regardless of whether an atomic weapon and the Russian naval code had been recovered, no one could forget the coffins stacked in the hold.

If Hawaii was heaven on earth, the citizens of Kauai privately regarded their island, located at the northern end of the archipelago, as the only true paradise. Their waterfalls were more spectacular, their vegetation more verdant, their beaches cleaner and less heavily populated than those found elsewhere in the state. Kauai, in fact, was perfect for people who sought isolation.

The cottage, sturdily built and boasting every modern household convenience, stood on a high rise overlooking the sea, and was cooled by the trade winds. It had its own private beach, a boat was anchored in its tiny, sheltered harbor, and the fishing in a river that raced to the ocean was easily as good as that in Cornwall.

Behind the house was a garden filled with banana and pineapple plants, breadfruit and citrus trees, all producing in such quantities it was impossible to eat everything that grew there. Rising high in the distance was the island's only peak, Mt. Waialeale, and every afternoon white clouds formed around the top of the mountain.

Porter and Adrienne made love and slept, ate and swam, fished and shared the chores of cooking and cleaning. Twice each week they drove in their little car to the nearby village for meat, bread, coffee and other supplies, and sometimes they stopped at a thatch-roofed tavern for a beer before returning home. Occasionally, too, they stopped at the local post office to pick up stacks of books they had ordered from Honolulu and San Francisco. They received no other mail.

Sometimes they paused, too, to chat with neighbors with whom they shared an evening every week or two. Like the other citizens of Kauai, Adrienne and Porter were bronzed by the sun, their hair streaked by it, and wearing only the clothes that society deemed necessary, they radiated good health. Porter had regained complete use of his arm, and only the fading scar on his shoulder reminded them of his fight on the Singapore dock.

Late one afternoon Adrienne was frying breadfruit when Porter returned from an offshore expedition with a large fish.

"I've never seen one like it," he said, "but we'll try it for dinner."

"Provided you clean it, dear."

"I'll clean it." He took a knife from a rack and went outdoors to perform the task.

The sound of the kitchen radio drifted out to him. "Here are the six o'clock news headlines. A new crisis is building in the Balkans, where—"

"Turn that damn thing off," he called.

Adrienne happily obliged.

As he returned to the kitchen with the fish, the telephone rang.

She eyed it. "It may have been a mistake to install that," she said.

Porter picked up the instrument.

"This is Brian Davidson, calling from Washington. How are you?"

"Doing beautifully until I heard your voice."

Davidson forced a laugh. "I don't suppose you people have heard the news, but hell is popping in the old cockpit, and we wonder if we can persuade you to undertake a very special mission for us in Bucharest. We simply know of no one else who can handle it."

"Davidson," Porter said, "my wife and I refuse to be separated ever again."

"So much the better! This caper is made for a husband and wife team, and you and Adrienne will be perfect for it."

"I'll call you back," Porter said, and went to a cabinet for

241

a little-used bottle of whiskey.

Adrienne dropped the fish into a pan.

"Bucharest," he said. "Together."

She sighed. "I knew this was too good to last."

"It'll be here when we come back," Porter said.

"We'll do it, of course," Adrienne said. "Even paradise is sometimes a trifle dull."